Something Motionless This Way Comes

BOOK 2

DARYL WALKER

Contents

CHAPTER ONE

Oz

"Lift her up carefully. She should be able to walk for a bit. I've stopped the bleeding for now. Just make sure you're supporting her the entire way," Nixx said.

Jamie was barely conscious as Abel helped Nixx lift her to her feet. They'd known that either Jamie or the Queen needed to be brought close to death to sever the connection between them, but the Queen had caught them all by surprise by pulling out a dagger and violently stabbing Matt in the thigh before plunging it deep into her own side.

Matt sat on the floor next to the green door, flinching as he bound the wound in his left leg. The Queen had been too quick for him and had escaped through the door into Oz.

"We good to go?" he asked, finishing up and looking around.

Nixx nodded and held out his hand. Matt grasped it gratefully, letting Nixx pull him to his feet. Matt leaned on the wall for support, and Chris winced as he watched him hobble a few steps.

Matt's annoyance was obvious to anyone watching, and Chris didn't blame him. They hadn't expected the Queen to stab anyone or get away from them, and Matt now couldn't move as quickly as he wanted to.

Once satisfied that he could kind-of walk, Matt grabbed the handle of the green door and yanked it open.

"Alright, let's get going," he ordered, holding the door open and leaning against it to take the pressure off his injured leg.

Abel and Jamie shuffled over to the door. One of Jamie's arms was draped over Abel's shoulder, and he kept a firm hold around her waist in case she collapsed.

Nixx moved past them both, gesturing impatiently to Chris, Ash, and Alex. Chris was the first to react, quickly following Nixx through the doorway, with Ash and Alex not far behind.

Chris blinked rapidly in the sudden light and instinctively shielded his eyes. It had been nighttime in Wonderland, but it was obviously still daytime in Oz. The bright sunlight was unmistakable as Chris tried to make his eyes adjust to the sudden light change. He hadn't considered that there might be some sort of time difference between the two counties.

Abel and Jamie came through the doorway, followed by Matt, who slammed the door shut behind himself.

They were standing on a grassy hill, and all Chris could see in any direction was a green, seemingly endless, field.

"We've got to get a move on," Matt said, limping ahead of them all to take up the lead. "It's going to be night soon. Oz is about four hours behind Wonderland, which makes it roughly three, maybe four, in the afternoon. We've got to find somewhere to hole up for the night. The last thing you want to do is get caught outside in the open in Oz when night falls."

"Dare I ask?" Chris sighed. He was getting tired of weird outside entities who wanted to kill him.

"You think Wonderland's scary in the dark, Chris?" Matt asked, glancing over his shoulder at him before heading off without waiting for anyone else to move. "Oz has its fair share of spooks, ghosts, and things that go bump when the sun goes down. Best to get somewhere to stay before they decide to come out and play."

Matt continued limping down the hill. They all hurried after him, not wanting to get left behind for spooks and ghosts and things that go bump in the night.

"Where are we going, Matt?" Abel called, sighing as he readjusted his grip on Jamie. She was getting heavier as she tired. "It's starting to get dark. We've been walking for hours."

Everyone was walking slowly now. Matt was a little way ahead, still limping, and he wasn't getting any better. Chris, Ash, and Alex followed him closely, while Nixx hung back, in case Abel needed help with Jamie.

"We'll find somewhere safe to stay the night," Matt called back. "Just trust me."

"We're getting nowhere!" Abel snapped. "We've been walking across the same damn field for nearly four hours, Matt! Where are we?"

Matt stopped abruptly and turned around, wincing as he jolted his leg. Chris, Ash, Alex, and Nixx stopped as well.

"If you know your own damn way around, then don't let me stop you from finding your own damn way!" Matt shouted at Abel. "How many times have you been in Oz, Abel? Once? Twice? How about none? I know my way around. I know where I'm going. I know what happens when the lights go out in Oz, so shut up, and let me find somewhere we can be safe for the night!"

"You don't know where we are, do you?" Chris asked skeptically.

Matt switched his glare to him as the last bit of light disappeared below the horizon. They were now in almost complete darkness and Chris could only just make out Matt's shape in front of him.

"I know exactly where I am, Chris. I just don't know where there might be somewhere around here that we can stay until morning," Matt said, sounding offended. "Now, if everyone would just have a little bit of faith in me, we need to keep moving. There's bound to be someone living around here."

Matt turned back the way they'd been going and limped off across the field again. Chris sighed as he walked after him, with everyone else following.

Abel shook his head as he readjusted his grip on Jamie again and continued moving. Nixx still stayed close in case he needed help.

Chris caught up to Matt who'd picked up his pace as much as he could, either no longer feeling the pain in his leg or trying to ignore it.

"Where are we going tomorrow, Matt? Like, what's the main place we're heading to?" Chris asked, feeling a few light drops of rain on his face. That was just what they needed right now: to be stuck in the dangerous dark and now the rain.

"We're going to the Emerald City," Matt said, keeping his voice down. The irritation and bitterness came through in his tone. "There's a guy there who can help Jamie."

"How far away is that?"

Matt shrugged. "Few days walk if we're lucky. The way we're going though, we either make it in about a week and a half since our pace is so slow, or Jamie dies before we get there. In all honesty, right now, I couldn't care which one it is. I just want to get somewhere safe for the night and then we can figure everything else out in the morning."

The two of them walked in silence for a while before Chris glanced back to make sure the others were still there. The rain was still falling but at least it was still light enough it just made them damp, rather than drenched.

"What do you think has happened to the Queen?" Chris asked, his focus back on Matt.

Matt shrugged and Chris saw him wince again.

"Hopefully, the bitch is dead," he began, then sighed. "But knowing her, she survived, and she'll be heading to the wicked witches' castle."

Chris frowned. "Where's that?"

"The opposite way to where we're going," Matt said. "She has an alliance with the witches. She'll probably turn up on their doorstep half-dead, tell them what happened, and what she wants to do about it. Put it this way, Chris: Marion's going to start a war, and she won't stop until we're all dead."

The Queen put her hand against the tree. Her other hand pressed tightly against her side, trying to stanch the blood flow and suppress the pain. She looked over her shoulder, back the way she'd come.

There was no one in sight. It looked like she'd gotten a decent head start. They were all most likely too preoccupied with other things right now. The thought was enough to bring a smile to her face.

If she was right, Jamie would most likely be dead. If she wasn't dead yet, she would at least be the main priority of the people she'd left behind.

Taking a short, sharp breath, she pushed herself off the tree, trying to ignore the pain. She needed to get to her destination. Her current condition would most likely add a few more days than this journey would normally take.

She continued on her way, moving as fast as she could as the sun slowly sank, and the darkness gradually took over the land.

She needed to find somewhere to spend the night. She definitely didn't want to be stuck outside here when the sun disappeared. She had nothing to defend herself with and the things that lurked in the Oz darkness wouldn't hesitate to try and get her, especially in her vulnerable state.

Her thoughts turned to Wonderland and all that she'd left behind. It was all for the greater good, but if Jamie died, it was only a matter of time before Abel came for her, seeking vengeance. Although, to be fair, whether Jamie lived *or* died, he'd probably do it anyway.

It made her wonder if they'd even come through the door into Oz. Knowing Abel and Shade, it was likely that they were already here.

She'd be safe enough if she managed to make it to the castle. The women would fix her up and then she'd be able to begin her plan for getting rid of the pesky convoy that she was sure was following her.

She was going to eliminate them all, preferably as a group, but if it meant doing it one by one, so be it. They were all going to die.

CHAPTER TWO

Refuge

"There, up ahead! Is that a house?" Chris called, trying to be heard over the sound of the pouring rain.

Of course, they had to get stuck outside in an unknown place in the dark during a storm. The rain and wind had picked up a while ago and, now, they were all soaked through. Alex wasn't liking it one bit and made sure Ash continuously heard about it.

Matt glanced behind. "Come on, guys. Pick up the pace!" he shouted as a crash of thunder tried to drown him out and lightning lit up the sky. "We're nearly there!"

"Nearly where?" Abel called. Jamie held onto him as he adjusted his grip on her again.

Chris pointed ahead as another flash of lightning lit up the surrounding area. He was walking just behind Matt and he turned and walked backwards for a few steps, shouting, "There's a house!"

The house was still quite far away, but it was at least something. Chris turned back to face the way they were going, only to find that Matt had disappeared into the dark.

Ash picked up her pace, holding her arms tight around herself, trying to stop shivering. She moved up next to Chris.

"Where's Matt?" she called. She had her head down and Alex held on tightly to her left arm, desperate not to lose her.

Chris shook his head as the harsh wind plastered his hair against his face and thunder shook the ground. "I don't know! He was here a second ago!"

Looking up again, he saw that the house was now close enough to see someone outside the door. Chris jogged the last few yards to the house, only to find Matt, pounding his fist against the door.

"No one's answering!" Matt shouted, looking at Chris. "The door's locked."

"Can't you just get inside and let us in?"

Matt shook his head, slamming his fist against the door a bit harder, trying to get someone to answer so they could get out of the storm.

"I'm not about to let myself into someone's inhabited house unannounced," Matt said, slamming his fist against the door again. "See, this is why we need Gates and Blaze. We wouldn't have needed to be let into someone's house if they were here."

Matt hit the door harder. "Open the goddamn door!"

Ash and Alex joined them. Ash was still trying to stop shivering and Alex continued to hold onto her.

The sudden, chilling scream that came from somewhere nearby made everyone stop. Another flash of lightning lit up the area, thunder not far behind it now.

Matt turned back to the door, pounding his fist against it again as another scream rang out. Chris was sure whatever was screaming was getting closer.

"Come on, open the door!" Matt shouted. "Please!"

Abel, Jamie, and Nixx finally made it to the door as another flash lit up the surrounding field.

"We've got to get inside!" Nixx called, water running off the brim of his hat like a waterfall. "Something's out here and it's getting closer, Matt!"

"You think I don't know that?" Matt shouted back. "I'm trying, Nixx. No one's answering the damn door!"

He slammed his fist into the door again as hard as he could.

Chris felt the dread building up inside himself as that blood-curdling scream rang out again, sounding closer still. At this rate, whatever was coming was going to get them and it would be game over for all of them.

Matt smacked the palm of his hand on the door one more time, before it finally opened, revealing a young boy holding a candle. He looked to be no more than ten at the most.

"You've got to let us in," Matt said, his tone desperate. "Please kid, we can't stay out here."

The boy looked at the seven bedraggled travelers before looking over his shoulder. "Father," he called.

A few seconds later, an older man appeared. He looked to be in his early forties, his beard already greying. The man leaned forward and studied the group standing outside his door.

"Please, you've got to let us in," Matt said, with a desperate look in his eye. "We can't stay out here. We need somewhere to stay, just until morning. Please."

The man looked them all over again before nodding. He moved aside and gently pushed his son out of the way.

Matt gave a grateful nod and ushered everyone in before himself. He closed and locked the door as the piercing scream sounded again, but it now seemed to be drifting into the distance, as if the screamer realized its prey had gotten away.

"Thank you," Matt said, shivering.

The little wooden house reminded Chris of the first house he and Abel had stayed in back in Wonderland before they'd made their home in the town.

"Go find these people some dry clothes and some towels," the man instructed his son. "Then straight back to bed."

The boy nodded and ran off up the stairs as a woman, presumably his mother, came down.

"We've a spare room upstairs," the man said. "My son will be back with dry clothes and towels to dry off with."

"We'll just take the towels, if you don't mind. We'll dry out by the morning," Matt said, looking around at the others before looking back to the man. "Hopefully."

"Why were you outside at night, and in such a bad storm?" the woman asked with a frown. She stood by her husband, inspecting the cold, soaking wet travelers.

"We're heading to the Emerald City," Matt explained as the boy came back, handing each of them a dry towel. "We came in from Wonderland."

The man and his wife both nodded in understanding. The boy stood just behind his mother, so he could still see the whole group.

"We've heard about what's been happening over there," the woman said. "It must be a terrible place to be living in this day and age."

"Guess it depends whose side you're on," Abel said as Jamie leaned against him, clearly tired. He looked at her before looking back at the family. "I'm sorry, but is there somewhere I can sit her down? She's exhausted."

"Has something happened to her?" the woman asked, directing them into what looked like the living room. The woman then disappeared into another room and the boy moved to stand behind his father.

"She's hurt," Nixx explained as Abel gently set Jamie down on the sofa, sitting down next to her. Jamie leaned against Abel's shoulder and closed her eyes. "That's why we're headed to the City."

"What happened?" the man asked.

"We had a bit of a run-in with the Queen," Nixx explained as Matt winced, clearly still feeling the pain in his leg. "It's a very long story."

The man nodded as his wife came back in with a dining chair, placing it in front of Matt.

"You're injured, too. Take a seat," she said, indicating for him to sit down. "Take the weight off it."

Matt did as he was told and painfully sat down. Chris could tell Matt had overdone it with all the walking today and had probably made his injury worse. The woman gave a satisfied nod.

"Go get some blankets," she instructed her son, getting a nod in return before the boy dashed off through the house again.

Matt slouched in the chair. He looked as exhausted as Jamie.

The man gestured at the four still standing. "Come with me and I'll show you to the spare room. We'll light the fireplace in there to help you all dry out."

They followed him out of the living room, and Chris heard his wife saying something softly to Abel as they left the room.

The wind and thunder were still loud outside as the man led them up the staircase. They reached the top and took a left turn. There wasn't anything lighting the way, so it was rather dark within the confines of the small house.

The man stopped outside one of the rooms, indicating that this was the one they would be spending the night in.

"I'll head down and get some wood to light the fire. There are some candles inside that you can light so you're not in the dark all night," he said to Nixx. "My son will bring up some blankets and you can dry out and get some rest. Make yourselves at home and I'll be right back."

He gave them a nod before disappearing back the way they'd come. Nixx cautiously went into the dark room, followed by Chris, then Ash and Alex.

Even though the curtains were closed, Chris could see the edges of the window as the lightning continued to flash outside.

"Well, at least we're not stuck outside anymore," he said with a sigh.

"Yes, well, I don't think I want to be out there during the dark hours," Nixx mused as he looked around the room.

There was one bed, two chairs and a sofa. It looked like no one had slept in here in quite a while.

The man returned with an armload of wood and stacked it in the fireplace. It took a few matches to get the fire to light.

"I'll bring up some more wood to keep it going for a few hours," he said as the fire finally sprang to life.

He lit the candles on the walls near the door, then left the room, leaving the door open. Alex headed straight to the fire and knelt in front of it.

"Give it a chance to actually warm up," Ash said, tiredly trying to dry herself off with the towel she'd had wrapped around her upper body.

"But I'm cold now," Alex complained, looking up at her.

The man came back in and dumped more wood on the floor next to the fireplace. His son trailed along behind him with an armload of blankets and dropped them on the bed.

"These should help you warm up," the man said. He and his son moved towards the door and looked around at them all.

Nixx handed Ash a blanket and held one out for Alex, but he was too mesmerized by the warming fire to pay attention.

"Thank you," Chris said as the man went to leave the room. "Seriously, we really appreciate it."

The man nodded. "Your friends will probably stay downstairs," he said. "Two of them won't be able to make it up the stairs."

The man ushered his son out of the room, closing the door once the two of them were gone.

Nixx sighed as he took off his top hat and coat. He dropped his coat on the floor and put his hat beside Alex who was still kneeling in front of the fire. He knew Matt could make it up here if he really wanted to. There was a lot of shadow in here, after all.

Chris removed his own soaked jacket, picked up Nixx's coat, and hung them both on the coat rack by the door. Hopefully they'd both dry out overnight.

"Well," Nixx said, looking around at everyone. "Today's been rather ... eventful."

"To say the least," Ash said. She wrapped the blanket around herself, removed her shirt, and put it on the floor near Nixx's hat.

"I don't know about you guys, but I'm sick of travelling already," Alex said, moving closer to the fire, happy to be warm again. "I assume we're heading off in the morning?"

"If Matt and Jamie are right to move," Nixx said, grabbing a blanket and wrapping it around himself. He pulled over a chair, sat down, and shut his eyes.

"Why wouldn't they be?" Chris asked.

"Matt's been on his feet too long today. He's probably done more damage than he'd like to his leg," Nixx said, opening his eyes and looking at Chris. "He might need a few days to recover properly. Hopefully the woman downstairs can help him."

"We don't have a few days. Jamie won't last that long," Ash said, sitting on the floor beside Alex.

Chris grabbed one of the blankets, removed his shirt, and put it in front of the fire. It was too cold with it on because of how soaked it was.

"She'll last longer than you think," Nixx said. "And, like I said, hopefully the woman downstairs can help. Rest will help too. She's exhausted."

Ash stayed silent, staring into the flames, as Chris sat on the edge of the bed, feeling pretty drained himself. Alex repositioned himself next to Ash, also just watching the fire.

"What if Matt or Jamie can't move on for a few days? How far is it really to the City?" Chris asked. "Matt said it might take us a week and a half to get there. Have we got that long?"

"We wait until Matt can go," Nixx said. "I don't know how far the City is. Matt's our guide, which is why we need him with us. Without him, we'd just be walking in circles."

CHAPTER THREE

Things that Go Bump in the Night

"You need to stay still," the woman said, as Matt winced and involuntarily pulled away from her touch. "The more you move, the longer this will take."

The woman sat opposite him, carefully cleaning his wound. Matt stayed silent. He knew she'd be stitching him up shortly and that wasn't going to be much fun.

Abel and Jamie had moved to an unoccupied downstairs room, while Matt was stuck with the living room sofa for the night.

"How did you say this happened again?" the woman asked.

Matt watched her pull out a needle and thread. This was going to hurt.

"Run-in with the Queen," Matt said. He knew she was trying to get his mind off what she was about to do. "It's a long story."

He flinched and gritted his teeth when the needle dug into his thigh, and she started stitching him up. Matt switched his gaze to the man, trying to take his mind off the pain. Hopefully, this wouldn't take too long.

"Your friends are upstairs for the night," the man said, standing by the fire watching his wife work. "Do you think you'll all be able to travel tomorrow?"

"I guess we see about that in the morning," Matt said, flinching again. He was surprised that he could even feel anything anymore, after the long walk and the cold and rain.

The woman finished stitching and looked at him. "And we're done. Take it easy for the next few days, OK?"

Matt nodded and gave her a pained smile. "Thank you."

She gathered up her items and headed out of the room.

"Get some rest," the man said as he followed his wife. "It's late and you've been walking all day."

When he was alone again, Matt dragged his damp jeans back on, then grabbed one of the blankets and wrapped it around himself.

He looked gratefully at the fire still burning in the fireplace, then sighed and took off his snapback, tossing it onto the floor. It slid to a halt in front of the fire where it would hopefully dry out overnight.

He painfully rose from where he'd been sitting on the sofa. He took off his shirt and placed it next to his hat before limping back to the sofa. He sat down awkwardly and sighed, before tipping over onto his side, pulling the blanket over himself. He lay there, staring at the blazing fire as he felt the tiredness finally set in. It had been a very long day.

Chris jumped awake as the same scream from earlier in the night came from the other side of the window.

He sat up and looked around. The fire was still going, and a small blue cat was curled up in front of it. It looked like Alex preferred to lie in front of the fire rather than sit on one of the chairs. Nixx had moved his chair over by the window and Chris could see that the scream had woken him, too.

"What the hell is out there?" Chris asked, keeping his voice down.

When the next scream came, Ash sat up from where she'd been asleep on the bed next to him. The cat also startled awake, blinking in confusion as he looked around.

"I don't know, but whatever it is, it doesn't seem to want to go away," Nixx said, standing up as Chris got off the bed and came over. Nixx moved the curtain aside, peering out into the darkness. "It's been circling the house for the past thirty minutes."

"Why?" Alex asked, transforming back into a person and coming over to the window to stand beside Nixx and Chris.

The three of them stood, looking out the window. A flash of lightning lit up the outside of the house, but there was nothing out there.

"I don't know," Nixx admitted as Ash joined them. "I've never heard anything like it before."

"Any ideas what it could be?" Chris asked. Another flash of lightning and, this time, he saw a figure outside. "OK, I'm not the only one who saw that, am I?"

The chilling scream rang out again.

"What the hell is it?" Ash asked, sounding freaked out but also intrigued.

"You're looking at a banshee."

They turned as one to find Matt stationed on the second, unused chair, just staring at the fire.

"I didn't think they still existed," he continued.

"Banshee?" Chris asked as Nixx moved the curtain back into place.

Matt nodded, looking over at them, his gaze no longer on the fire. Chris could see just how tired he was.

Ash went back over and sat on the bed, next to Matt's chair, and Alex moved back to the fire. Nixx sat back down on his chair and Chris stayed by the window.

"Normally banshees scream when death is near. It signals someone's going to die," Matt explained. "It used to be like that anyway, way back when, or whatever you want to call it."

"So, what happened?" Alex asked.

Chris flinched as the scream rang out again and he moved to join Ash on the side of the bed. Ash shifted her position so her leg was touching his.

"I didn't think banshees circled houses," Nixx commented, with a hint of skepticism.

"It knows we're inside and it can't get in uninvited if the door's locked," Matt said, adjusting the blanket he had around himself before linking his fingers together and slouching in the chair. "But if you leave the door unlocked, well ... that's a whole different story."

Chris and Ash exchanged looks, and Matt glanced at them before continuing. "I locked the door when I came in, so we should be OK. But this one's not going away. This is one reason why you don't want to be outside in the dark."

"So, what happened?" Alex asked again. "Why did they change?"

"Curiosity killed the cat," Matt said with a smirk, but Alex didn't rise to the bait. "But, yeah. My understanding is that there was some sort of change. Banshees used to only *signal* death, now they *are* death.

I actually thought they died out long ago. No one's seen them in years."

"They kill?" Chris asked.

"Oh, they kill alright," Matt said with a nod. "As in, tear-you-limb-from-limb kill and that's only after they've nearly drained you. They keep you alive long enough to feel the pain as they tear off your arms ... or your legs. Or, if you're really unlucky, both."

Alex looked at Matt, wide-eyed and obviously freaked out. Matt smirked at him again.

"We'll be safe once we're in the City," he explained. "Nothing can get through those walls unless it's let in. Sure, it happens every once in a while, but not very often. The Wizard doesn't stand for it."

"Why do the banshees kill now?" Alex asked, getting Matt's attention again. "You said they never used to. Why'd they change?"

"You ask a lot of questions, kitty," Matt said. "I can tell you what I know. There are a lot more evil entities out there now than just banshees. The food chain's evolved. Survival of the fittest, you know. Banshees do what they've got to do to survive, same as all the others."

"Like a human," Chris spoke up.

"Exactly," Matt said with a nod. "You're right on the money, Chris. It'll be gone in the morning. They only come out under cover of darkness. Well, unless that's changed as well. Just hope you never come face to face with one. You won't know what's happened until it hits you, believe me."

Chris could see that Matt really needed to sleep and was struggling to keep his eyes open.

"What happens when we leave here?" Ash asked. "What if we don't come across another house?"

"I'll sort that out, don't you worry," Matt said. "Hope you don't plan on getting any sleep tonight. That banshee probably won't shut up for a good while."

"It sounds pretty quiet out there now," Alex said, cocking his head and listening. "Maybe it's gone?"

The silence was broken just a few seconds later by the blood-curdling scream again, making Matt smile in amusement at Alex who just shrugged.

"How's Jamie?" Nixx asked, trying to change the subject.

"I don't know. They moved her and Abel into one of the downstairs rooms," Matt said. "The woman was going to see if she could do anything to help us get her to the City, but I don't know."

Nixx nodded. "What about you? How are you doing?"

"I'm just fine, thanks," Matt said with a hint of sarcasm in his voice, sitting up straighter in his chair. "Slept like a fuckin' log."

"Matt," Nixx sighed. "You need to try and sleep. You're exhausted. We can all see it."

"Speak for yourself," Matt said harshly. "You lot look like the goddamned walking dead."

"You look worse than us," Chris said. "You clearly haven't seen yourself recently."

Matt scoffed and was gone, presumably back downstairs. At least they now knew their abilities worked here in Oz, too.

"He'll be fine," Nixx said, shaking his head as he looked at Chris. "Just needs to stop putting on the tough façade and actually get some rest for once in his life."

"He said we'd be OK if we don't come across a house tomorrow," Chris said. He smiled at Alex who had changed back into the cat and was snoozing in front of the fire again. "How's he going to guarantee that?"

Nixx shrugged. "My guess is he'll disappear sometime during the day, or even tonight, and go fetch Gates and Blaze."

"What can they do?"

"You'll find out soon enough."

CHAPTER FOUR

Backup

C hris trudged downstairs, rubbing his eyes.

The front door of the house was wide open, revealing the bright mid-morning sunlight outside. There was no sign of the banshee or the storm that had been raging last night.

Nixx, Ash, and Alex were still upstairs. Chris was fairly sure they were all still asleep and he was wishing he was too. The banshee had hung around for a few hours after Matt had disappeared back downstairs, and it had disrupted everyone's sleep.

Chris went into the living room, frowning as he found it empty. There were still blankets on the sofa, and the pillow was on the floor, but there was no sign of Matt.

Chris dismissed it and headed back to the open door. The man who owned the place looked up and signaled for Chris to come out and join him.

As he stepped outside, Chris realized the storm had actually left a lot of damage in its wake. Trees were down everywhere, but there were also marks in the ground that didn't look like they were made by the weather.

"Is this all from the storm?" Chris asked.

"Not all of it," the man remarked with a shake of his head. He pointed to the marks in the grass beneath their feet. "That there was the banshee. We don't normally get them around here."

Chris wondered how one banshee could do so much damage. But then he thought, maybe he didn't really want to know.

"Your friend wasn't in the living room when I came down this morning," the man continued, still looking around at the storm damage. "He's not in the house anywhere. I assume he'll be coming back?"

"I sure hope so," Chris responded with a wry smile.

"You're back early," Gates said.

Matt shrugged as he walked past him, heading for the bar. Gates was sitting in his usual place at the table, but there was no sign of Zeke.

Gates frowned, abandoning what he was doing and staring at Matt, who was now on the opposite side of the bar.

"And you're limping," Gates noted. "Care to share?"

Matt glanced at him as he filled a shot glass, not caring that some of it splashed onto the bar. It was too early for this.

"Not yet," he said. "Where's Zeke?"

Gates shrugged, watching Matt down the contents of the glass in one gulp. He was clearly far from in a good mood today.

"He's around somewhere," Gates said, pushing his chair out and getting up. He walked over to the bar and leaned against it, gesturing for Matt to pour him a shot too. "You check his room or the club?"

"Not yet. Just got here," Matt said, pouring a shot for Gates and sliding it across to him. "I need your help with something. You and Zeke."

Gates frowned again, swigging the shot and wincing.

"Forgot how strong that shit is," he said, indicating for Matt to pour him another. "What do you need help with?"

Matt poured a shot for himself as well as Gates as he spoke. "The Queen got away, disappeared into Oz."

"Wasn't she at the castle?" Gates asked, watching Matt down his shot in one gulp again. "There's no way through to Oz unless you go north."

"That's what we thought," Matt replied as Gates downed his own shot. "But the bitch somehow managed to manufacture a door and have it conveniently placed in the castle. She disappeared through it, but not before stabbing me in the thigh and herself in the side to severely injure Jamie."

Gates sighed. "So, what do you need help with?"

Matt looked at him for a few seconds while deciding what to say. "I need you and Zeke to come with us. Help us get to the City and then help us take the Queen down once and for all. We were just lucky we found somewhere to stay last night, else I wouldn't be here right now."

"Why's that, dare I ask?" Gates said with an unamused expression.

"Damn banshee found us and followed us," Matt said. "Circled the house we stayed in all night."

"I didn't think banshees still existed."

Matt shrugged. "Neither did I, but there was no mistaking that scream. There's a ton of dangerous shit out there now. If we don't find somewhere to stay along the way, there's no way we're making it to the City. Jamie's slowing us down enough as it is."

Matt watched Gates as he thought about what he was saying.

"Alright, I guess we can help," Gates said after a bit of thought, bringing a smile to Matt's face. "I'd love to see the Queen gone for good. This shit's gone on way too long as it is, and too many horrible things have happened. Wait here and I'll go find Zeke."

Gates pushed off the bar and headed to the door that led into the club. There wouldn't be anyone around this early in the day, but he was pretty sure that's where Zeke would be.

Matt filled his shot glass again as he waited.

"Seen any sign of Matt this morning?" Chris asked.

He was in the upstairs room, sitting on the bed next to Ash. Nixx sat in his chair by the window, and Alex stood in front of the fireplace, disappointed that the fire was out and missing the warmth of the flames.

They all shook their heads.

"He's not downstairs?" Nixx asked.

Chris shook his head. "No. The guy said he wasn't there this morning when he came down. He's taken off somewhere."

Nixx frowned, not saying anything.

"Has anyone checked in on Abel and Jamie this morning?" Ash asked, looking at Chris.

"I didn't when I was down there before," Chris admitted as Ash rolled her eyes. "I'm sure if something's happened, we'll be told straight away."

Ash shook her head, stood up, and headed out of the room before anyone could say another word.

The house was quiet as she headed downstairs, listening to the stairs creak under her feet. This entire house seemed to creak with any movement, as proven by the overnight storm.

No one was around as she made her way through the living room to the room Abel and Jamie had been moved to. The door was closed, so she knocked quietly, hoping she wasn't disturbing them.

After a few seconds, the door opened slightly, revealing a very tired-looking Abel. "What?"

He kept his voice down and sounded like he could use a lot more sleep than he'd managed to get. He was obviously worried about Jamie, and the banshee wouldn't have helped either.

"Just came to check in with you, see how everything's going," Ash said.

Abel looked at her blankly, then opened the door just enough for him to slide out, making Ash move back a step. He shut the door behind himself, not wanting to disturb Jamie.

"How's she doing?" Ash asked, still keeping her voice down.

Abel crossed his arms and shrugged.

"Honestly, I don't know," he sighed, looking down. "She's just lucky she's lasted this long. The woman that lives here couldn't do anything except try to clean it up a bit. Jamie's probably not going to make it through tonight at this rate."

"I'm really sorry to hear that, Abel," Ash said, reaching out and touching his arm. "When Matt comes back, we'll talk to him and let him know we need to get moving."

Abel shook his head. "The City's still days away. She won't make it."

"We'll make sure she does," Ash said seriously, seeing that Abel didn't have much faith left in what he now thought of as a pointless journey.

Abel looked at her sadly, not saying another word as he turned his back on her. He went back inside the room, again shutting the door behind him.

Ash shook her head, turning away, planning on going back upstairs. She jumped as three people who weren't there a minute ago stood in front of her.

"What the hell's your problem?" Ash snapped, shoving Matt, which just made him laugh.

Apparently sneaking up on people and scaring the living daylights out of them was funny.

"Oh, lighten up, princess," Matt said.

Ash angrily crossed her arms across her chest. She didn't appreciate people scaring her like that. Ash looked at Gates and Zeke who were looking around, minding their own business.

"What are you two doing here?" she asked with annoyance.

Gates switched his gaze to her. "Here to help."

Matt looked at Ash. "They're backup. Believe it or not, they can help us out, and the more people we have who will stand against Marion, the better."

Ash looked between the three of them before looking back at Matt.

"Fine," she said, bitterness back in her tone. She was going to be mad all day at Matt's antics. "But I swear, you scare me like that again and I'll end you. We need to get a move on. Jamie's not doing well."

Matt smiled as she pushed roughly past him, shooting both Gates and Zeke a glare on her way back upstairs.

CHAPTER FIVE

The Orchard

"Alright, we're going to head on out," Matt said, addressing everyone in the upstairs room.

Matt had already spoken to Abel before suddenly appearing out of thin air upstairs, once again startling Ash who wasn't the slightest bit happy. But was she ever?

Matt looked around at everyone. He was about to say something before he was rudely interrupted by an irritated Ash.

"Why are we even still here when we could be at the City by now," she said, crossing her arms as Matt switched his gaze to her. She indicated to Matt. "You can shadow-step, why haven't you just stepped her to the City, or even taken all of us by now?"

"Well, Ash, what a wonderful question," Matt replied. "Seeing as you asked so nicely, I'll take a bit of time out of what we could be using to travel to explain it to you. Yes, you're right when you said I can shadow-step. Gold star for you. But you forgot to take into account that you know fuck all about Oz and what goes on here. The City is warded. You can't get within ten miles of it. If I shadow-stepped, I wouldn't be able to get any closer than that. And, that boundary also happens to fall within the poppy fields, which is equally as bad. So, to answer your stupid question, I could try to step us all there, but it would probably mean we wouldn't make it very far at all. I don't know this area as well as I do Wonderland, and I need to know where I'm stepping to. Don't want to end up in a wall or a hole, do we? Better to walk and stay together. Everyone, and every ability, has limits, Ash."

Ash stayed quiet as Matt gave a vague, satisfied nod before continuing to address the rest of the room.

"As I was saying, it's going to be a very long walk, and it will take a few days. I can only go so far with the shadow-stepping as I said, and for the most part it's all open fields, which is another reason I can't do much. There aren't a lot of villages on this side of Oz. No shadow, no step."

Chris felt his heart sink a bit. Exercise was about to happen. He had been OK with the travelling part, up until Matt had said he couldn't go very far due to these damn fields.

"Hang on," Nixx suddenly spoke up, making everyone look at him. He looked around at everyone as he spoke. "We can't be out there during the dark. We only just managed to stumble across this homestead as it was. There's no way we're going to survive a night out in the open, let alone a few days, Matt. How are we meant to combat the creatures out there?"

"Yeah, I know I don't particularly wish to run into a banshee," Chris input, making Ash nod as Nixx indicated his point. "Or something worse..."

"You never know what kind of dog-like evil is out there," Alex said seriously. "I don't think I'd like to be eaten alive while trying to sleep."

Matt rolled his eyes as everyone started talking about what they didn't want to happen. This was all becoming one serious mess. Maybe he should've just left them all in Wonderland and done this himself. At least Jamie wouldn't be complaining about every little thing.

"Everyone shut it!" Matt suddenly snapped, causing the noise to settle down. Four people certainly made a lot of commotion when they were concerned for their lives. "You all need to shut up and actually listen to what I have left to say. You all keep interrupting and at this rate we won't be going anywhere today. Now, are you going to stay quiet and listen to me?"

When no one spoke, Matt looked around again before finishing.

"Alright, I was going to explain all this shit, but you all keep jumping to conclusions. Yes, there are horrible things out there, but we will get through this," he said, not talking directly to any one person. "Now, I've taken care of what we can do and that's why I went and got Gates and Zeke. We need both of them. Without them, we won't be making it to the City."

"Oh, it's Zeke now, is it? I thought it was Blaze?" Ash said demeaningly, before looking at Matt with a skeptical look. "How? How can they possibly help?"

Matt looked at her with a slight smirk on his face. "Guess you're gonna find out once it gets dark."

"Be very careful. Move her to a sitting position and we'll work from there," Nixx said.

Abel stood in the doorway. His fists were clenched as he watched Nixx and Matt work on trying to move Jamie without causing her too much pain. Chris stood next to Abel who didn't once glance away from what was happening. The husband, wife, and their son had left for the markets, so they had the house to themselves for now.

"She's going to be OK, you know," Chris said, glancing at Abel before turning his attention back to Matt and Nixx. This looked like it could take a few minutes. "We're going to get her to the City and whoever's in charge there is going to help her."

Abel looked at him, then reluctantly pushed away from the doorway and walked away.

"Chris, come here," Matt said, indicating for him to join them.

"Everything OK?" Chris asked.

Jamie was finally sitting on the edge of the bed and Nixx crouched in front of her.

Matt looked at Nixx, who was frowning as he checked Jamie over, making sure she was OK to move. Nixx spoke to her quietly as Matt looked back at Chris, keeping his voice down as he spoke.

"We have a couple of problems," he said. "First problem is that we might not be able to move her. She was OK until we got her sitting, now I don't think she can make the journey. A couple of us might have to go to the City and leave the others here with her. I'm thinking maybe we'll do a half-half type of thing. Everyone I can use on the trip will come with me, while the others will stay here until we can get back with some help."

Chris nodded. "So, what's the other problem?"

Matt glanced over at Nixx and Jamie again before lightly grabbing Chris's arm and moving him further away to the other side of the room. He quickly shut the door and came back over to where Chris was standing.

"When it was just me, Nixx, and Jamie in the room, Nixx said he could feel the presence of four," Matt said, his voice barely audible as he leaned in to keep the secret. "He wasn't sure, and I don't know how accurate he is, but it looks like Jamie might be pregnant. Which means she needs help, like now."

Chris stared at Matt, at first unsure of what to say. "Does Abel know?"

Matt shook his head. "No, and no one outside of this room is going to find out. You can't tell anyone. This is serious. If someone else knows, then that could cause more panic, and panic leads people to doing reckless things. Do I have your word, Chris? You won't tell any of the others, especially Abel?"

Chris nodded and Matt nodded back in satisfaction.

"Matt," Nixx called, making both men look at him. "Get a group of people together and head straight out. Jamie's not going anywhere. It's too risky to move her now."

Matt nodded, indicating for Chris to open the door. "I'll take Gates, Zeke, and Chris."

"I'll do what I can here to try and keep her stable until you get back," Nixx said, nodding at Matt. He looked at Chris who was standing by the door. "And not a word to anyone."

Both Chris and Matt nodded as they left the room and headed to the living room where everyone else was waiting. All except Abel, who was nowhere to be seen.

"Are we leaving? What's going on?" Ash asked, getting straight to the point.

Matt was once again in charge. At least he knew what he was doing and had it all planned out.

"We can't move Jamie. We can't risk it," he began, noting the displeasure on Ash's face. "If we move her off that bed, she won't last the day. Nixx is going to stay with her and do what he can. I'm taking

Gates, Zeke, and Chris and we're going to get as close to the City as we can, and bring back help. The less we have the better."

"You are not going without me," Ash said, crossing her arms and frowning at Matt. "I'm not hanging around here any longer than I have to."

"You're staying here," Matt snapped, making her flinch at his harsh tone. "The more people we have here who can help keep Jamie safe, the easier things are going to be. You and the cat aren't leaving until we get back. Abel and Nixx are staying here, too. The less I have with me, the better chance we have. Anymore and we'll be slowed down."

Ash looked like she wanted to say something, but Matt kept talking.

"I am not about to argue this. The longer you yell or snap at me, the more time we're wasting. We need to leave and we're leaving now."

Ash wisely chose to stay quiet.

Matt pushed past her, heading for the door. Zeke followed and Gates indicated for Chris to follow as he headed out after the two.

Alex wandered over to the sofa, minding his own business. At least he was content with staying behind for the time being.

Ash grabbed Chris's arm, making him stop.

"What's going on?" Ash asked, her voice down as she kept a tight grip on Chris's arm. "What happened to everyone going?"

Chris shrugged. "I don't know. Just go with it. Matt knows what to do. Trust him."

Ash seemed unamused and reluctantly let him go. "You'd better come back."

"You took your damn time. Get over here," Matt grumbled.

Chris jogged over to where Matt, Zeke, and Gates stood in the field under a few trees that had managed to survive last night's storm.

"Sorry, got held up," Chris said.

"I don't care," Matt said, leaning against a tree and still sounding annoyed. "Alright, so the plan is this: we're going for a bit of a walk further down into the orchard. Hopefully, there's enough shade down there that I'll be able to shadow-step us down the path a bit. After that, we go on by foot. I don't know a lot of this area of Oz, so it's a bit of a guessing game at where we're going to end up when we step."

"How does shadow-stepping even work?" Chris asked. "I've never had the chance to ask. Did it take long to master?"

"Right now, I don't have time to explain. Maybe if you ask again along the journey, I'll have time to tell you about it," Matt said. "Now, let's get walking."

He pushed off the tree, the other three following along behind him. Chris hadn't even known there was an orchard here. It looked like Matt had already done a bit of scouting.

Chris trailed along behind as they descended the steep hill. Now he could see the orchard. It was large and impressive, with the trees closely packed together. It was almost a sight to make Chris smile. Almost.

The banshee tracks from the previous night were still indented in the ground. It had done more than just damage to the front yard of the house. The bright green grass was still evident, but next to the tracks it was dead and black, looking almost charred. This mess would take a very long time to clear up.

Chris followed Matt and the other two into the orchard. When Matt came to a sudden halt not very far in, Gates nearly ran into him.

"What?" Gates asked.

"You feel that?" Matt asked, a frown on his face as he looked around.

Gates frowned, looking around as Zeke and Chris joined them. "Feel what?"

Matt held up his hand for a few seconds before suddenly flinching.

"That," he insisted. "I haven't felt that before."

"Matt, what are you talking about? None of us can feel anything," Chris input, looking around uneasily.

If Matt was uneasy about something, then there was most likely something rather wrong, even if no one else felt it.

The frown stayed on Matt's face as he moved further into the orchard, taking step after careful step before he suddenly stopped again.

"Nah, there's something seriously wrong here," Matt said, flinching again. "I don't know what it is, but this orchard isn't right."

"Like what? Matt, none of us can feel anything," Chris tried again. "What are you talking about?"

Matt paused. "That. Something's in here."

"Matt, if there was something here, we'd all be able to see it," Gates said.

Zeke and Chris nodded in agreement.

Matt finally turned to look at them. "Seriously, I'm not kidding, there's something here. Something that shouldn't be in here. Also, this orchard is very dark. Even with this many trees, there shouldn't be this much shade."

Matt suddenly flinched again, turning back the way he'd been heading. "There is definitely something here, further in."

"Wait, you can feel this ... thing?" Gates asked as Matt kept walking further into the orchard.

"I don't know. All I know is that something's wrong," Matt said, beginning to keep his voice down as they all moved deeper into the orchard, following along behind him at a reasonable distance. "Whatever's in here ... it's dark."

Matt continued on his way, and the other three followed along.

"Matt, we don't have time for this," Gates called, causing Matt to signal for him to shut up by holding his hand up.

The deeper they went into the orchard, the more Chris looked around. It hadn't looked this big from the outside. It was like its own small forest in here, and it was also starting to make him feel uncomfortable. Matt was clearly on edge as well, as the further he went, the more he kept flinching.

It looked like they were getting close. Or something was getting close to them.

"We've really got to turn back," Chris said, his voice down as Matt suddenly stopped.

The others caught up to him and watched him crouch down to look at something on the ground.

"You see something?" Zeke asked as Matt brushed a few leaves out of the way.

"No, but I can feel it," Matt replied with a frown, placing his hand directly on the ground. "Whatever's in here, it came this way and isn't far up ahead."

"Please tell me we're not going to find out what 'it' is," Chris said.

He didn't want anything to happen, and he just wanted to leave before it was too late. Maybe it already was.

Matt ignored him and got to his feet, picking up his pace, stepping cautiously again. By the time the other three had caught up, Matt had stopped again.

"What is it?" Gates asked.

Under one of the trees was what looked like a large burrow, much like the rabbit hole Chris had originally fallen down in the first place. The one that had taken him into the heart of Wonderland.

"We've got a problem."

CHAPTER SIX

Options

Matt quickly made the other three back up until they were about ten yards away. "Keep your distance, this isn't good. Wait here a second."

Before anyone could argue, Matt was walking back towards the burrow.

"What the hell are you doing?" Gates hissed, as Chris and Zeke just watched in silence. Matt didn't respond. "Matt? Dammit, Matt, get back here!"

Matt signaled for him to be quiet and wait and carefully approached the burrow. The only sound was the soft crunch of leaves under his feet. He crouched down in front of the hole, frowning as something caught his eye.

There was a mark carved deeply into the base of the tree, just above the large burrow. He reached out and ran his hand across it to make sure he wasn't seeing things. It was a letter 'B' with a deep cross slashed across it. The entire mark looked rushed, as if someone had tried to carve it quickly. Next to it were the initials 'CL' with a cross slashing over them too.

"We've got to get back to the house," he said, his focus still on the carvings. He ran his hand over them again just to make sure.

"Why?" Chris asked.

But Matt still stared at the burrow and the marks.

"Matt, what's going on?" Chris tried again.

Matt looked over his shoulder at them. "We've got to get everyone out of that house. When did the family leave?"

"Ah, I don't know. Maybe an hour or so ago?" Chris said. "Why?"

"Chris, you and Zeke go back up to the house and start getting everyone out of there. You all start walking and Gates and I'll catch up."

"But we can't move Jamie," Chris protested.

"Well, you're going to have to," Matt said. "I don't have time to explain right now, but you've got to trust me on this, man. We're going to get everyone to safety first and then we're going to come back and deal with this before that family gets home."

Chris nodded, knowing he didn't have much choice. He certainly wasn't about to argue with Matt. Matt flinched as he indicated for Chris to head back up to the house with Zeke.

Chris and Zeke started to jog back the way they'd come, quickly disappearing into the trees, heading towards the house.

Matt looked back at the burrow in front of him. He linked his fingers together as Gates crouched down next to him.

"That bad, huh?" asked Gates.

"That bad."

Chris burst through the door, startling Ash and Alex. Alex had been dozing on one end of the sofa, not as a cat this time, while Ash sat on the other end, reading a book she'd managed to find in the house. She didn't look very interested in it.

"Thought you boys had gone," she said disapprovingly as Zeke joined Chris in the doorway. "Did you forget something?"

"Everyone needs to leave this house now and come with us," Chris said urgently.

Ash frowned even more, while Alex stood up, rubbed his eyes, and stretched.

"Why, what's going on?" Ash asked, her tone suspicious.

"No time to explain. Just take Alex and wait outside while we get Nixx and Jamie," Zeke said, already heading over to the room Jamie was still in.

Ash looked at Chris as she closed the book and put it down beside her.

"Chris, what's going on?" she asked, getting off the sofa.

"I'll explain when we're outside. Right now, the main thing is that you guys get out of this house and a good distance away," Chris said.

Zeke came back out of the room and gestured for Chris to come over. "Nixx needs your help to move Jamie. I'll start walking with Ash and Alex and we'll wait a safe distance away for you. You'll be able to see us."

Chris nodded as Zeke passed him, heading to the front door to follow Ash and Alex.

Chris went into the room and Nixx looked at him from where he stood in front of Jamie. She still sat on the edge of the bed where Chris had last seen her.

"I assume you're going to explain all this once we're out of here," Nixx said, moving to Jamie's side and indicating for Chris to stand on her other side.

"Well, when we get out of here, you can ask Matt to explain. He wasn't very descriptive, but he was adamant that we all get out now."

Nixx shook his head, then they both helped Jamie to stand. She automatically leaned on Nixx more than on Chris. It was clear that she had no strength to even slightly carry her own weight. They slowly helped her out of the room and to the front door. This was going to be a tough journey, Chris thought.

"Where's Abel?" Chris asked, pulling the front door open while trying not to let Nixx take all of Jamie's weight.

Nixx shook his head again as they maneuvered Jamie out of the house as gently as they could. "No idea, haven't seen him."

They headed around the back of the house and Chris sighed as he saw Ash, Alex, and Zeke standing there waiting for them. Ash stood with her arms crossed, refusing to move any further without the rest of them.

"Why are we all out here? What exactly is going on?" she asked as they stopped next to her.

Chris motioned for Alex to come and take his position, helping to support Jamie.

Chris looked at Zeke, ignoring Ash and her questions.

"Matt was pretty clear that we should get these guys a safe distance away, but I think we should head back down to the orchard and see what's happening," he said. "I don't like leaving Matt and Gates there on their own."

Zeke nodded. "Agreed. Might as well go see what's going on."

Chris nodded and looked around at their group.

"We all good to move down to the orchard?" he asked. Everyone except Nixx and Jamie nodded. "Alright, but you guys should probably stay outside it, though. I'm not sure how safe it will be."

"Before we move," Nixx spoke up, resigned to the fact that they were moving. "Has anyone seen Abel?"

Everyone shook their heads and Nixx just sighed before beginning to help Jamie move down the steep hill to the orchard.

"What are you doing?"

Matt and Gates looked behind them. Abel stood with his hands in his pockets a few yards away, looking back at them.

"I could ask you the same question," Matt said, standing up. Gates followed suit. "Didn't think you'd be the type to skulk in orchards."

Abel shrugged as he walked over to where they were.

"Needed to clear my head," he said quietly as he stopped next to them. Matt flinched, bringing a frown to Abel's face. "Everything OK?"

"Yeah, just seem to have developed this annoying flinch in here for some reason. It got worse as we got closer to this one spot," Matt said, looking back to the burrow. "Well, closer to this anyway."

The frown remained on Abel's face as he followed Matt's gaze. "What is that exactly?"

Before Matt could answer, Chris and Zeke appeared next to them, causing the three to look at them. Matt looked behind and saw everyone else trailing behind.

"What did I tell you to do?" Matt said harshly to Chris. "Why the hell have you brought them in here?"

"I told them to stay out, but they all kind of just ... ignored me and kept following," Chris said as Nixx came to a halt off to his side.

Alex and Ash stood back supporting Jamie.

"Next time I tell you to do something, you damn well do it," Matt growled. "Just be happy if we all get out of here alive now."

Nixx looked at the burrow. "Is that what I think it is?" he asked.

"Depends what you think it is."

"Banshee burrow?"

Matt nodded and Chris's expression fell. Gates looked uneasy, Abel just frowned, and Zeke moved back a step.

"But it's worse than that," Matt said, indicating for them to come over as he crouched down in front of the burrow again. They all crowded around, and Matt pointed to the hastily carved marks in the tree base. "The reason I got you all out of that house before the family comes back is that someone's bound it. Usually that's only done by necromancers. I've never seen anyone game enough to do it, though. Banshees don't stay still very long."

"You think it's someone in the house? Is that why the banshee was circling the house last night?" Abel asked.

Matt glanced at him and nodded, before running his hand over the marks again.

"That's my best guess," Matt said, linking his fingers together as he shifted and looked at Abel. "Probably why it didn't attack us when we were out in the open. It had the chance, but it didn't strike. We all heard how close it was."

"What's the point of binding banshees?" Chris asked. "What does it do?"

"Most times, it's for dark magic, rituals, or revenge," Matt said. "Normally they don't stay bound for long. Most of the stories I've heard say that they eventually turn on their captor. They're wild animals and it's not wise to hold a banshee very long. By the looks of this mark on the tree though, this one's been bound for a while. It's not new. Maybe at least a year. I don't know why it hasn't turned on its captor yet. It's very uncommon for them to stay this docile with whoever they're bound to."

"Well, let's just leave," Abel said, glancing back at Jamie.

Matt shook his head. "We can't do that."

"Why not? It's not like it's out here now and trying to kill us. It's not here and we can just leave it alone."

Matt shook his head again and looked back at the burrow.

"It's already got our scent," he explained. "If we leave now, we're all as good as dead. Once it gets dark, no matter where we are, it'll hunt us down. Once it's been denied food the first time, that's when it'll start disobeying and go for the last scent it latched onto, which is ours. We can't risk it."

"Then what do we do?" Zeke asked.

"We have to kill it."

CHAPTER SEVEN

Knife Hunting

"You're joking," Chris said.

"Does it even remotely look like I'm joking, Chris?" Matt snapped. "This is serious, and until we deal with it, we can't keep going. We'll be stuck in that house until that banshee decides to turn on its binder, and then we're all dead! And if someone in that house has bound it, we don't know if, or when, they'll decide to let it in."

"How do we kill it?" Abel asked quietly.

Everyone became quiet and looked at him.

"Silver blade to the heart," Matt responded.

"Where are we meant to find one of those?" Gates asked. "And does it have to be pure silver?"

"Hopefully, there's one in the house and, yes, it does have to be pure silver. You'd be crazy not to have one if you're binding banshees. Someone needs to go back and search the house."

Everyone exchanged looks, but no one moved. Matt looked around at everyone, waiting for someone to step up and volunteer. He wasn't about to leave his post, so it had to be someone else.

"How will I know if it's pure silver?" Chris sighed, knowing no one else was about to do it.

"You'll know," Matt said.

"We don't really have time for this," Abel spoke up. When Matt looked at him, he lowered his voice. "What about Jamie? She's gonna die, Matt. We can't take time to do this. Hell, she can't even stand. What are we doing about that, huh?"

Matt sighed, readjusting his snapback as he thought about the best course of action. He looked back at Chris.

"You and Abel go up to the house and see what you can find. If there's rope or something, grab that too, but make sure it can hold weight," he instructed.

Chris nodded, but Abel just looked at Matt with bitterness and disapproval.

Matt continued. "I'll take Jamie and the cat further away, so they won't get hurt. He can help get Jamie a bit further along the way, while we take care of this. Then we all catch up. Sound fair?"

Abel looked Matt over briefly before meeting his gaze and nodding reluctantly. Abel and Chris headed back up to the house.

Matt walked over to Alex, Ash, and Jamie. Jamie and Alex were sitting on the ground, leaning back against a tree. Ash was standing, also leaning against the tree, waiting to be told what was happening.

"Alright, kitty, let's go. On your feet," Matt ordered, making Alex jump to his feet. "You and Jamie are going to get a head start on the rest of us."

Alex frowned, looking at Ash before looking back to Matt. "What does that mean?"

Before he could say another word, Matt grabbed Alex's wrist and put his other hand on Jamie's shoulder. Suddenly, Alex and Jamie were under a lone tree, with no house and no orchard in sight.

Alex shook his head, feeling dizzy, caught off guard by the sudden shadow-step. He turned around and saw Matt crouched down in front of Jamie, saying something to her quietly.

"What did you do? Where are we?" Alex demanded to know as Matt got to his feet.

"I need you to help Jamie get as far along the way as you can," he said seriously. "We've got other pressing matters that can't wait. This has to be taken care of now, but Jamie can't be anywhere near what we're doing. So, you're responsible for Jamie until we catch up."

"When will that be exactly?" Alex asked, glancing at Jamie.

Matt saw that Alex was starting to panic. He sighed and walked over to Alex, coming to a halt in front of him.

"Once this is taken care of, then we'll catch up," he said. "Now, I need you to listen to me very carefully. You have to hear everything I say and don't miss a thing, got it?"

Alex nodded hurriedly, torn between panic and not wanting to let Matt down. He knew that Matt could get very mad and that was something he wanted to avoid.

"OK," Matt began. "You need to head in the direction I'm facing. You'll keep going until you hit a road. You can't miss it. It's made of yellow bricks. Once you reach that road, you need to go to your right. Keep following that road and do not ever stray from it once you're on it, especially when it gets dark. Under no circumstances do you step off the Road once you're on it."

"What happens if I do?" Alex asked, the worry clear in his tone and on his face.

"Let's just say you don't want to know," Matt said. "You need to stay on the Road and keep going. We'll find you there before it gets dark. If there are any turns, do not take them. You keep going straight forwards. Do not stray down the wrong way. You have all that? Do you understand?"

Alex nodded.

"Relay it back to me," Matt instructed. "So I know you're not lying and you won't fuck this up."

"Keep going forwards until I hit the Yellow Brick Road," Alex began, as Matt nodded along. "Then go to my right. Don't step off the Road and don't take any turns. Straight forward and you'll find us before it gets dark."

Matt nodded again, satisfied. "Good, now get going. I'll bring everyone else once we're done."

With that, Matt was gone.

"Find anything?" Abel asked as Chris rummaged through the kitchen drawers.

"Nothing," Chris sighed, violently shoving the drawer back in. He looked at Abel. "Any luck on your end?"

Abel shook his head. "No. I don't think there's one in here."

Chris sighed again, leaving the kitchen and heading into the living room, trying to think of where someone would keep a pure silver blade. Surely it wouldn't be too hidden, right? What if they needed to use it?

"Where else, besides the kitchen, would you hide a blade?" Chris asked himself out loud. "A blade of pure silver, nonetheless."

Abel stopped on the other side of the sofa; his thoughts clearly written all over his face. If they weren't able to find anything in the kitchen, where else would it be?

"Maybe you'd hide it somewhere that only you know to look," Abel said. "I mean, like, somewhere no one would think of looking for it. If it's in your house, where's the one place you don't let guests go?"

Realization crossed Chris's face. "The bedroom."

Not needing to be told again, both men rushed out and to the staircase. Chris took the steps two at a time, with Abel following.

"You check the room we were in last night and I'll check one of the others," Chris instructed.

Abel nodded and veered to his left as Chris went right down the hallway.

There was a room at the end of the hallway, and two other rooms off to the left side. Chris figured that his best shot was the room at the end. If there was nothing in there, then he'd check out the other rooms.

The door was slightly ajar. Light coming through the window in the room streamed down the hallway as Chris approached the room. No one else was in the house, besides himself and Abel at the present time, but that didn't mean he wasn't going to be cautious.

Reaching the door, Chris carefully pushed it open. The old hinges creaked, making him grimace at the sound.

He stood in the doorway, looking around at what was obviously the master bedroom. A perfectly made double bed sat on a dull grey rug, directly under the window. A breeze came in through the open window, moving the curtains slightly. A chest of drawers stood on the right side of the room. Several paintings and framed pictures were placed around the room, some on the chest of drawers and some on the walls.

He went over to the bed and crouched down. If there was one thing he knew about hiding anything, it was that most times whatever was hidden was either under the bed or under the mattress.

On his knees, Chris placed his hands on the floor and looked under the bed. It was clear.

He sighed, having hoped that there was going to be something under there so he didn't have to lie down, crawl under the bed, and look under the mattress. But apparently not.

He lay on his back and moved himself half under the bed. Luckily this bed frame wasn't one solid board that the mattress sat on. There were a few pieces of timber making up the base, which made Chris's job easier.

"Chris? You in here?" Abel's voice sounded from the doorway. At least, that was where it sounded like it was coming from.

"Under the bed," Chris called back.

He heard Abel's footsteps cross the hard wooden floor. Then he saw Abel's face on the other side of the bed, looking under to see what Chris was doing.

"What are you doing under there?"

"Looking to see if there's anything under the mattress," Chris said. "Nothing in the other room?"

Abel shook his head as Chris shifted further under the bed to continue his search, having found nothing yet.

"Nothing," Abel sighed, lying on his front as he watched Chris. "Want me to look somewhere else in this room or have you got it covered in here?"

"Maybe go check the chest of drawers while I look under here?"

Abel nodded and pushed himself up off the floor as Chris continued on with his search. Abel sighed as he reached the chest of drawers, picking up one of the framed pictures. It was a family photo, the four of them all smiling. The picture looked quite old.

"They seem like such a normal family, maybe Matt's wrong," Abel said, still looking at the photo.

"Why do you think that?" Chris asked, his voice muffled as he kept looking under the mattress.

"I dunno. Like they don't look like they'd be necromancers."

"Well, even the nicest people can end up evil. Some are already corrupt and just playing the part."

"Yeah, I guess."

Abel put the picture back in its place on top of the chest of drawers. He pulled the first drawer open.

"I don't think there's anything under here," Chris said, dragging himself out from under the bed. He sat on the floor and looked at Abel. "Anything there?"

"Hopefully," Abel said, moving aside a few items of clothing. Something cold and metallic touched his hand. "I think I've got something."

He pulled something out of the drawer and they both smiled when they saw the dull silver blade.

"Well, I think we've just found our murder weapon."

CHAPTER EIGHT

The Burrow

"**Y**ou find anything?" Matt asked Chris and Abel as they came back and stood next to the group.

Everyone had been keeping a watch on the burrow. Even though it was daylight and banshees were nocturnal, they weren't about to take any chances.

"We found the blade and I also found some rope," Chris said, handing the heavy blade to Matt who nodded in approval as he looked it over. "The rope's pretty strong, so it should be able to hold some weight."

"Where did you find these?" Matt asked, looking at Chris.

"In the master bedroom," Chris said, causing Matt to smile in amusement.

Chris just rolled his eyes at the immaturity in Matt's thoughts. Abel dropped the rope on the ground, and Chris started unraveling it. He still didn't know what it was needed for.

"How are we going about this?" Ash asked.

Matt pulled his gaze away from the blade and looked at her.

"At least two of us are going down into the burrow. The banshee should be asleep since it's still daylight," Matt explained, examining the silver blade again. "That's what we need the rope for: to get down and then out again. No one will even know we were here."

"You sure this is a good idea?" Abel asked, making Matt look away from the sharp object in his hands.

"Why wouldn't it be? You keen to get killed by a necromancer or his banshee bitch?"

"How do we even know someone in that family is a necromancer?" Abel asked seriously. "All four of them look like perfectly normal people, Matt. They helped us last night. You really think one of them is capable of harnessing a banshee to do their bidding or kill their enemies? None of this makes sense to me."

Matt frowned as he looked at Abel. "What did you just say?"

"That it doesn't make sense to me?" Abel tried, making Matt shake his head.

"Before that."

Abel frowned, trying to think what he'd just said.

"That none of them look like they'd be necromancers?"

"Did you say four?" Matt asked. The frown remained on Abel's face as he nodded. "Why did you say four?"

"Because there's a family photo of four people in the master bedroom," Abel said. "Why?"

Before anyone could move or say anything, Matt stepped into a shadow and disappeared.

"Where's he gone now?" Nixx sighed.

Chris dropped the rope, not bothering with it anymore. "I'm sure he knows what he's doing."

Matt picked up the framed photo. The picture was old, rather faded, and looked like it hadn't always been in this frame. But this frame had been moved and picked up a fair few times, judging by the light scratches in the top of the chest of drawers and the wear marks on the edges of the frame.

"Goddamn it," Matt swore to himself, looking the picture over.

He threw the frame to the ground and the glass smashed as it hit the floor. He bent down and carefully picked it back up, brushing glass fragments off the picture before pulling it out of the busted frame.

He turned the picture over and read the neat handwriting on the back of it: 'Colin, Mara, Angel, and David Lindell. 2011.'

"Seriously?" he mumbled to himself.

He dropped the frame and picture back onto the floor, moved back into the shadow, and stepped back to the orchard. Everyone jumped and stared as he suddenly appeared in front of the burrow.

"That picture was dated five years ago," Matt said, ignoring the looks from the others. "Looks like there used to be four, but I know for a fact that there's only three in that family now."

"So?" Chris asked, still not quite understanding what he was talking about.

"I think I know why this banshee's remained docile for so long."

Everyone frowned, exchanging looks with one another before looking back at Matt.

"What do you think?" Abel asked, crossing his arms.

"Necromancers generally deal with bringing spirits back to life, more to project the haunted to the person wanting to see it. Very dark magic that shouldn't be touched. Sometimes novice necromancers, or people who don't quite know what they're doing, slip up. Some necromancers do it on purpose when they're dealing with clients. They still get the money, and they can do what they want. Comes with the dark job description."

"You think someone in that house was just trying out dark magic?" Nixx asked. "On a family member?"

"I think someone in that house fucked up more than once," Matt said, continuing on with his theory. "I think something happened to their daughter and this banshee is the result."

Everyone was quiet as they took in what Matt was saying.

"Can you even do that?" Ash asked.

"It's probably the reason it's so docile. You use dark magic wrong and there can be a lot of unwelcome consequences. That's why it's so dark around here. I think this girl—their daughter—died and they tried dark magic or necromancy to try and bring her spirit back, or even her physical body back. But there was a slip up and now this has happened."

"But why would it be bound?" Chris asked, still trying to get his head around it. "Why bind it if it was a person?"

Matt shook his head. "Because it's still a banshee, Chris. Dead person or not, it's a banshee. It could kill everyone if not dealt with accordingly."

"So, we're going to kill this banshee that was once a little girl?" Ash asked, horrified. "Matt, you can't be serious. You're actually going to do this?"

"There's no other choice," Matt said, sounding sad. "If this banshee gets loose, that's a whole new problem. It's got our scent, and it knows who's bound it. If we don't take care of it now, then someone else will or we all die."

Ash shook her head, not saying another word.

Matt looked around at everyone. "So, who's coming down with me?"

"I don't like this at all," Chris said.

Matt had the silver blade with him, and he was going down into the burrow first. Abel, Gates, and Chris were going with him, and Chris was far from happy with this decision. If he was going to die, this wasn't the way he wished to go.

Zeke, Nixx, and Ash were staying top-side to ensure nothing happened and to help get everyone out when it was done, or in case something went wrong. Chris hoped it was the first option.

"Alright, let's get this shit done," Matt sighed. "We all know our role?"

Everyone nodded. Matt had assigned everyone their own individual role so there would be no confusion about who was doing what.

Matt nodded back, glad that everyone knew what was going on. He handed one end of the rope to Zeke and indicated for Ash to help him.

"How long's this gonna take?" Abel asked. "We really don't have all the time in the world here, Matt. That family could be back at any moment, you know."

"I know, that's why we're going now," Matt said, keeping hold of the other end of the rope as he stood in front of the burrow. "I'll go down first, then the rest of you make your way down. I don't care which order you come down in, as long as there are a few of us in case something happens. And for the love of God, don't let go of the rope, no matter what. We don't know how far down this burrow goes and the last thing we need is someone else getting hurt."

Abel gave a nod of understanding and Matt looked at Zeke, who also nodded, indicating he was ready.

Matt looked around at everyone once more before shaking his head slightly. "Alright, let's go."

Matt moved and Chris could see the uncertainty on his face as he headed into the burrow. If Matt was unsure, then Chris was feeling even more uncertain about this whole thing.

Matt quickly disappeared into the burrow as Zeke carefully lowered him down.

"How do we know when he reaches the bottom?" Ash asked, standing next to Chris as they all watched the rope disappear further into the burrow.

It was running out rather quickly.

Chris shrugged, not having an answer for her. Zeke was standing very close to the burrow now, having nearly reached the end of the rope. How deep did this go?

"Matt, that's the end of the rope," Zeke called. "Either you come back up or let go."

The rope suddenly lost all tension, causing Zeke to stumble backwards from the sudden slack. He shook his head and sighed as he pulled the rope back up for the next person.

"Careful. There's a bit of a drop."

Chris looked at Matt with no amusement, wincing as he hit the ground hard.

"Could've warned me before I let go," Chris muttered, dusting himself off. He heard someone else starting to be lowered into the hole above him and he moved out of the way.

Matt was looking around, even though there wasn't a whole lot to see, as it was quite dark down here. All Chris could make out was dirt walls and floor.

"I think we need Zeke down here, can't see a damn thing," Matt mused. "But it might be better to leave him up there..."

"Well, I'd like to see where we're going. I don't know about you, but I don't think it would be wise to suddenly stumble across a sleeping banshee," Chris input as someone landed hard just behind him.

Abel appeared next to Chris, dusting his jeans off like Chris had just done.

"How far in do we have to go?" Abel asked.

"Once Gates is down, we'll start moving. We most likely have to go the entire way in," Matt said, not turning around to talk to them. "Banshees usually reside right at the end of the burrow, away from prying eyes, so they can get the upper hand when someone hunts them."

"How come you know so much about this?" Chris asked, crossing his arms as Abel looked around. "You said banshees were thought to no longer exist."

Matt glanced over his shoulder at him before looking back to the area in front. "I've had a lot of time to myself over the past few years."

Chris didn't argue the point, knowing not to ask Matt any more than he already had. Gates suddenly appeared next to Abel, startling both of them.

"Everyone's good top-side," Gates said, making Matt finally look over to him and away from whatever had been holding his attention. "Are we good to go? Sun's starting to go down, so we'd better get on with it before we run out of time."

Matt nodded and indicated for everyone to follow him as he started walking, not waiting for anyone. If they weren't coming along, then that was their problem, not his. Gates was the next one to move, following Matt into the dark.

"This is crazy," Chris sighed as he and Abel both reluctantly started walking. They were only just able to see Matt and Gates up ahead.

"Yeah, well, we didn't seem to have much of a choice," Abel replied, keeping his voice down as he walked close by Chris's side. "Matt's got this all planned out and he seems to need us down here instead of the others. By the way, any idea why he decided he needed Gates and Zeke along on this whole trip?"

Chris shook his head, not sure if Abel could see it or not in the dark. They fell silent, and continued to walk, hoping they weren't about to lose the two men in front of them.

It wasn't long before they reached Matt and Gates, who'd come to a halt. Matt had a frown on his face, head tilted to the side as he listened to the silence.

"Everything OK?" Abel asked, his voice down but still echoing off the dirt walls.

Matt shook his head and Chris saw him flinch.

"It's a lot worse down here," he said, flinching again and keeping his voice down as well. "I think we might be dealing with more than one banshee."

CHAPTER NINE

Wicked

A lex sighed, supporting Jamie as they slowly continued moving. It felt like they'd been walking forever.

They still hadn't seen any sign of the Yellow Brick Road and Alex was starting to believe there was no such thing. Well, here at least.

Maybe Matt had gotten it wrong. Maybe they were in the wrong place. And for that matter, where was Matt? He'd told Alex that everyone would be joining them, but he hadn't specified when that would be, apart from 'before dark'.

Alex was worried because it was definitely starting to get darker. The sun was slowly sinking below the horizon, which heightened Alex's anxiety. What if Matt and the others weren't coming? What if something had happened to them? He and Jamie wouldn't even know, since they were on their own with the light fading and the terror setting in.

"I'm sure they're on their way," Alex said, mostly trying to make himself feel better, but not really achieving it. "Matt will keep to his word and find us before it gets too dark."

Jamie remained silent.

"You're lucky our scouts found you when they did, otherwise you'd probably be dead."

The scowl remained on Marion's face. "You don't say?"

Carmen shrugged and walked across the room. Marion watched her closely the entire time. Even though she knew Carmen, she wasn't about to take any chances. Witches could be rather unpredictable, especially the wicked ones.

"So, what brings you here this time?" Carmen asked. Her back was to Marion as she went about organizing things on the table in front of her. "It wouldn't happen to be due to a couple of ... intruders, would it?"

Carmen turned back to face Marion, leaning back against the table as she waited for an answer.

"I'll take it they're still moving towards the City, then," Marion said as she shifted her position on the hard chair. She winced at the pain in her side, glad that one of Carmen's servants had cleaned and tended to the self-inflicted wound.

"Two of them are: the girl and the shapeshifter," Carmen said. A bitter look crossed her face as she looked over to the door on her right. "Vivian! What the hell is taking you so long, girl? Get in here!"

Carmen shook her head, far from pleased as she looked back at Marion.

"Which girl? Ash or Jamie?" Marion asked with a frown, watching a woman enter the room. "And what do you mean 'shapeshifter'?"

The woman crossed the room silently, walking with her head down, making sure not to make eye contact with anyone.

"How long does it take you to do as asked?" Carmen snapped, slapping the woman's cheek. "You've been here, what, a few years now, Vivian? I asked you to do one simple thing. How hard can that be?"

"Sorry," Vivian mumbled, causing Carmen to shake her head.

"Is the bedroom made up for Marion?" Carmen asked. Vivian nodded. "Good, now get out of my sight and back to your duties. You come straightaway next time I call you, got it?"

Another nod and Vivian left the room. Carmen shook her head and switched her gaze back to Marion.

"Sorry about that. That stupid girl apparently still hasn't learnt."

"She's been doing everything, though?" Marion asked as Carmen turned back to what she had been doing.

Carmen shrugged, not looking up. "Ever since you sent her over here, she's been doing alright. Well, once she learnt the ropes, which luckily didn't take her too long. But she has days where she forgets or slips up. I don't tell her this, but she's good for the most part."

Marion nodded and they both fell silent for a few minutes.

Carmen looked over her shoulder briefly before looking back at the table and what was in front of her. "Just before, when Vivian came in, you asked about something. What was it?"

"You said 'the shapeshifter and the girl'. Which girl and what shapeshifter?"

Carmen stopped what she was doing again and turned back to look at Marion. "Not the whore, the other one."

Marion nodded slowly, assuming Carmen meant Jamie.

"And the cat, the little blue one, the shapeshifter," Carmen continued.

Marion frowned. This was news to her.

"Alex?" she asked, but Carmen just shrugged. She didn't know his name. "That little bastard. You mean to tell me he was a person this whole time?"

Carmen nodded, going back about her business. She was preparing something.

"Thought you would've known," she said, as Marion shook her head in irritation. "Your castle slut knew."

"Of course, Ash would know," Marion said with annoyance. She sighed. "I swear, I'll kill all of them, even if it kills me too."

"Couldn't help but notice Abel was with them too," Carmen said. "I can't lie. I'm a bit sad he's not dead yet, if I'm being honest here."

"Believe me, I'm working on it," snapped Marion. "As long as we stop them from getting into the City, we should be fine."

"You know I can't get any closer than the warding," Carmen said. "Which also means that your little group will be travelling on foot for a good few miles. But you'll need to stop them soon if you're going to. The cat and the girl aren't at the Road yet and your other friends are quite a way away from them, too."

"They're not together?"

Carmen shook her head. "Just give me one moment and I'll be able to tell you where they've ended up. Some dark magic has been blocking my view. I only know where the cat is because of that damn shadow-stepper. He'll be one of the hardest to get rid of."

"He's been a pain in my side for quite some time," Marion confirmed, the displeasure clear in her tone. She needed to get rid of Shade first, and then she'd focus on Abel and the rest of the group. She looked back to Carmen. "My champion's back in Wonderland. Any chance you can go and get him and bring him back here?"

"I'm sure Heather will be up for a bit of travel. She's been complaining lately about not going anywhere. When she gets back, I'll let her know. After that, we'll try and catch up to your friends."

"Believe me, they're far from being my friends," Marion said bitterly. "I'd rather watch them all burn than be 'friends' with any of them. I must say, I am slightly disappointed that Jamie's managed to survive this long."

"Well, if her and the cat don't get to the City soon, you won't need to worry about that. She won't be surviving," Carmen said. She added a handful of something into the stone bowl in front of her, causing a cloud of gray smoke to rise up. "She's suffering, that's for sure."

"Well, at least one good thing's come out of today."

"Hopefully more than one good thing will come out of the day if I can get past that damn magic barrier," Carmen said. "I don't take too kindly to being blocked out of areas of my own county."

Marion frowned. "Who set up the barrier?"

Carmen shook her head, adding something else into the bowl before looking through the different vials spread out on the table.

"There's a family a few miles out—the Lindells.. They lost their daughter about a year ago. The man of the household, Colin, went and sought out Dusk, wanting his daughter back."

"As in, Dusk the necromancer?" Marion raised one eyebrow.

Carmen nodded. "That's the one. He's still up to his old tricks. He gave Colin a spell that he said would bring his daughter back, but instead it created quite the opposite. Created quite the aggressive banshee. Colin had to go back and get a protection spell off him and now look, the barrier is in place."

"So, what does this barrier do exactly? Apart from not letting you see into the area?" Marion asked, feeling as though she wasn't quite keeping up.

"There's a very powerful dark energy barrier now around that entire field. That's where I think your intruders are camping out," Carmen said distractedly, still unable to find the correct vial she was after. "It's in place to keep the banshee away from the Lindells, but it can take whoever else it wants. It can't physically touch the family, it's been blood-bound. The banshee is pretty docile around that family anyway because it still has a bit of its humanity left. It was an eight-year-old girl turned into an evil creature, but it still recognizes its family house and the people inside it knew as a child."

"Why can't you see through the barrier?"

"Because Dusk deals with very dark magic, dark enough that it can counter mine and block my vision," Carmen said with annoyance as she picked up a small, dark blue vial. "And as I said, I don't take too kindly to people shoving me out. This isn't their land to do so. It's mine and if I wish to block someone, I certainly will. But nobody is going to block me."

"I didn't think this land was yours," Marion said, getting a scowl from Carmen before she went back to her work. "The Wizard seems very much in control of what goes on within Oz."

"Vincent doesn't own anything!" Carmen exclaimed petulantly, leaning back as more smoke rose from the bowl. "I was here first. He took over my land and exiled me out here. You know I've been trying for years to get my land back but all I have to show for it is this barren landscape on the edge of Oz."

Marion shrugged, not saying anything more as Carmen continued on with what she was making, beginning the search for another vial.

"You look exhausted," Carmen noted, glancing over her shoulder at Marion who returned the look briefly. "I'll get Vivian to help you up to your room. Get some rest. I'll finish up here and let you know what I find."

"Are you still able to go and find my champion?" Marion asked as she painfully sat up properly in the chair.

Carmen nodded. "I'll get Heather onto it when she gets back."

"Where is she?"

Carmen shrugged. "She's around somewhere. She didn't trust the servants to get the right stuff she needs, so she went out to get it herself."

Carmen glanced over at the open door. "Vivian! Get in here and help Marion up to her room. Get her anything she needs, whenever she needs it!"

Vivian appeared, head down again as she went over to Marion and helped her stand up.

"Just call if you need anything," Carmen said as Marion and Vivian left the room.

Chapter Ten

Banshees in the Backyard

"What are you doing down here? Where are the others that were with you?"

Ash, Nixx, and Zeke all turned around in surprise on hearing the voice behind them. The man from the house was standing a few yards away, with a shocked look on his face. The sun was almost down, but all three could see the worry etched into the man's face, even in the darkness of the orchard.

"You're not meant to be down here," he said, warily stepping forwards. "You need to leave."

"You need to stay where you are," Nixx warned, pointing at him.

Zeke handed the end of the rope to Ash who took it without question.

"You all need to get out of here now," the man said, taking another step forward, holding his hands out in front of himself in a non-threatening way. "It isn't safe to be down here when it gets dark."

"We've noticed," Nixx said back in annoyance. "And I'm going to warn you again: stay where you are. We know what's down there. You don't need to tell us."

"You don't understand what I'm trying to say," the man tried again, sounding desperate as he stepped forward once again.

Just as he went to step forward for the fourth time, a wall of flames suddenly spread out across the man's path, forcing him to back up in alarm.

"He told you to stay back. So, if I were you, I'd stay back," Zeke threatened.

Ash and Nixx both looked at Zeke as he repositioned himself, crossing his arms across his chest.

The man moved backwards again, and Zeke stared him down, not saying a word. The wall of flames had spread so fast there was no way the man was getting through to them now.

Ash went back to her job of keeping a watch on the burrow, still holding the rope in case something happened and the others needed a way out.

Nixx frowned at Zeke, but it was obvious he wasn't about to move. "Did you do that?"

Zeke switched his gaze to him as the man on the other side of the burning wall tried to see if there was a way around. "He wasn't listening to you."

Nixx shook his head. "Just don't burn down the whole orchard while we're here."

Zeke shrugged, uncrossing his arms and putting his hands in his pockets instead. "Outta my control."

Nixx shook his head again, turning his focus back to the man who'd finally stopped where he was, seeing there was no way around.

"All of you need to get out of here before it's too late," the man said, speaking directly to Nixx, not wanting to acknowledge Zeke. "I know you all think you know what's going on here, but you don't."

"We know you're harboring banshees in your backyard," Zeke input, making the man and Nixx look to him.

"It's not that simple!" the man snapped. "Nothing's as simple as you think!"

Zeke rolled his eyes but didn't say another word.

"Then explain it to us," Nixx said, crossing his arms this time, trying to take control of the situation. "If you're so sure we don't know what's going on, then tell us. We've got all night."

"At this rate, none of us have all night," the man said with a shake of his head. "We've only got a few minutes until the sun fully goes down. We have to leave and get up to the house, otherwise we're all gone."

"Well, our guys are already down in that burrow, so you'd better start explaining this now. No one leaves this orchard until we're told exactly what's going on."

"At this rate, we're all gonna burn alive," Zeke input helpfully. "He doesn't seem to want to talk about whatever's going on, and that fire isn't slowing down any time soon."

"Well, maybe you should have thought about that before you started it," Nixx scolded. He shook his head at Zeke's shrug and looked back at the man on the other side of the flames. "Are you going explain what the hell's going on?"

The man glanced at Zeke before looking at Nixx and, again, talking directly to him. "Yes, there are banshees down there," he began.

Zeke was about to say something, but Nixx signaled for him to keep his mouth shut for a few minutes.

"But there's one of them you can't kill, please," the man continued. "One of those banshees is my daughter. She hasn't caused any harm to anyone. She's bound, you see, so she won't hurt us. It's the other ones that need to be killed but we haven't had the courage to go down there ourselves or ask anyone to help us get rid of them."

"Wait, did you just say there's more than one down there?" Zeke suddenly spoke up.

The man nodded. "There are four, including my daughter. For some reason, they all banded together here."

Nixx and Zeke exchanged looks.

"Someone else needs to go down there and find the others," Nixx said, making Zeke nod. "If we're dealing with four, we've got a very serious problem."

Zeke gave another nod. "Alright, I'll go down and find them."

"Be careful," the man said. The flames were still burning but were now slowly dying down in front of him. "And please, don't kill my daughter. I can't lose her again."

Zeke looked him over briefly, before turning away. "No promises."

"If we're dealing with more than just the one, how the hell are we going to pull this off?" Abel asked in a harsh whisper.

There was no other sound within the dark depths of the burrow. Matt shook his head as he thought.

"I don't know," he responded eventually, also keeping his voice down. "We thought there was only one but there's definitely more than that."

"How many are we dealing with?" Chris asked, really wishing they had a light of some sort. He didn't particularly like wandering around in the dark, especially when dangerous creatures lurked in the vicinity.

Matt shook his head again, straining to hear something, anything, as he flinched. "No idea, but it's more than the one we originally came down here for."

Chris and Abel exchanged looks before returning their gazes to what was in front of them, not that they could see much. Chris frowned as some of the ground and area behind him seemed to gain a bit of light. He turned around to see someone headed their way, holding what seemed to be a small flame above their left hand.

Matt turned around as well, having seen the gradual light making its way towards them.

"You're dealing with four," Zeke said as he came to a halt next to Chris. His voice was low, so it didn't echo off the walls. "Which, in short, means we're fucked if we don't get out of here right now."

"Sun gone down?" Matt asked. Zeke nodded and Matt nodded in return, before turning his focus back to the way they'd been heading. "Alright, let's turn back then. Let the owners of the house deal with this shit. I'm not risking any of us for four banshees."

The corridor in front of them split off three ways and Chris was glad they weren't going any further. At least now with Zeke's light, they could see what was actually down here and awaiting them.

Matt turned to head back the way they'd originally come, but an ear-piercing scream rang out from one of the corridors, making everyone halt in their tracks. It sounded like the banshees were awake for the night.

"Alright, we need to move, now," Matt instructed, not bothering to keep his voice down anymore. "Everyone head back the way we came, don't veer off or lose sight of anyone. We get out of here and we do it now."

Everyone did as told, not waiting to be told twice. Another scream sounded, echoing around the burrow, followed by another two screams. Chris was sure the first one was louder this time.

Matt stayed at the back of the group with Gates while Chris, Abel, and Zeke quickly headed in the direction of the burrow's entrance. They were a lot further in than Chris had realized.

"Is that getting closer?" Abel called over his shoulder to Matt.

Matt didn't say a word as two screams sounded out, one of them getting dangerously close as Chris and Zeke came to a very sudden halt, Abel nearly running into them. Matt and Gates both slowed down, making sure they weren't about to run into their companions.

"This wasn't here before, we've gone the wrong way," Chris said as the burrow fell silent.

It was a dead end. The dirt wall stopped them all in their tracks, and there was no way to go but back the way they'd just come from, towards the banshees.

Matt shook his head, a confused look on his face as they faced him.

"No, this is the right way," he said. "We didn't veer off the path, we went straight and didn't turn at all. This isn't right, something's wrong here."

Seeing Matt confused certainly didn't make Chris feel any better. If he didn't know what was going on, then there was definitely something wrong.

"I literally just came down here less than five minutes ago," Zeke said with a shake of his head.

"Well, what do we do?" Abel asked as Zeke started inspecting the wall to see if there was any way through or around it.

Matt shook his head, looking down the length of the wall and back as he tried to come up with a solution or even an explanation. "I don't know."

"Well, you'd better figure something out soon or we're all gonna die down here."

A frown crossed Matt's face. He looked around, back the way they'd come, before looking back at the others again. "Is it just me, or has it gotten really quiet?"

That made everyone look around as panic started to set in. Even Matt was looking worried.

A sudden loud crash sounded from the way they'd come, causing everyone to look back down into the darkness. There was still a bit of light, thanks to Zeke, but not enough to see what was going on.

"Matt, we need to move," Zeke said, his voice down. "We can't stay down here."

Matt didn't even glance back, keeping his focus on what was headed their way.

"Alright, everyone back up," he instructed, taking a few steps back. Gates didn't move from his place a few paces away.

"We can't go any further back, we'll hit the wall," Chris said as Zeke moved back as instructed until his back was against the wall.

"That's the plan," Matt said, looking over his shoulder as Gates kept a cautious watch as another crash was heard. He flinched. "It's closer than we thought."

Before anyone could say another word, a scream echoed off the dirt walls and shook the ground slightly, with a second scream following moments later.

Gates suddenly put his hands out and a clear, glass-looking barrier appeared in front of him. Something moving very quickly hit the barrier hard, forcing Gates back a step, but the barrier stayed in place.

"I can't keep this up for long against four of them," Gates said, dropping his hands. The barrier disappeared just as quickly as it had appeared. He readjusted how he was standing, trying to get a bit more of a balanced stance so he wouldn't be easily knocked over. "Just that one was enough to knock me back and we don't where the others are."

Sensing something, he quickly put his hands back out in front of him and the barrier appeared again. Moments later, something hit it hard again before disappearing from sight. Gates looked at Matt briefly, seeing that he was trying to figure out the best way to go about this.

"Alright, we've got to find where we came in," Matt spoke up as something hit Gates's barrier again. Gates dug his heels in as he got pushed back slightly by the force.

"But this was definitely where it was," Mat continued. "We never veered off, so I don't understand where this wall's come from."

"Maybe wonder about that later, Matt," Gates said through his teeth as he was pushed back more when his barrier was hit again. "We can't afford to think right now, except for how to get out of here."

Matt abandoned his post a pace behind Gates, walking the few yards back to where Chris, Abel, and Zeke were. Zeke still had his back against the wall. Matt stopped in front of the wall and placed his hands against it to try and find a way through.

"Matt, there's no way we're getting through that wall," Chris said, hearing another, harder, hit smash against the barrier.

Gates wasn't going to be able to hold them off for much longer. It now made sense to Chris why Matt had insisted on fetching both Gates and Zeke from Wonderland, and he was glad he had.

"There's got to be a way," Matt insisted.

"Matt, we seriously don't have time for this," Gates stressed, his tone very urgent.

They all looked over, watching something hard hit the barrier but not disappearing this time. It was one of the banshees, just like everyone had assumed.

Chris had never seen a banshee before, and now he was wishing he never had. It was one of the worst things he'd seen in his life, and that was saying something.

The banshee looked humanoid, but not quite fully human. It was twisted, in a way. It probably wouldn't have been so bad if it weren't for the sharp teeth, fangs, and long claws. Seen up this close, it was the stuff of nightmares.

This particular banshee had a feminine look to it. It had long, flowing hair and was levitating a couple of feet above the ground. It reminded Chris a little bit of what people depicted vampires to be in some horror movies. Maybe they were from the same creature family tree?

The banshee screamed, making everyone flinch as it began pushing against the barrier. Gates dug his heels in again to try and stop it breaking through. If he faltered, the barrier would too, and then they were all gone.

Matt quickly turned back to the wall as the banshee continued to force itself against the barrier. Chris could see Gates slowly slipping back towards them, all the while trying to keep the barrier intact.

"We can't stay here," Abel said. "Matt, we have to get around the banshee and keep going."

"How?" Matt snapped, looking to him now as Gates pushed hard against the force of the banshee, managing to somehow force it back a pace or so. "Abel, we're stuck, we don't have anywhere to go because of this wall."

"You've still got the blade," Chris noted. "Can we use that somehow?"

He watched Matt think while Gates was still occupied with the banshee. It was a constant battle to keep his ground and keep the banshee back.

"Maybe," Matt said, still thinking as he spoke. "If we can distract it, we might be able to."

"How are we going to do that?" Abel asked, making Matt shrug.

"You'd better figure it out pretty damn soon," Gates remarked, slipping back more, the dirt under his feet shifting with him.

Another scream sounded out, this time not from the banshee that was pushing against the barrier.

Chris looked at Matt with worry as he thought about how they could distract the banshee.

"Anything?" he asked.

Matt shook his head. He was clueless.

Chris sighed. This was it, the end of the five of them. It certainly wasn't the way that Chris wanted to go out.

A second banshee hit the barrier, joining the first one in pushing against it. Gates strained harder to keep his footing against the doubled force.

This banshee looked a lot like the first one, apart from a few minor details. This one wasn't quite as terrifying as the first, but it looked a lot older. It had shorter hair, with a grey tinge to it, and its fangs were not as long.

Chris was pretty sure by now that banshees were part of the vampire family.

"Matt, if we don't do something now, we're all gonna die," Gates stressed, slipping back further as the banshees pushed against the barrier as a single unit. "This isn't gonna hold forever."

The look on Matt's face suddenly changed as he thought of something. He looked at Gates.

"I need you to keep them occupied for just a few more minutes," he said.

Gates growled in annoyance as a third banshee joined them. It was nearly identical to the first one.

"I don't think I can," Gates said through his teeth.

"Well, you're going to have to."

With that, Matt grabbed Zeke and was gone, sending the other three into darkness.

CHAPTER ELEVEN

Locations

"Hey, you still with me?"

Alex looked at Jamie from where they were currently sitting on the Yellow Brick Road. They'd made it about an hour ago and it was now dark. Alex had been staring up at the moon for the past ten minutes. It was a nice view from here.

Jamie nodded tiredly. She'd been leaning against him and hadn't said anything all day since they'd left. Alex was just hoping she was going to be alright.

Were they meant to keep walking towards the City or just wait? Matt had said they'd catch up before it got dark, but it had been dark for about half an hour now and no one else had shown up.

Alex didn't even know which way the City was. Was it left, or was it right? Which way had Matt said.

"Maybe we should continue on," Alex said, feeling like he was speaking to himself for the most part, but he didn't mind. "They'll all catch up eventually. I'm sure they're not far off now."

He was trying to convince himself more than he was trying to convince Jamie of that fact.

Alex sighed and Jamie moved off him as he got to his feet, planning on continuing to make their way to the City. He was determined to make it one way or another, with or without Matt.

He helped Jamie up before pausing when he heard a growl. It sounded close and it made him uncomfortable.

Alex shifted his weight, making sure he still had a good hold on Jamie and was still supporting her, when something appeared out of the darkness.

The light from the moon illuminated a medium-sized, vicious-looking black dog standing on the edge of the grass and the Road, growling as it stared at them.

Alex stayed exactly where he was, not daring to move even slightly. The dog suddenly went for him, making him step back in fear.

He frowned as the dog knocked into what looked like thin air. Something was stopping it from getting the two travelers.

The dog growled louder and started pacing up and down, its gaze fixed on Alex the entire time. Alex cautiously put his hand out in front of him, seeing a bit of a shimmer as his hand reached the edge of the road.

There was what seemed to be a magical barrier in place, and he hadn't even known.

He was sure that it hadn't been there when they'd stepped onto the Road in the daylight. Maybe it was something that was in place during the dark hours, stopping anything from the outside getting in.

Alex felt his heart sink a bit. If this dog couldn't get in, did that mean that neither could the rest of their small group? Did it stop everything or just the evil that lurked in the fields during the night?

Did it mean they couldn't get off the Road until the morning? Not that he wanted to.

"I'm sure Matt knows what he's doing," Alex said, beginning to walk and forcing Jamie to walk as well. The black dog continued to stalk them on the other side of the Road, watching their every move. "Either way we'll see them once the sun comes up. It's either that or we just continue on towards the City and they'll meet us there."

"Ash, I need the rope."

Ash jumped and turned to seeing Matt looking at her, Zeke beside him. Nixx looked over from where he was, the wall of flames still there but slowly dying out. It had spread a bit further than when Zeke had originally caused it.

"What's going on?" Nixx asked, ignoring the man who still couldn't get to them.

"We've run into a problem," Matt said. "I've just got to test something before we get back down there."

"What's happened?" the man asked.

Matt ignored him and took the end of the rope from Ash who just handed it to him, not saying a word. He'd once again startled her, and she wasn't impressed.

Matt indicated for Zeke to go back down the rope into the burrow. He had a source of light, so he was the best option for now.

"Has anyone been hurt?" Nixx asked.

Matt kept a firm hold on the rope as he lowered Zeke down. He glanced over his shoulder as Zeke disappeared back down the hole.

"Not yet," Matt said. He looked down into the burrow. "Zeke, I need you to see where you are and when you're ready to come back up just let me know."

Matt stayed where he was, all of them staying silent as they waited. A few minutes passed before Matt felt a pull on the other end of the rope. Without a word he began hauling Zeke back up.

"Nothing," Zeke said as Matt helped him up, grabbing his hand and hauling him out. "About five yards and then a wall. We've been blocked off."

Matt swore to himself as Zeke dusted himself off.

"What's happened?" Nixx asked seriously, still near the man on the other side of the flames.

Zeke looked at him while Matt was off in his own world, thinking.

"We were backtracking, got cut off by a wall that wasn't there before," he explained. "The others are still down there."

"Why didn't you just shadow-step them out?" Ash asked as Matt handed the rope back to her.

"Because I only just managed to get us out of there," Matt said. "There's some serious dark energy down there and it's stopping my shadow-stepping. It's interfering and almost like it's sapping my ability."

Ash frowned. "I didn't know that was possible."

"Neither did I, but it's happening. I don't know if it's just me or everyone," Matt said, sounding very tired. "That took a hell of a lot out of me, and I've still got to get back in there."

"Well, what do you propose to do?" Nixx asked.

He could see just how drained Matt already was from that small shadow-step. Matt switched his gaze to the man on the other side of the flames.

"You're Colin, right?" he asked, making the man nod. "What does your daughter look like?"

"You don't need to worry about her, it's the others you need to watch for."

"Yeah, well right now there are three men down that damn burrow about to be killed because of this," Matt snapped. Colin looked down briefly before making himself meet Matt's gaze again. "You can't keep banshees here. Three of them are trying to get to the others and they need to be stopped. Which one's your damn daughter?"

"Why do you need to know?" Colin asked seriously.

"Because that's the reason the others are here," Matt said harshly. "You bound your daughter when she was brought back as a banshee. Others sense it and they come to protect it until they die. Not to mention the amount of dark magic that's been used in this area. Banshees are attracted to dark magic rifts and to top this off they're protecting a bound one. Even if it was created via dark magic, it's still a banshee, and it will break free of the bond once it's strong enough."

Colin looked at Matt for a bit longer before sighing, giving in.

"Alright," he said. "She's right at the back of the burrow. When you come to the three separate ways, you take the far left one. After that there are a few more turns but you'll find her at the back of the burrow. You do what you have to in order to stop this once and for all. I don't plan on having anyone else hurt."

Matt nodded, satisfied with the answer. He looked at Zeke. "Let's go."

"Did you hear that?" Alex said.

He stopped, looking around in the dark. He'd heard something and he wasn't sure what it was. It had sounded like someone else was on the Road with them, but he wasn't too sure. The black dog was still stalking its way down the grass on the edge of the Road, coming to a stop as Alex did.

"I'm sure if it was important, it'll happen again."

He began walking again, hoping that he'd imagined the sound or that it was nothing. It would be just his luck to run into something terrible on the Road. The sound came again, causing Alex to halt in his tracks once more.

He definitely hadn't imagined it this time.

"Is someone there?" he called, looking behind, then back to the front. He wasn't about to take any chances.

"You seem to have a follower."

Alex jumped upon hearing the voice. It was a bit unsettling. He looked behind himself again before returning his gaze to the front. Someone was in front of him now, making him jump again.

"Who are you?" Alex asked straight out.

Running into strangers in the middle of the night in the dark wasn't something he'd planned on doing.

An area of bright white light lit up the Road between the figure and Alex. It was so bright Alex had to shield his eyes. Jamie stayed against him, too exhausted to be fazed by anything anymore. Alex couldn't see a thing, but he knew whoever was in front of him was a man.

"The dog is a death omen," the man said. "Means someone hasn't got much time left, twenty-four hours at the most. It won't go away until the dawn."

"Who are you?" Alex tried again, still shielding his eyes as he strained to see who was in front of him.

"Someone who can help."

CHAPTER TWELVE

Backs Against the Wall

Gates pushed back as hard as he could against the banshees, but none of them let up or shifted in the slightest. He was pushed back again and again, unable to dig his heels into the ground anymore, until he was dangerously close to where Chris and Abel stood with their backs against the wall.

"What are we going to do if Matt doesn't come back in time?" Chris asked, not caring which of his companions was going to answer him.

"We die," Gates managed to say as he, once again, used all his strength to hold the three banshees at bay. "I can't keep this up much longer. They're going to break it."

"Break what?" asked Chris, pushing himself back against the wall more in the hope that it would somehow protect him as Gates was continually pushed back.

"The barrier!" Gates snapped, slipping back again. The force on the other side was too much for him. "What else would I be talking about?"

Chris shrugged and looked at Abel, who just shrugged back at him. "Breaking your spirit?"

"I could use a bit of help, you know," Gates continued, choosing to ignore the comment and pushing against the banshees again. "Instead of just standing there, how about you two make yourselves useful?"

"What do you want us to do?" Abel asked.

"Just ... I don't know, do something!" Gates exclaimed, looking very worn out. The barrier flickered ever so slightly. Gates was faltering. "I don't care what you do, just do something!"

"I hate to be the bearer of bad news," Abel said. "But Chris and I don't know how to control our abilities yet."

"Well, you'd better learn real fuckin' quick."

Abel and Chris looked at each other again, before looking at Gates again. Both men had the same expression and neither knew what to do.

Gates shouted in annoyance, slipping back until there wasn't much distance between them now. "Today would be nice, guys!"

"Alright, we have to do something," Chris said, tearing his gaze away from Gates as one of the banshees screamed, causing the other two to join in.

"What? How are we going to do anything?" Abel exclaimed. "We don't know what triggers our abilities!"

Chris looked around, trying to quickly think of how they could help out. "Yours seems to work when you get mad. So, I mean ... get mad?"

"How am I meant to do that?" Abel snapped.

Chris felt the darkness shift and move, like he'd felt back in Wonderland when Abel was angry.

"Whatever you're doing, keep it up," Gates said, managing to move a step forward and somehow push the banshees back.

The dark feeling suddenly disappeared, and Gates was pushed back the step he'd managed to gain.

Abel looked at Chris. "I can't. I've got nothing to be mad about."

"You just had it!" Chris said. "Can't you be mad that we're going to die?"

"Well, you could always try yours."

"I don't know how I did it the first time."

"Then figure it out!" Gates suddenly shouted, slipping further with the barrier flickering again. "Because I'm about to lose it. And we're about to die."

Abel looked at Chris. "You just ... just try!" he said, starting to sound desperate.

"You try too, then. This is a team effort, Abel."

"Both of you shut the fuck up and do something," Gates snapped, slipping again. His back foot was nearly at the wall. "One more push like that and I'm gone. We're all gone."

Chris nodded, trying to psych himself up to get his ability to work. He still had no idea how he'd done it when the doctor had been coming for them. It had been purely a self-defense act.

But now was not really any different, he thought. Without another thought, Chris put his hand out in front of him, trying to get something to happen. When nothing happened, he shook his head, trying to figure out what was going on.

"Anything?" he asked Abel.

Abel shook his head too, also clearly unable to tap into his ability.

"You're doing real great, guys," Gates said through his teeth. His foot slipped back and finally hit the wall. "Keep up the hard work!"

"We're trying!" Abel snapped back, and Chris felt the darkness move again. "Maybe if you gave us a few seconds, we could figure this shit out!"

"We don't have a few seconds!"

"Then, I guess we're all gonna die then, right?"

Gates glanced over his shoulder at them, the barrier flickering again as he tried to readjust his position so he didn't get knocked off balance. He was already nearly against the wall with them.

"Well, I could literally leave you two down here," he said, using all his strength to try and move the banshees. "I don't have to have this barrier up. If you'd prefer, I can easily shield myself and leave you both down here to die."

"Well, you kind of need us," Chris said, feeling the oppressive dark disappear again as Abel calmed down.

"Not really," Gates said.

With one last effort, Gates shoved against the force from the banshees and the barrier flickered again.

Chris was sure he could see a few cracks in it now, like cracks in a glass windowpane. Abel moved back, making sure his back was definitely against the wall, when the banshees suddenly heaved hard against the barrier, sending Gates back into the wall.

The barrier disappeared.

Without a second's hesitation, Gates had his hands back up, his back fully against the wall now as the barrier managed to flicker back to life in front of the three of them. The banshees didn't waste any time. Within a second of the barrier being back, they were on top of them again.

"What now?" Chris asked urgently.

Gates was trying his hardest to keep the barrier in front of them. There wasn't even a couple of feet of space in between them and the banshees now.

"I don't know!" Gates yelled. "Either Matt hurries up or the barrier fails. Depends which comes first. Goddamn it!"

One of the banshees suddenly turned and disappeared, leaving just the two. But, before any of them could speak, the banshee returned, banging hard into the barrier before disappearing again.

"They're gonna break it," Gates said, sounding strained as he tried to extend his arms to give them a bit more space.

"What happens if it breaks?" Abel asked, never taking his eyes off the banshees as the same one came back, bouncing off the barrier and disappearing again. "Besides the obvious, that we die."

"I don't know, it hasn't ever happened before," Gates stressed, once again trying to get them more space. "They're trying to wear me down and, believe me, it's working. I really can't keep this up much longer."

The barrier flickered again, this time a lot more and for longer than it previously had. The other two banshees suddenly took off, disappearing back into the darkness. In less than a second, one of them hit the barrier hard again.

Gates suddenly collapsed to his knees and the barrier was gone as he finally gave in.

Chris and Abel exchanged looks, as all three banshees screamed from the darkness.

"You've got to get up," Chris said urgently, keeping his voice down as another scream rang out getting closer. "Gates, you've got to get up."

Gates shook his head, staying on his knees with his head down and hands flat on the ground. His whole body was shaking from the effort of holding the banshees off.

"I can't," he managed to say.

"If you don't, we're all gonna die," Abel stressed.

Gates stayed silent, unable to say anything in his exhaustion. Chris and Abel exchanged looks, knowing it was only a matter of time before the banshees came back at them.

Chris looked down at Gates, deciding in that split second what to do. He grabbed Gates and hauled him to his feet. Gates instinctively put his hands back up and the barrier flickered weakly back to life. It was very damaged, and it was clear it wouldn't hold for long.

Gates moved forwards unsteadily, taking a few steps to get some space back between them and the wall.

Suddenly, a banshee was up against the barrier again, causing it to flicker, but it managed to hold. Then, a second banshee was beside its companion, also pushing against the barrier. The third was only moments behind.

"You've just got to hold it a bit longer," Chris said, really wishing he knew how to use his ability so he could help. It was frustrating not being able to be useful in some capacity.

"That's the plan," Gates managed to wheeze, using all his strength to hold the banshees back as the barrier continuously flickered and another crack appeared in it. "When this falters, just run."

"You'll be coming too, right?" Abel asked.

Gates slipped back a pace again. He'd be against the wall again within moments.

Gates stayed silent, looking to his right as he thought. Chris could see his mind ticking over his options before he glanced back at Chris and Abel.

"When I say go, you go," he instructed, the tiredness evident in his voice. "You go find Matt and you don't stop."

"Gates, we're not about to go anywhere. We're in this together," Chris said with a frown. "We go down together or not at all."

Gates glanced at him before turning his gaze back to the immediate threat in front of him. Very quickly, he moved his right hand out to his side. The barrier flickered and reluctantly extended around to the side of the burrow, giving them a bit more space.

Chris could see how hard Gates was now trying to stop the banshees, having used what he had left to give him and Abel a bit of protection on their way out. He was shaking and the barrier was shimmering from the effort.

"Go," Gates said. "I've got your back for as long as I can see you, as far as it can reach. Find Matt and finish this."

"Can't you come with us?" Abel said.

Chris and Abel carefully moved away from the wall.

Gates swore to himself. "OK, fine, just move. I'll do the rest."

CHAPTER THIRTEEN

Help

The white light continued to blind Alex. He didn't know what was going on.

The black dog growled, not liking the light either. It suddenly took off, disappearing into the night. The light faded and Alex cautiously removed his hand from where it had been shielding his eyes.

"What's going on?" Alex asked, blinking to try to get his eyes to adjust to the darkness. He'd been fine until this suspicious man had shown up out of nowhere and blinded him. "Who *are* you?"

The man moved forwards into a beam of moonlight illuminating the Road. Alex took a step back, moving Jamie with him. He wasn't about to take any chances with strangers in a strange place.

"Look, I'm not going to hurt you," the man said, holding his hands out in front of him in a non-threatening manner. "My name's Jacob. I'm from the Emerald City. I work for the Wizard."

"How do I know you're not lying to me?" Alex asked suspiciously, not liking this one bit. "How do I know you don't work for the enemy? How do I know you don't work for *her*."

Jacob moved to get something out of his pocket, causing Alex to step back again. Jacob just looked at him for a few seconds before continuing with what he was doing. He pulled something out of his pocket and threw it so it landed in front of Alex.

"Just look at it."

Alex reluctantly bent down and grabbed the item off the ground, trying to keep his gaze on Jacob the entire time. Jamie kept hold of Alex's arm as he looked at what had been thrown to him.

It was an ID card, confirming what Jacob had said. The pale moonlight only just allowed Alex to see what was written on it. The card had Jacob's picture, a number near it, and his occupation. It said he was from the Emerald City and did, indeed, work for the Wizard. Alex wasn't sure what an 'ability instructor' was.

"Alright, you've got my attention," Alex said, tossing Jacob's ID back to him. "What are you doing out here?"

"We're alerted whenever someone's on the Road," Jacob explained, putting his ID back in his pocket. "No one else was available at this time of night, so I've been sent out to see what's going on. Not many people use the Road much anymore."

Alex gave a nod to indicate he was keeping up and he readjusted his grip on Jamie, who was still leaning against him.

"But now, I've got to ask who you are," Jacob continued. "And why the Death Omen was following you. He isn't seen much anymore."

"I'm Alex. This is Jamie," Alex introduced them both. "We've come in from Wonderland. Jamie's hurt and we're heading to the City to get her some help. We have others with us, but I don't know where they've gotten to. We were at a homestead, but I don't know where that is now."

Jacob nodded. "Have either of you got any ID on you?"

Alex shook his head, and he saw Jacob thinking.

"We never had that system in Wonderland," Alex explained. "The Queen didn't care who was who. She knew who she wanted to know."

"Alright, well, we can fix that when we get back to the City," Jacob said. "Everyone has to have an ID before they enter the City, but the Wizard will sort all that out for you and your friends. How many of you are there?"

Alex did a quick count, making sure he didn't miss anyone. "Nine, including me and Jamie."

"OK, we'll go to the City and I'll inform the Wizard what's going on."

"How are you going to get us there? It's days away, isn't it?" Alex said with a hint of confusion. His voice suddenly rose in excitement. "Wait, how did you get here? You just appeared out of nowhere. Oh my God, do you shadow-step, too?"

Jacob frowned. "Ah, no, sorry to disappoint. I actually haven't heard of that ability before."

"Really? You haven't heard of shadow-stepping?" Alex exclaimed. "Oh, it's really cool. One of the guys that's in our group does it and, man, is it handy. Shame he can't shadow-step us to the City or else we'd be there by now. It's the warding that's stopping him, so he says."

Jacob nodded. "He's not lying. The warding works against pretty well everyone. It keeps the evil out, but it also stops anyone from using their abilities to get to the City. Only those who work under the Wizard can get through it with abilities. I don't know much about how it works, but that's what happens."

Alex nodded slowly as everything started to make sense. "So, you can get through the warding?"

Jacob nodded and Alex's face lit up with a grin.

"We'll get you into the City and to the Wizard. Once the day breaks, we'll send someone out for your friends. Then we'll sort everything else out. Sound good?"

"Sounds excellent!" Alex exclaimed cheerfully. "So, how does this work?"

Jacob smiled, moved forwards, and stopped directly in front of him. He held his hands out to his sides, palms facing down. Alex shielded his eyes as the bright white light returned and a circle appeared around the three of them.

A minute or two passed before the white light faded, and Alex could see again. He blinked a few times, looking around to see where they were.

They were on the sidewalk of an empty street. Some streetlights were on, and Alex could see the houses and buildings around them. It was nice.

There was no one out and about at this time of night, even though Alex didn't actually know what time it was.

"Welcome to the Emerald City," Jacob said, spreading his hands out to his sides. "It looks a lot better during the daylight, believe me."

Alex smiled, getting a smile back from Jacob.

Jacob turned to face the building they were standing in front of and fished around in his pocket. He produced his ID card and held it upside down under something on the door. A light scanned across it and the door clicked open as Jacob put his ID back in his pocket.

"A lot of benefits to working for the Wizard," he said, opening the door and indicating for Alex to take Jamie inside. "ID card gets you in anywhere. He employs a few people, mainly safety and whatnot, which is why we can get into any building or house in the City."

Alex nodded as Jacob followed them in, shutting the door after himself. It locked behind them and Jacob moved past them, gesturing for the two of them to follow him as he headed off down the corridor.

Alex quickly started walking after him, supporting Jamie the entire way. He slowed down when he realized she was struggling to keep up.

"Where are we going?" he called, his voice echoing off the walls.

"We're off to see the Wizard!" Jacob said, laughing at his own joke. Alex didn't get it. "This corridor leads into the castle. Bit of a back entrance, if you'd like. Only those who work for the Wizard can access it, so we won't be running into any … unwanted guests."

"Right…"

"Look, all you need to know now is that everything is going to be sorted out by morning," Jacob said. Alex saw a door up ahead. "He should still be awake at this hour. Most times you can get in to see him any time of the day or night. We'll get Jamie the help she needs, and then we'll deal with the rest in the morning."

Alex stayed silent as Jacob reached the door, scanning his ID again before opening the door. A light streamed through, once more blinding Alex. It wasn't as bright as the light Jacob had produced earlier on, and it was clearly from some other source. It certainly wasn't candlelight, but it was very bright.

Alex cautiously went in, being careful when maneuvering Jamie through the doorway. Jacob followed and shut the door once he was inside.

They were in a large room and the light made Alex blink a few times to try to get his eyes to readjust. He looked up at something attached to the ceiling that was holding the light. He frowned. He'd never seen that before. He was used to candles and dull candlelight.

"It's called a light fitting," Jacob explained, hands in his pockets as he looked up at what had caught Alex's attention. "We've got electricity here."

Alex was mesmerized but he managed to tear his gaze away from the shining light and look at Jacob. "Electricity?"

Jacob nodded, watching Alex look around the large room. There were a few more 'light fittings' around the room, making it quite bright so Alex could see everything clearly. There seemed to be a lot of doors here, too.

"The Wizard should be around somewhere," Jacob said, watching Alex marvel at the room and its fancy technology. "Wait here for a few minutes and I'll see what I can do. Take a seat and the Wizard shall see you shortly."

Jacob headed over to a door on his left, scanned his ID, and stepped through the doorway. The door closed and locked behind him.

Alex sighed, looking around some more. There were some sofas placed around the open space, and a table with chairs sat right in the middle of the room.

Alex slowly moved Jamie over to the closest sofa and carefully sat her down before joining her.

"Well, we made it," he said quietly as Jamie leaned against him. "Don't know how, but we did."

He sighed, hoping they weren't going to be kept waiting too long.

Chapter Fourteen

End of the Line

"So, your cat and the girl made it to the City."

Marion looked up and glared at Carmen, who leaned against the door frame with her arms crossed. Marion sighed and shut the book she'd been reading. She'd been unable to sleep even though she was exhausted.

"Well, isn't that just wonderful," she said bitterly. It was late and she was starting to really feel it now. "How did they get there in such a short time?"

"Our good friend Vincent sent someone out. The cat and the girl were on the Road," Carmen said, watching Marion carelessly throw the book onto the bedside table. "I still can't see the others, though. They must still be at the homestead and within the barrier. Once they leave there, I'll be able to find them."

"What are you going to do when you find them?" Marion asked, wincing as she shifted her position in the bed. She planned on getting a bit of sleep once she had her answer.

Carmen shrugged and pushed away from the door frame. She came into the bedroom and sat on one of the chairs.

"They'll probably head to the Road, get past the warding, and then into the City," she said, inspecting her painted nails as she spoke. "So, as soon as they're in my vision, I'll send a couple of people out. Maybe your champion too. Heather's on her way back now, actually."

"Hunter will take care of them," Marion said with a wave of her hand. "Seeing as only a few of them know how to use their abilities. For the most part they can't. They're useless."

A slight scowl appeared on Carmen's face. "Yes, well, some of us aren't lucky enough to have abilities, hence why we become witches."

"Nothing I can do about it," Marion said with a careless shrug. "I don't control the world and what it does."

Carmen rolled her eyes, crossed her arms, and leaned back in the chair.

"I plan on sending your champion out with a few of my people. I'm down on men at the moment, due to one reason or another," she continued. "I'm sure Heather would like to get out too, see what your boys can do."

"Well, just make sure something's done about them," Marion said, dismissing Carmen with a wave of her hand.

Matt looked around. Zeke stood next to him, producing some light so they could see.

"He said the far left," Zeke said, his voice down but echoing slightly. "So, I guess we go to the far left."

Matt nodded. There wasn't a sound within the burrow, which struck him as a bit odd. He was hoping the other three were doing alright without them. They'd heard the banshees scream a few times, but that seemed to have stopped about five minutes ago. The silence was making both men uncomfortable.

Matt began heading off to his left with Zeke following along. They were about to step into the tunnel when they both stopped, having heard a noise behind them.

"You hear that?" Zeke asked quietly.

Matt nodded and they both looked back at where the noise had come from. He and Zeke exchanged looks as the noise grew louder. Someone was headed their way at a quick pace.

Abel suddenly came to a halt, nearly running straight into Matt, with Chris not far behind.

"Where's Gates?" Matt asked, hearing a scream ring out.

That wasn't good and it was very close.

Before either of them could answer, Gates appeared, knocking into Chris as he deflected an oncoming banshee, somehow sending it back a few paces.

Matt could see the barrier flickering from the previous damage. There were more cracks in it than he remembered from when they'd been down here earlier. It looked like it would shatter like glass if it took any more hits.

"I'm right here, keep moving," Gates said, the barrier disappearing briefly before flickering back on.

He kept his back to them as they quickly moved off, Matt in the lead with Zeke keeping the light going so they could see where they were walking. Gates glanced over his shoulder as he backed up before turning his full attention to the banshees again, which were beginning to show signs of being irritated with his constant deflection.

"What are we doing?" Chris asked as he caught up to Matt who was walking at a fast pace, almost about to break into a run.

"We're going to the back and we're killing the girl," Matt said, hearing Gates get hit again. "We going to stop this once and for all. We've been down here too long already."

"How's killing the girl going to stop the other banshees?" Abel asked.

Gates swore to himself as his barrier was hit once more. He'd taken quite the beating over the last half hour or so.

"She's the reason they're congregating here," Matt explained, taking a turn as the corridor curved. "And more will come if we don't kill her. They're drawn to dark magic, and they protect bound banshees if they're in the same area. Kill the girl and they'll disperse. Simple. Kill the reason and they go back into hibernation until they need to come out again. They'll be back to being rare sightings."

Abel nodded. Chris went to say something but was interrupted as a noise behind them forced them to stop.

"Guys, keep moving," Gates shouted, back to his original stance and trying to get the banshee to back off. He was using all he had to keep this one at bay and the other two were nowhere to be seen. "We're about to be in some serious trouble."

Before he could say anything more, the banshee disappeared, came back fast, and smashed into the barrier. The force of the blow knocked Gates flat onto his back. He managed to react quickly, keeping the barrier above himself as he put his left hand out and a second barrier flickered into life in front of the others.

"I'll keep this one here. You guys keep going," he called, desperately pushing against the banshee as it screamed. "But I can only keep this up for you if you're in my sight. Once you're gone, you're on your own."

Chris wondered where the other two banshees had disappeared to, and the thought crossed his mind that they should probably be worried about them.

Matt quickly turned and continued on the way they'd been heading. In less than a minute, Gates was nowhere to be seen. All they could hear were screams, followed by a few other unidentifiable noises which made Chris rather uncomfortable.

The tunnel turned again, and Matt slowed his pace as they finally reached their destination.

"This is it," he said, his voice low as another, very close, scream sounded out. "End of the line."

No one said a word as they looked at what was in front of them. They were in an underground cavern. A stone altar had been built right up against the wall and a glass coffin was placed in front of it. Chris didn't like it one bit.

Matt hesitantly moved forwards, while the others stayed where they were.

"You're really gonna do this?" Abel asked.

The silence was making Chris uncomfortable again. It shouldn't have been so quiet.

Matt stopped and looked back at them with a hint of sadness in his eyes. "There's no other choice."

Matt turned back to face what was in front of him. Chris was glad he didn't have to do this. He didn't think he'd be able to go through with it.

Matt halted in front of the glass coffin, carefully looking to see what was inside. As he'd expected, the little girl was lying there, completely motionless. It looked like she was sleeping.

Matt shook his head, trying to psych himself up enough to go through with this. Even though he knew what he had to do, it was hard to make himself do it.

But, before he could do anything, a close scream sounded out, causing everyone to look back the way they'd come. Gates suddenly appeared, sliding to a halt. He quickly raised his barrier again as a banshee slammed into it, causing him to lose more ground.

"Whatever you've got to do, you'd better do it now!" Gates shouted as the barrier and the banshee disappeared.

Gates tried to get the barrier back up, but it didn't seem to work. Gates looked over at Matt. "Matt, do it!"

Matt turned back to the glass coffin, knowing there was no other choice but to open it and kill the girl.

"Someone get over here and help me get this open," Matt instructed as Gates tried again and again to get his barrier up, but to no avail. "Gates, you'd better get that damn barrier back up!"

"I can't!" Gates snapped. "I'm done, man. I'm fucking done!"

"Just a few more minutes!" Matt shouted at him, making Chris flinch at his harsh tone. "For fuck's sake. Chris, get over here and help me!"

Chris did as he was told, jogging over to the coffin. Abel and Zeke both stood back watching, while Gates growled in annoyance and kept trying to get his barrier back up.

"You'd better hurry up," Gates warned, backing up as a scream sounded out.

Chris looked over his shoulder to see all three banshees loitering in the entrance to the cavern, ready to attack at any moment, but holding off for some unknown reason. When the next attack would be, none of them knew.

"Alright, we've got to work fast," Matt said to Chris, already trying to get the coffin lid off. "We get this off and we'll be out of here in no time."

Chris repositioned himself as he tried to help slide the coffin lid off. He noted that Matt was looking rather worn down and like he needed to stop for the night. But there was no hope of that right now.

"You'd better be lifting," Matt growled. "I'd better not be doing this entire thing myself."

"I'm trying," Chris hissed back.

"Guys, they're beginning to circle," Gates said, backing up a bit more to where Zeke and Abel currently were.

"Just give us a minute," Matt snapped, using all the strength he had left to try to open the coffin. "We can't get it open."

"Well, try harder!" Abel said urgently, not taking his eyes off the banshees.

Gates once again tried to get the barrier back up but still couldn't. He was done. Gates looked at Zeke who just returned the look without saying anything.

"Care to help out at all?" Gates asked.

Zeke shot him an annoyed look before switching his gaze back to the banshees. A wall of flames suddenly erupted, sending the banshees back into the wall, screaming in the process.

"Should keep them back for a minute or two, won't be lit for long down here," Zeke said, shaking his hands out. A thoughtful look crossed his face. "Whole orchard's probably on fire by now..."

Gates shook his head. "Could have done that a while ago," he grumbled.

The banshees tried to make their way around the wall of fire, but they were unable to find any gap in it.

"Anyone else care to help?" Matt asked. "We can't move it. Won't even shift a little bit."

Abel, Zeke, and Gates moved over to help. Luckily the girl inside the coffin hadn't moved.

Gates leaned over the coffin ever so slightly, not wanting to get too close, but wanting to see what was inside. "Creepy."

Matt rolled his eyes, signaling for them all to help. Everyone took a place around the coffin.

"Alright, on three we'll try to shift it," Matt said, adjusting his position as one of the banshees screamed again. He glanced over his shoulder and saw the flames slowly dying. They didn't have long. "If we can't get it, someone's breaking the glass. Alright, one, two, three!"

The coffin lid shifted slightly, and everyone pushed against it again.

Zeke realized the wall of flames had suddenly dispersed behind them, so he abandoned his post, making Matt swear to himself. The flames appeared again, this time a bit closer, keeping the banshees back once more.

Zeke quickly moved back into his original position.

"Bit more," Matt said, sounding strained from the effort. Why was a glass coffin so hard to get into? Glass wasn't that heavy, was it?

With one last heaving effort, the coffin lid slid off, hitting the ground hard and leaving a mark in the dirt floor.

Everyone but Matt backed off and the banshees screamed louder as they saw what was happening, but they were unable to get to them.

Matt suddenly stopped. Something was wrong. He quickly looked around the cavern, patting his pockets as he realized something was missing.

"Matt?" Abel said cautiously, while Zeke kept the wall of flames up. "What's wrong?"

Matt looked at the group in front of him, his expression unreadable.

"The dagger's gone."

CHAPTER FIFTEEN

Finished

"What do you mean the dagger's gone?" Abel said, appalled. "You had it with you the whole time!"

"I thought I did," Matt said, back to looking around the cavern. "It's got to be around here somewhere."

"What do we do now?" Chris asked.

Zeke still kept the banshees occupied, while Gates put his hands on his hips, looking at Matt judgmentally and not saying a word.

Matt looked around at everyone, trying to decide what the best course of action was. "Alright, just keep them occupied and I'll be back."

He suddenly disappeared, leaving the other four in the cavern with the banshees still trying to get past Zeke.

Gates went back to trying to get his barrier back up.

Chris shook his head, looking at Abel. "Great."

"Matt, oh my God, are you OK?"

Matt looked over at Ash from where he was on his knees, having appeared a couple of paces away from her in the orchard.

The flames in the orchard were nearly out now and Nixx and Colin stood together.

Matt pushed himself up off the ground, steadying himself as he stood upright.

"What's happened?" Nixx asked. "Where's everyone else?"

"Just hang on a sec," Matt said, holding his hand out to signal Nixx to stop. "Head's spinning from the shadow-step. Haven't had that happen in years."

"Must be the dark energy," Ash said, unimpressed now that she knew Matt was alright.

Matt shot her a glare before looking at Nixx. "The dagger's gone. I had it with me when we went in, and it's gone."

He looked at Colin. "Was it the only one you had in your house?"

Colin nodded and Matt swore softly to himself.

"What are you going to do?" Nixx asked.

"There's not really anything else we can do," Matt said with a sigh. "All that's left is either find the dagger or let them be. Personally, I'd rather the first option. You absolutely sure it was the only one you had?"

Colin nodded.

Without another word, Matt was gone.

Nixx exchanged looks with Ash who just shrugged in return.

"You think he's coming back?" Chris asked, standing with his back to the open coffin, Abel by his side.

"I'd like to think so," Abel said in response. Neither of them was overly concerned about the banshees anymore. If they were going to die, then so be it. "Makes me wonder where he's gone this time."

"Probably to see if there are any spare daggers somewhere. Either that or he's backtracking to see if he dropped it."

Abel nodded, crossing his arms as he watched Zeke keep the banshees back with his fire.

Gates was also just standing back now and watching, having come to the conclusion there was no way he was getting his barrier back up. He'd been overworked and was completely done.

"You ever wonder how they managed to get a hang of their abilities?" Chris asked, keeping his voice down as he watched Zeke easily play with his fire.

Abel nodded. "Yeah. Guess they're self-taught."

Chris nodded and both men fell silent. One of the banshees suddenly disappeared again, leaving two of them fighting against Zeke and his walls of fire.

"Did you see that?" Chris asked, a bit of worry setting in now.

Gates nodded. "Yeah, clearly found something else to go after instead of working against us here."

"Think it knows where Matt is?"

Gates nodded again. "Without a doubt."

Matt crouched down, unable to see anything in the darkness of the burrow. He knew there was a wall in front of him, as that was where he'd shadow-stepped to. This was his best chance of finding the dagger. Either it was here, or he'd lost it when they'd come back this way to try and get out.

Suddenly flinching, Matt stood up, and without a thought, he disappeared, appearing again a few yards back.

Something hit the wall hard.

He winced as the scream rang out. It was obviously one of the banshees that had hit the wall. Served it right.

Matt was only just able to see the banshee in the darkness. It was staring him down from where it stood next to the wall.

"You really wanna fuck around with me?" Matt snapped. The banshee screamed in response. "Alright, fine, bring it on then."

Before the banshee could move, Matt disappeared again. This time he reappeared in front of the three-way tunnel split. He crouched down again, carefully looking for any signs of the dagger and where it could be. Before he could move again, something pushed past him.

Matt swore, feeling a sting on the side of his face. "Oh, it's on. You wanna mess with me? You've got the wrong guy."

Disappearing, Matt quickly backtracked to where they'd come down. The wall was still in place. He wasn't about to put up with the banshee. It was all a scare tactic, and he wasn't about to stand down.

He retraced his steps again, flinching again before disappearing. He smiled as he heard the banshee hit the wall again as he reappeared in the same place moments later.

"They never fucking learn."

He moved back a bit more, making sure to keep tabs on the banshee as he tried to find where he'd dropped the dagger. It had to be here somewhere.

A minute later, something pushed past him again and he felt another sting on the same side of his face.

Ignoring it, Matt continued on, quickly shadow-stepping out of the way as the banshee came back through, luckily missing him again.

It screamed, trying to intimidate him, but he ignored it again, picking up his pace as he made his way back to the three-way split.

It had to be here.

His foot suddenly hit something, and he stopped and crouched down. He moved his hand around over the dirt floor until he felt something cold and metallic. He picked up the blade, smiling to himself as the banshee screamed again, very close now.

He stood up slowly and looked back the way he'd come, only just able to see the banshee a few paces in front of him. He was sick of having to deal with this damn banshee. The fewer there were, the better. It was about time this ended.

The banshee suddenly went for him, also sick of playing games.

Matt wasn't quick enough. The banshee knocked him to the ground and was on top of him within seconds.

The dagger slipped out of his grip, sliding a few feet away as the banshee held him down, its long, sharp claws digging into his right shoulder. It raised its right hand, screaming as Matt tried to move and grab the dagger from where it had landed.

It was just out of his reach.

With one last effort, Matt pushed the banshee back, catching it off guard. It released its grip on his shoulder, and he quickly scrambled for the dagger. He grabbed it, turning back over as the banshee went for him again.

This time he was prepared. He held the dagger above himself as the banshee moved, forcing it straight into its heart. He winced as the banshee's final scream rang out.

The banshee suddenly burst into ashes, spreading everywhere over the ground and over Matt.

Matt sighed, pushing himself up to a sitting position. "One down, three to go."

—◦⊸✦⊷◦—

"You find it?" Gates asked.

Matt held up his hand from where he'd appeared on his knees back in the cavern. Chris and Abel were staring at him.

"Just hang on a sec," Matt said. "This whole place has me messed up. Give me one moment for my head to stop spinning. Shadow-stepping here has its downside."

Neither Chris nor Abel said a word as Matt slowly got to his feet, a bit unsteady once he was upright.

Gates glanced over before looking back at Zeke who was starting to tire.

"Yes, I found it," Matt began, feeling better now. He produced the dagger from where he'd had it tucked under his belt. "And we're one banshee down."

"You killed one?" Abel asked.

That got Gates's attention.

Matt nodded, looking drained. "Even if it almost killed me first."

"Zeke's got the other two occupied," Gates said.

Matt glanced at him before turning his attention to the glass coffin. A frown crossed his face. "Where's the girl?"

Chris, Abel, and Gates turned and stared at the coffin. It was empty.

Matt looked at the three of them, confusion etched across his face.

"She was just here a minute ago," Chris said.

Matt looked around the cavern. "Alright, fuck this, we're going back up top."

He grabbed Chris and Abel and disappeared. Before Chris could even blink, they were back up top.

Nixx looked at them as Ash joined them. They clearly no longer needed the rope.

Matt was back with Zeke and Gates before anyone could say a word.

"Zeke, you block that entrance off, make sure they can't get out," Matt instructed, sounding tired and desperate. He looked at Colin. "Man, we're out, you can deal with this shit yourself."

He threw the dagger onto the ground in front of Colin who stepped back in alarm.

"What?" Nixx said, not understanding what was going on. "You said you were going to kill the girl."

"The girl's gone!" Matt snapped as the banshees screamed from inside the burrow. "We found her, I lost the dagger, and now she's gone! We have to get to the City. We have more important things to do."

"So, we're just going?" Ash asked, not clear on what was happening.

"Yes, we're just going," Matt snapped. "We're moving out of this damn orchard and we're going. I'm not shadow-stepping anyone again while we're still here. I can hardly function here now as it is. Fuck this orchard and fuck the banshees."

"Won't they keep coming for us, though?" Abel asked as Matt began making his way out of the orchard. "You said they won't stop, Matt, once they get someone's scent."

"They will once we make it to the Road for the night. Once we make it to the City, it won't matter and we'll be long gone."

Abel shook his head as Matt disappeared from the orchard. It seemed he had enough energy to shadow-step himself out but no one else.

"Guess we just follow before he disappears on us," Chris said as Gates and Zeke both began moving out of the orchard.

"They're on the move."

Marion looked over as Carmen came into her room again, sitting on the chair like she had previously.

"They're out of the barrier, should be on the Road in about half an hour," Carmen continued. "I'll send some people out and we'll grab them for you. Your champion's here too, by the way."

Marion nodded and Carmen smiled back.

"How are you planning on dealing with them when you run into them?" Marion asked. "I honestly don't care if you bring them back or kill them. The choice is yours."

"I'll let Heather decide. She can choose what's best. She might want to keep a few and kill a few, depends on her mood."

Marion nodded. She didn't particularly care what happened now. She knew Alex and Jamie were out of reach in the City, but the others were free game for whatever Heather wanted from them.

"Actually, I do have one request," Marion said. Carmen raised her eyebrows. "Bring Shade and Chris back. I don't care about any of the others, but those two are the ones I need kept alive."

Carmen nodded, not bothering to ask why. "I'll inform Heather."

CHAPTER SIXTEEN

Roadblock

"Once we get on the Road, don't stray from it until daylight," Matt informed the group as they walked. He, of course, was out in the lead.

"Why?" Chris asked.

"Just don't."

"You know, maybe you should actually tell us what's going on instead of just assuming we can figure it out," Abel said with annoyance.

Matt sighed, stopping and turning to face his companions. They'd been walking for nearly half an hour and Chris was sure he could see the Yellow Brick Road up ahead.

"Look, I don't mean to keep things from you but, right now, I don't want to explain," Matt said. "We're all tired and beaten up and the main thing is that we get onto the Road and we get to the City. I told Alex we'd be here before dark, and it'll be morning soon. We just need to keep walking and meet up with Alex and Jamie at the City. They've already got hours on us."

He turned and continued walking. Everyone else stayed silent and followed along.

It wasn't too long before Matt stepped onto the Yellow Brick Road, coming to a halt as the others caught up and joined him.

"Just remember, stay on the road, OK?" Matt said, sounding exhausted. "If you need to veer off it for any reason, wait until daylight and you'll be OK."

Everyone nodded, seeing that Matt wasn't about to say any more.

"Well, well, what do we have here?"

They all paused as Hunter and a woman walked up to them from the opposite direction they'd been about to head. A small group of people hung back as Hunter crossed his arms, eyeing off Matt's group.

"Didn't realize you were still around," Matt growled. "Was hoping you'd died on your little Alice hunt."

"Look who's talking," Hunter growled back, the dog at his feet snarling like always. "But no, your little bitch got away. Shame really."

"Oh, such a shame."

"Alright boys, get over yourselves," the woman next to Hunter said, rolling her eyes. She stepped forwards, a bit of a smile on her face. "I'm Heather. Are you two done with your macho act now? Ready to shut up and let the grown-up talk?"

Hunter and Matt stayed silent, and Heather nodded with approval before speaking again.

"Now, I'm after a Chris and a Shade. The two of you care to step forwards?" she asked, linking her fingers together and stepping forward again as she surveyed the group of travelers in front of her. "How about you make my job a little easier and give yourselves up willingly?"

"It depends why you want to know," Nixx said, crossing his arms and getting Heather's attention.

"Where's the fun in telling?" she said with a wicked smile. She switched her gaze to Matt, moving forwards a bit more and stopping just in front of him. "What about you, handsome? Know where I can find someone named Chris and someone named Shade?"

Matt stared her down, no amusement on his face at all. "No idea."

The amused smile stayed on Heather's face as she moved back a few steps, giving Matt his space. She sighed, looking around at them all.

"Well, I don't think you really want disappoint dear Marion," she said.

A scowl appeared on Abel's face. "She's still alive?" he asked, getting Heather's attention.

"You seem sad about it," Heather pouted as Abel glared at her. "Which must make you Abel."

"What makes you so sure?" Ash asked, Heather shooting her a disapproving look. "You don't know who any of us are, so how do you know who he is?"

"Sweetheart, if I were you, I'd shut that pretty little mouth of yours," Heather said sweetly. "I don't have time for sluts like you, got it? Let the adults talk and shut it."

She gave her a bit of a smile before looking back at the others, a thoughtful look on her face.

Hunter and Matt continued to glare at each other. The tension between the two was palpable.

Heather looked at Hunter. "You know who's who. Be a sweetie and tell me who I'm after."

Hunter took his time, looking everyone over. Matt stayed silent and Chris hoped that he had a way out of this.

"That's Shade," he said, pointing at Matt. He then pointed at Chris. "That's Chris."

"Why only us?" Chris spoke up.

Heather looked at him as Hunter took up his usual position, arms crossed and serious expression on his face.

"Just doing as I've been asked," Heather said.

Chris rolled his eyes. Not exactly the answer he'd been after.

Heather looked around at them all again, clearly trying to make up her mind on something.

"If you two would be so kind as to come with us, that would be much appreciated," she said, directing her words mostly at Matt. "Or we'll have to use force and, believe me, you don't want that."

"You're right, we certainly don't," Matt said, glancing at Chris. "Do we, Chris?"

Chris shook his head, wondering what Matt was up to, hoping he had a plan.

Heather gave them a triumphant smile. "Well then boys, if you'd be so kind."

She gestured for them to come over and join her. Matt and Chris looked at each other.

"Guess we do as the lady says," Matt said.

Chris frowned.

"Today would be nice," Heather said, getting impatient with how long they were taking. "Wouldn't want to use that force now, would we?"

"Not at all," Matt said.

He grabbed Chris by the wrist and moved quickly, dragging him off the edge of the Road. They both disappeared from sight as they went through the shimmering barrier.

Heather screamed in frustration. Hunter smiled to himself as he stayed where he was. Abel and Nixx exchanged looks.

When Heather looked back at Hunter, he was back to being his usual serious self.

"Why didn't you stop them?" she snapped. "Where the hell did they go?"

Hunter shrugged and said nothing. Heather looked back to the five remaining travelers.

"Well, this is an inconvenience," she said, trying to regain her composure as she glared at them. "Guess I'll have to deal with you lot, then."

She went to move forward towards them, but a sudden white light appeared in between the two groups. Everyone shielded their eyes from the blinding light.

"You need to get off this Road, Heather," someone said. The light disappeared, leaving a man in its place. "You know you're not allowed in this area."

"I'm allowed where I want, Jacob," Heather snarled. Jacob stood his ground in between the groups. "You're not the Wizard. You don't say what I can and can't do."

"You and Carmen are under strict rules and you know what happens if you break them," Jacob said harshly. "Get off the Road and go back to where you're allowed. Be grateful you're allowed anywhere."

Abel looked at Nixx, who just shrugged in return, the others staying quiet too. Gates and Zeke were the only ones who didn't seem confused, but they knew a bit more about things because they spent a lot of time around Matt.

Heather glared at Jacob, clicked her fingers, and her entire group disappeared.

Jacob turned to look at the remaining five.

"I'll take it you guys belong to Alex's group," he stated. A frown crossed his face. "Shouldn't there be seven of you? He said there were nine all up."

"We don't where Matt and Chris disappeared to. They were here and now they're gone," Nixx said. "They stepped off the Road when that woman demanded they go with her."

The look on Jacob's face fell. "Oh."

"Is that a bad thing?" Abel asked with worry in his voice.

"I'll explain later. Right now, we need to get you guys to the City."

"Did Alex and Jamie make it?" Ash asked, standing next to Abel now that Chris was no longer around.

Jacob nodded. "Yeah, I found them a little way from here, heading in the wrong direction. They're fine. Got them to the City just in time."

Ash nodded, as relief made itself known on Abel's face.

Jacob looked around at them all, realizing something.

"Sorry, where are my manners. I'm Jacob," he said, properly introducing himself. "I work for the Wizard in the Emerald City. I would've interfered earlier, but we had a bit of an issue, and I had to deal with that first. Can I just ask who each of you are, since I assume none of you hold any ID?"

Everyone exchanged looks, no one knowing where to start.

Nixx looked at Jacob, seeing that no one else was going to speak up first.

"I'm Nixx. This is Abel," he said, indicating to Abel who gave a nod of greeting. Nixx pointed to each person as he introduced them. "This is Ash, Gates, and Zeke. Matt and Chris are the ones that we lost off the Road a few moments before you showed up."

Jacob nodded. "Well, it's nice to meet you. We'll deal with everything when we get back to the City. We'll have to get you all ID cards and whatnot so you can move around freely, and I'll explain what's going on when we get there. I don't know if you'll get in to see the Wizard today since it's so late now, even though he's usually available all times of the day and night. He's been dealing with Jamie tonight and probably won't have any free time until the morning."

"Whenever's fine," Nixx said, taking charge of their small group now.

Jacob gave a nod again, not saying anything as the blinding white light returned, everyone instinctively shielding their eyes from the sudden light change. A minute or two later, the light faded, everyone blinking to try and get their sight back.

"Welcome to the Emerald City," Jacob said, sounding like he was bored with saying that line. "Now if you'll follow me, I'll show you where you'll be staying.

CHAPTER SEVENTEEN

The Emerald City

"Guys! You're OK!"

Alex rushed over, grabbing Ash in a tight hug, making sure she couldn't get out of it. He suddenly let her go, looking around at everyone.

"Wait, where's Matt?" he asked, confusion on his face as Jacob stood off to the side, leaning against the wall with his arms crossed, watching the reunion. "And Chris? Where's Chris?"

The five of them either shrugged or shook their heads, not having an answer for him. Alex looked at Ash, worried when he saw the look on her face.

"They disappeared off the Road when we ran into Hunter and some woman named Heather," Ash said.

"Heather's a witch," Jacob spoke up, everyone switching their gazes to him. "She and Carmen were exiled many years ago by the Wizard. There was a bit of a war at the time, but it's settled down over the past few years. They now mainly keep to themselves."

"Witches?" Abel queried, sounding unimpressed. He sighed. "Just keeps getting better and better, doesn't it?"

"They shouldn't be too much of a hassle," Jacob said, indicating for everyone to take a seat at the table in the middle of the room. "We haven't really seen much of them over the past, I don't know, three years or so it's probably been. It was a surprise to see her on the Road."

Everyone took a seat and Jacob joined them, sitting in the remaining chair.

"Why witches?" Nixx asked, intrigued. "If people have abilities, they shouldn't need to turn to magic, should they?"

"Not everyone develops abilities," Jacob explained. "And that's where the witches come in. They don't have an ability, so they use magic to fill that space. It's rare but it happens. Carmen and Heather are well known witches too, mostly in Oz but also in some other counties. The witch count isn't very high around here, but they're the two that everyone knows about and reads about in the history books."

"Why were they exiled?" Gates asked.

Jacob looked at him. "Carmen and Heather tried taking over all of Oz. It was a hard time for everyone, but the Wizard stepped in and now they're exiled into the barren land at the edge of the county. They're allowed in that immediate area, but no further. Heather should not have been out on the Road, and she knows that."

"We think Marion's with them," Abel said.

"The Queen of Wonderland?"

Abel nodded.

"We don't know if she is or not," Jacob said. "We only have alerts in certain areas of Oz. If she *is* around, then she'll be in the barren land with them."

"Is there anything you can do about her?" Abel asked. "She'll be healing up from what happened back in Wonderland. We can't afford to have her at full strength."

"You'll have to run it by the Wizard. I'm not the one in charge," Jacob said with a shrug. "I'd love to help, but I can't do anything. It's not my place to step into these kinds of affairs."

"You said we could see the Wizard in the morning?" Nixx said.

"Most likely," Jacob said, standing up. "But worry about that later. For now, you should get some sleep. You all look exhausted.

"Do you know what happened to Chris and Matt?" Alex asked as he sat cross-legged on the bed, watching Ash look around the room.

Jacob had shown everyone to their individual rooms for the night. Alex had insisted on being in the same room as Ash, not wanting to be by himself.

It was very late, and Ash was sure it must be nearly morning. She shook her head, peering at something on the desk that caught her attention.

Abel had been denied access to see Jamie until the morning and had been sent to a different room nearby. He'd been far from happy with it and had protested loudly until Jacob explained that it wasn't his rule, it was the Wizard's decision and what was best for Jamie.

Nixx was in his own room, a few doors down from Alex and Ash, with Zeke in another on the opposite side of the hallway.

Jacob had taken Gates to the infirmary when he'd seen that he needed medical attention after the encounter with the banshees. He had purple-black bruising around his wrists from the amount of force he'd had to use to hold the banshees back. It looked like there was a downside to most people's abilities, and Gates's one happened to be physically feeling the effects.

"We don't know where they've gone," Ash said, picking up a small decorative piece from the desk and beginning to inspect it. "Matt dragged Chris off the Road, and they just disappeared. I don't know if Matt shadow-stepped them out of there or if something else happened."

"But Matt told me not to leave the Road once we were on it, especially in the dark," Alex said, a frown on his face as Ash put the item down and went back to looking around the room.

"He told us the same thing and now look. He's gone and done exactly what he told us not to do."

"I'm sure he had a reason," Alex said. He trusted Matt to know what was best for them all. "He wouldn't have just done it."

Ash wandered over to the window. The curtains were shut tight, blocking any sort of light. She moved the curtains aside and looked down at the street below. They were quite high up in the castle and there was no sign of life outside. It was still dark, even with the streetlights on.

"Sometimes Alex, I don't think Matt knows what he's doing at all. He's smart in some ways but, other times, I don't think he even stops to think about what's best. Now we don't know where he and Chris have ended up or if they'll be back."

"I'm sure they will be," Alex reassured. "They'll be back in no time."

Ash looked over at Alex, who was smiling to try and reassure her that Matt and Chris would indeed be back. She didn't look convinced, and she returned to looking out the window.

"Guess it's just a matter of when that is."

"Morning."

Jacob glanced over as Abel and Nixx came into the small kitchen. Each floor of this building had rooms, its own kitchen, and a few other things.

"Any chance of seeing the Wizard today?" Nixx asked straight out.

Jacob went over to the table, placing his cup on it before taking a seat. He shook his head as Abel joined him at the table.

"He had to take off early this morning, had some business to attend to a few towns over," Jacob said as Nixx sat next to Abel. "He should be back by tomorrow."

Alex wandered in, happy as usual. He thought it was a lot nicer here than in Wonderland. He started to look around to find out what there was to eat this morning.

Ash wasn't far behind Alex. She came in and took a seat between Nixx and Jacob.

"And what if he isn't?" Nixx asked Jacob.

"Then you have to wait until he's back."

Nixx sighed.

"Any chance I can see Jamie today?" Abel asked hopefully.

Jacob shrugged. "We'll have to wait and see what the nurses have to say."

Neither Zeke nor Gates were anywhere to be seen this morning.

"How did Gates pull up after last night?" Abel asked, directing his question to Jacob. He seemed to know what was going on, when it was going on.

Jacob nodded. "He was alright when I showed him to his room after he'd been down at the infirmary. He had severe bruising on his wrists and was totally spent, but apart from that he seemed to be OK. What caused that exactly? He didn't say."

"We had a bit of a run-in with some banshees," Abel said awkwardly. "Gates can put up barriers, but it really took it out of him. We were trying to hold off three of them, and it took its toll."

"Banshees are very rare nowadays," Jacob said, eyebrows raised. "So is seeing physical signs from using abilities. It'll take him a few days, but he should heal up fine."

Alex joined them at the table, sitting next to Ash, having given up his search for food.

"So, wait," Alex said, making everyone look at him. "Where *are* Gates and Zeke today? I thought they'd be here with us."

"They were around earlier on," Jacob said. "Had a bit of a chat with them and got their IDs and stuff sorted. They went for a walk to see what the City's like. Said they hadn't been here before. Once you're ready, we can go and sort all that out for you too and then you're free to wander around for the day. Kill some time while you wait for the Wizard to get back. It's the first Thursday of the month which means the markets will be running."

Everyone looked around at each other, nodding before looking back at Jacob.

"How will we know when the Wizard's back?" Nixx asked, clearly eager to see him.

"By the time you get back later tonight, he should be ready to see you," Jacob said. "If you need any help with anything, come find me. I'll either be here or over at the training arena. Someone can point the way if you need it. Got a bit of a busy day ahead of me, but if you need anything just come find me."

⋯⋙✦⋘⋯

"This is weird. Why do we even need these?" Ash asked as she, Alex, and Abel began walking down the street.

She was looking at her new ID card and was confused as to why it was needed. She was rather unimpressed with it. It had a number just above her picture, no occupation, and said she lived in Wonderland.

Each of them had their own ID now. Jacob had even funded them a handful of money in case they found something at the markets they wanted to buy.

"Apparently, it's the law here," Alex said, happily looking at his card, turning it this way and that. "You need it everywhere you go. I think they're cool and a good idea."

"Sure," was Ash's deadpan response.

A few people walked by, heading in the same direction as them. They nodded at them as they passed.

"So, what's the plan?" Alex asked excitedly, putting his ID card into his pocket so he wouldn't lose it. Ash did the same.

Abel shrugged.

Nixx had stayed back at the castle, planning on having a look around for some reason. None of them had bothered questioning it. If he wanted to stay indoors, then he would.

"Guess we just wander around for a bit," Abel said, nodding at a couple more people passing by. "Go find these markets and then just hang around."

Ash and Alex both nodded.

"Wait, we never asked where Matt and Chris might have ended up," Ash suddenly realized as Abel started following a few people, figuring they knew their way around. "Jacob said he'd explain it and he never did."

"That can wait," Abel said with a shake of his head as they turned a corner, hearing a lot of commotion. They must be getting close to the markets. "They'll be fine. All that matters right now is that we're here and we'll be in to see the Wizard within the next twenty-four hours. After that we can ask, if they haven't come back by then."

The town square was up ahead and there were a lot of people milling around. Ash hadn't realized there were this many people. This was only one area and most of the occupants of the Emerald City seemed to be here today. It was still early, too.

Abel continued towards the markets, Ash and Alex trailing along behind. He began making his way through crowds of people, intent on keeping himself occupied by looking at what people had to sell.

Alex made sure he had a tight hold on Ash's arm, so he didn't get lost in the crowd. "I hope they have something nice," he said, looking around.

Abel came to a stop at one of the stalls.

"Feel free to wander around by yourself," Ash said to Alex, stopping next to Abel.

Alex just looked around as he stayed with her. "Uh-uh, I'm not letting you lose me in this crowd."

Ash shook her head, not saying a word, and continued on her way, leaving Abel to look at what he wanted to. Alex tightened his grip on her arm, feeling like he was being dismissed. Ash pushed past a few people, coming to a halt at one of the stalls.

Alex eagerly looked at what she'd found.

"Find something?"

Ash looked up, startled. Gates gave her a bit of a smile before looking at what she'd been eyeing off. Ash looked him over, seeing both his wrists were bandaged tightly. She hadn't spent much time with him, so she didn't really know him, but he seemed OK.

"Not really," Ash said. "Alex wanted something nice, so I thought maybe this was the place to start."

Gates glanced at her as he continued to look at the stall, the guy behind it giving them a welcoming smile. Alex continued to hold onto Ash as he also looked at the bright things arrayed across the stall.

Gates gave a bit of a nod and picked up a necklace, before looking back at Ash.

"I think you should start with this one," he said, handing her the necklace as the man behind the stall watched.

Ash looked the necklace over, smiling. She looked back at Gates who gave her a bit of a smile in return.

"I might just do that," Ash said.

"You won't be able to buy just one."

Ash gave a bit of a laugh, handing the necklace to the man behind the stall and reaching into her pocket to get out some of the money Jacob had given them.

Gates put his hands in his pockets, looking around as Ash handed the money over, the man giving her some change before carefully wrapping the necklace up.

"Everything OK?" Ash asked Gates as she took the wrapped necklace and put it in her pocket.

Gates gave a bit of a vacant nod before indicating that he was heading off. Ash quickly walked off with him. Alex clung onto her, not saying a word.

"Just doesn't feel right here," Gates said as he moved past a few people who were looking at things on other stalls, as more people made their way around them.

"What do you mean?" Ash asked, making sure she kept pace with him. She saw Abel over at one of the other stalls, talking to the woman behind it. She hadn't seen Zeke yet, but if Gates was here then he'd surely be somewhere nearby too.

"I don't know," Gates said, coming to a halt at a stall as something caught his eye. "Just feels too ... tame. Used to be like this back in Wonderland before everything happened. It's just too safe."

Ash frowned as Gates picked up a bracelet and tried to decide whether he actually wanted it. Alex finally let Ash go, seeing something on the stall as well.

"But isn't being safe a good thing?" she asked.

"Not when it's too safe," Gates replied, having made up his mind about the bracelet. He handed some money over, getting a nod from the woman behind the stall. "Means that if something happens, no one will know what to do. Everyone takes the higher powers for granted and when that higher power isn't there, it causes dysfunction if something happens."

Ash nodded and followed as Gates walked off again. As he carefully moved the bandage off his wrist so he could tie the bracelet on, Ash saw the bruising and winced.

"How are you holding up?" she asked.

Gates glanced at her, then back down at his wrist as he moved the bandage back into place.

"I'm fine," he said, avoiding her gaze. "Hurting, but fine."

Gates sidestepped some people and headed towards a stall bit further out of the way, on the edge of the town square. Ash's expression saddened a bit.

"Look, I don't know if anyone's actually thanked you yet," she said. "But they'd all be dead without you. You really put yourself on the line for them."

Gates shrugged, not looking at her or saying anything. He stopped at the stall and looked over the wares, before picking up another necklace.

"Really, Gates. They all appreciate what you did for them," Ash continued. "I know they do. There's just been a lot going on, what with Matt and Chris and everything else. You're the only reason we're here right now."

"I don't need anyone's thanks," Gates said, finally looking at her. He smiled and held the necklace out to her like he had before. "You can't buy just one."

"I shouldn't," Ash said, suddenly realizing that Alex had disappeared. She assumed he was still back at the previous stall.

Gates shrugged, putting the necklace back down on the stall. "Your loss. It suited you."

Ash sighed as Gates went back to browsing. She reluctantly pulled some more money out and handed it to the man on the other side of the stall, before taking the necklace.

"Happy now?" she asked, putting the necklace on and enjoying Gates's smile.

"Ecstatic."

Ash rolled her eyes, not saying anything as he wandered off yet again. He didn't seem to be able to keep still.

"You sure you're OK?" Ash asked, making sure she kept up with him as he pushed past people who were standing around in the middle of the crowd. She couldn't see Alex or Abel anywhere.

"Why do you ask?" Gates asked, not even glancing at her as he made his way through the crowd.

"Just want to make sure, I guess."

Gates stopped and stared at her when she stopped in front of him.

"I'm fine. Like I said, just hurting," he said. "Also, kind of wish Matt was around."

Ash looked at him sadly, receiving the same look in return. She sighed.

"I'm sure wherever he's ended up, he'll be fine," she reassured, understanding that Gates was worried for his friend. "I'm sure you're not the only one who misses his horrible presence."

Gates laughed and Ash smiled in return.

"He's not that bad. You've just gotten yourself on the wrong side of him, young lady," Gates said with amusement. "He'll be back. I don't doubt that. It's just a matter of how and when."

"Well, let's just hope it's soon," Ash said. Gates nodded in agreement. "He has Chris with him. Hopefully, without them, Marion can't do whatever she was planning on doing."

CHAPTER EIGHTEEN

Parallel

"What the fuck?"

Matt and Chris shielded their eyes against the sudden harsh sunlight.

Chris was confused. It had been night, and now it was day. They were no longer on the Road, and it was nowhere to be seen.

His eyes finally started to adjust to the light, and he looked at Matt.

"What did you do?" Chris asked, feeling slightly angry but still dazed.

Matt adjusted his snapback, turning it the right way around while he tried to get his eyes to focus. He looked around, trying to figure out where they currently were. It didn't look or feel like anything like Oz.

"Matt, where are we?" Chris asked urgently, looking around as well.

Matt shook his head. "I don't know."

"What? How do you not know where we are?"

"I just don't!" Matt snapped, finally looking at him. He went back to looking around, shaking his head. "This is not Oz."

"Then, how do we find out where we are?" Chris asked, wishing he had a hat like Matt's to keep the sun off his face. "And why is the sun out?"

"I don't know," Matt repeated slowly.

He sounded very unsure, and it didn't fill Chris with confidence.

They were standing in an open field. A few trees were scattered around and there was a lake further in the distance. A heap of flowers lay in amongst the green grass. There were no people in sight.

"This isn't right," Matt said, shaking his head as he put his hands on his hips. "Honestly, this looks like Wonderland."

Chris frowned, still shielding his eyes from the sunlight. It was getting to him and starting to make his head hurt.

"How? Wonderland's destroyed. It didn't look anything like this."

Matt nodded. Chris saw some of the damage he'd taken from the banshee. He had two red cuts on the side of his face, and his shirt was ripped over his right shoulder. Matt didn't seem too bothered by it, though.

"This is what Wonderland used to look like, before everything happened," Matt said.

"How did we get here?" Chris asked. "What time period are we in?"

Matt shook his head. "We're not in our Wonderland."

"What do you mean?" Chris sighed. "Matt, what's going on?"

Chris wasn't sure what the look in Matt's eyes was. It seemed to be a mix of things, but he wasn't sure what.

"When you step off the Yellow Brick Road at night, you go through the magic barrier that keeps the evil out," Matt said. "But it's only active during the dark. If you step off it and go through the barrier, you can end up literally anywhere. Not necessarily in Oz, not in Wonderland, but absolutely anywhere."

Chris frowned. "I'm not following."

"Parallel universes, parallel times," Matt emphasized, using hand gestures to try and get Chris to understand what he was saying. "Problem is, once you're here, you've got a very low chance of getting back to your own time."

Chris's expression fell as Matt shrugged.

"So, we're stuck in some alternate universe, and we can't get home," said Chris.

"Well, don't think of it like that," Matt said awkwardly. "We'll get out, just got to figure out how."

"I'll take it you don't know much about how this kind of thing works, then," Chris accused, crossing his arms across his chest as he stared at Matt.

"It was on my list to look into," said Matt, looking around again. "Just hadn't got to it yet."

Chris sighed, looking down briefly before looking up again. Matt was watching him, clearly feeling bad about their current circumstances.

"Wait, I remember someone telling me about parallel universes and whatnot," Chris said, piquing Matt's interest. "When we got stuck in the castle, a man in a mirror said something about it."

"Well, what did he say?"

Chris shrugged, not really remembering.

Matt sighed. "Alright, I guess we just start walking in some direction and find out whereabouts we are."

"Well, you should know. You know Wonderland better than I do."

"Things could be different here," Matt explained, heading off to his right. "It might be parallel, but things are usually different in each of them, different to our world."

"Like what?" Chris walked alongside Matt, already sweating in the heat of the day.

"Anything," Matt said with a shrug, wincing as he felt pain in his shoulder. "Like, literally anything. People, times, events, layouts. You name it and it could be different."

"Right..."

"So, for example, in this particular world we're in, neither of us might actually exist," Matt tried explaining as they walked. There was still no one and nothing of interest in sight. They couldn't even shadow-step because there was so much sunlight, and Matt was wary about doing it in places he didn't know. "Or, maybe Marion never took over with her evil ways. The possibilities are endless."

Chris nodded, not saying anything else as they continued on their way.

"Is that someone? Matt, I think that's a road."

Matt looked up from where he'd been sitting. Chris could see how exhausted he was from the events of the night, and now the constant walking wasn't helping. Chris had been keeping a watch while they rested, hoping to see something or someone, and now he had.

Matt got to his feet, wincing again from the pain in his shoulder. He rubbed it and held it as he joined Chris and looked at where he was pointing.

Sure enough, there was a dirt road and someone walking along it pulling a cart.

Matt indicated for Chris to move with him, quickly heading towards the person on the road. Right now, anyone was good enough to talk to.

"Hey, hey, wait!" Matt called as he and Chris picked up their pace.

The person stopped as they approached.

Matt and Chris halted on the side of the road and the man with the cart looked at them.

"Can I help you two with something?" he asked.

"Can you give us directions? We're a bit lost. We're looking for the closest town," Matt said.

Chris nodded to confirm his statement as Matt held his shoulder again.

"You two look rather worse for wear," the man noted, looking them both over. Matt and Chris exchanged looks. "I'm heading into town anyway, so you can just keep pace with me if you like. I'll show you where to go. You two not from around here?"

"No," Chris said. Matt chose to stay quiet for once, which was a rare feat for him. "We're not from here at all."

The man nodded. "Well, I'll be more than happy to show you to the closest town. It's Monday so the town markets will be on. That's where I'm heading. My name's Kyle, by the way. It's nice to meet you."

Matt frowned, looking at Chris.

"It was nearly Thursday when we left," he said, his voice down so as not to alert the traveler.

Chris shrugged. He didn't know what day it was anymore.

"Been traveling a few days, hey?" the man said. "Time does go by rather fast around here. Say, where are you headed besides the closest town? Any particular destination?"

"Ah, no, not really," Matt said, looking the man over. "Just the closest town. No particular destination."

The man nodded and began walking again. "Well then, this way."

Matt and Chris kept up with him at first, then dropped back slightly, but the man didn't seem to notice.

"What are we going to do when we get to this town?" Chris asked Matt, being sure to lower his voice. "We've got to find a way back home. We can't stay here forever, you know."

"Yeah, I know," Matt said back with a hint of annoyance. "Look, just give it a bit of time and we'll look into it. Maybe someone in town can help us."

"Here we are!" the man said.

Matt and Chris looked at the town spread out in front of them. The gates were currently open, inviting everyone in.

There were some guards on duty, which reminded Chris of Wonderland's main town where Marion had lived and held her tournaments.

"Welcome to Woz, OzLand's main town," Kyle said.

Matt raised his eyebrows. "OzLand?"

Kyle nodded, as Matt looked at Chris with a hint of doubt. It seemed they'd ended up in a place where reality had mixed the two counties from their own world together.

"Yes, OzLand. You two really are clueless about where you are, aren't you?" he said as they headed through the gates and into the town.

To Matt, the place looked like a mix between the Emerald City and the main town in Wonderland. Chris hadn't ever seen the Emerald City, so he didn't recognize the resemblance.

The sidewalk was bustling with busy people and families enjoying a day out in the fine weather.

"Is there somewhere we can stay here?" Matt asked Kyle as they began climbing a hill. "We've been walking for a few days."

"The Candlelight Inn is in the middle of town, near where the markets are held. They have electricity if you need to charge your phones," Kyle explained. "Just go on in and they might have a room for you. Although, it does get very busy this time of year."

"This time of year?" Chris said skeptically.

Electricity and phones? This was getting weirder by the minute.

Kyle nodded. "It's a very important time. The King returns this time every year."

Matt and Chris exchanged looks, not sure what to say. They finally halted just outside the busy town square. The markets and celebrations were well under way.

"If there's no room left at the Inn, come and find me," Kyle said, getting a piece of paper and a pen out of his back pocket. "I always have a spare room if you need it or can't afford to stay at the Inn."

He wrote something down on the piece of paper and handed it to Matt.

"Thanks," Matt said, nodding gratefully, pocketing the paper without even looking at it.

Kyle smiled before tipping his hat to them both. "Enjoy the markets and the town."

With that, he headed off down one of the side streets.

Matt and Chris stood there for a few minutes, just watching the markets and the ebb and flow of people.

"What now?" Chris asked. "We don't have any money on us. We don't even know what they use for money here! We can't really stay at the Inn."

"I know," Matt said with a nod, keeping his voice down as a group of young girls passed by. "But we might just have to change that."

CHAPTER NINETEEN

Disturbance

"I wouldn't buy that one. It doesn't suit you."

Ash looked at Gates as she admired a dress someone was selling.

"You think?" she said, holding the dress against herself. "I think it looks nice."

Gates shrugged. "Your money. You want it, then don't let me stop you from buying it. Just stating what I think."

Ash smiled at him, receiving one in return.

The smile suddenly faded from Gates's face, being replaced with a frown as he removed his hands from his pockets and looked behind himself.

There were still a lot of people around, but nothing looked out of the ordinary.

"What's up?" Ash asked, glancing at him in between browsing the different clothing items on sale.

"Something's wrong," Gates said, still looking behind himself, that same expression on his face.

Ash stopped what she was doing and looked at him. "Like what?"

Gates shook his head slowly, not saying anything.

Alex chose that moment to suddenly reappear, looking relieved to find Ash. Ash glanced at him before going back to looking at the clothing as another item caught her eye.

"There you are," Alex said with a sigh. "Thank God. I thought I'd lost you when you disappeared on me with *him*."

Alex pointed at Gates who was staring at something over the other side of the market. He didn't acknowledge Alex or what he'd said.

"You just didn't keep up," Ash said, admiring a shirt she'd found. She held it against herself, looking at Alex. "What do you think?"

"It's not your color," Gates spoke up, not even looking at her, making both her and Alex look at him.

"How would you know? You're not even looking," Ash said, slightly offended, but she put the shirt back. She looked at Alex. "Apparently he knows everything about clothes shopping."

Alex smiled at her before looking at Gates who was still rather distracted.

"Hey, you alright?" he asked.

"Something's seriously wrong," Gates said with a shake of his head, looking back at Ash and Alex. "Do you guys sense that too, or is it just me?"

"Just you," Ash said, still browsing and hoping she was going to find something she liked, and that Gates approved of. She'd had no luck so far. With everything she'd liked, Gates had told her it wasn't right for her. But she'd get something yet.

Gates shook his head. "Whatever then."

"Hey, you're the one being snappy," Ash said, finding another shirt she liked. She held it against herself, seeing she had Gates's attention briefly. "What about this one?"

Gates looked at it, looking her over briefly.

"I don't know. Turn it around."

Ash rolled her eyes, doing as asked. Gates gave a bit of a disliking look to the shirt before shrugging and going back to watching something over the other side of the market.

"Your money," he said.

"You're so damn hard to please, you know that?" Ash said with annoyance, putting the shirt back and continuing. There were a lot of choices at this stand, but if there was nothing here, she'd move onto one of the others.

Gates looked back at her, raising his eyebrows. "You're really trying to please me?"

Ash looked at him with no amusement, making him smile at her briefly. She shook her head and couldn't help but smile back.

Alex looked over Ash's shoulder, admiring the different colors of the clothes.

Gates frowned and looked away again.

"You seriously can't sense that?" he asked, looking to his left now. A group of people had caught his attention. "Like, seriously. You can't sense it?"

"Sense what?" Ash asked with a sigh. "None of us can sense anything, Gates. It's just you being all City-paranoid."

Gates scoffed. "City-paranoid? Please."

Ash stopped, crossed her arms, and looked at him. Alex moved around her to look at the clothing for sale.

"Seriously, ever since we got here, you've been all 'oh, it's too safe'," she said. "You're City-paranoid. It happens to the best of us."

"I am not 'City-paranoid'," Gates said defensively. "There's like a ... disturbance in the air, and you can't feel it?"

"Nope."

Gates shook his head, not saying anything more on the matter.

Alex held a shirt out to Ash who took it, looking it over.

"I like this one. I think you should buy it," Alex said as Gates glanced back at him. "Even if he doesn't like it, he doesn't have to wear it."

Gates held his hands up in his own defense. "I'm just trying to help."

"You've been denying her everything she likes!" Alex exclaimed as someone rushed past them.

Gates rolled his eyes and put his hands back in his pockets. "I just don't want her wasting her money on something she won't ever wear."

"Whatever. Ash, next thing you like, you buy," Alex said sternly. "If you want it, buy it. Don't let some know-all stop you buying nice things."

"He's not stopping me from buying anything," Ash said, feeling offended again. "Gates is helping, Alex. He has an opinion too, you know."

"Yeah, well, his opinion is wrong."

Ash shook her head, looking at Gates and indicating to the shirt. Gates gave a short shake of his head, so Ash put the shirt back while Alex rolled his eyes.

"Alright, I think I'm done here," Ash said. "Next one?"

"Sure," Gates said with a nod.

Ash smiled at him and Alex automatically latched onto her.

"You're not leaving me again," he stressed, keeping a tight grip on her so she couldn't escape from him. "No more leaving me at stalls."

"That was your own fault," Ash said as she began walking. Gates walked next to her and Alex clung onto her arm. "You just didn't see us walk off."

"They had shiny things at that stall…"

"You find anything good?" Gates asked as they wandered over to the next clothing stall. "Did you find your 'nice things'?"

Alex nodded and a smile appeared on his face as they stopped at the next stall. He reluctantly let go of Ash's arm as she started to look through the clothing.

"I did! I actually found some very nice trinkets."

Gates nodded and was going to say something but stopped. Alex tilted his head to the side, watching Gates look around again.

"You still sensing something wrong?" Ash asked, seeing that Gates had become distracted again. He gave a brief nod. "I'm sure it's nothing."

"No, it's definitely something," Gates said, ignoring the look he was getting from the lady behind the stall. He looked at Ash. "Just wait here a minute, I'll be right back."

"But what if I find something?" Ash called as Gates headed off.

Gates turned, walking backwards for a few steps. "I don't know. Just wait for me?"

Ash sighed, watching him disappear into the crowd and then into a side alley.

Alex looked at her, making her return the look. He pointed in the direction Gates had gone. "Should we go see what's up?"

Ash nodded, abandoning what she'd been doing and she and Alex followed Gates's path through the crowd.

Both were curious now that Gates had actually taken off. Turning down the alleyway, they saw Gates leaning against the wall of one of the houses, a suspicious look on his face as someone passed him.

"You OK?" Ash asked, stopping next to him.

"Keep a watch for me, please," Gates said, looking up and down the alleyway. "I don't want people intruding."

Ash nodded, indicating for Alex to keep a watch on the way they'd come in. No one was around or coming down the alleyway, but it looked like Gates wasn't about to take any chances.

Once he was sure it was clear, Gates crouched down, trying not to draw any unwanted attention to himself and to make sure no one could see him past Alex.

"What are you doing?" Ash asked, crouching next to him.

"I don't know if it's going to work, since I'm still pretty spent, but all I can do is try," Gates said, his voice down. Ash frowned as Alex looked over his shoulder at them. Gates sighed. "If you hadn't already guessed, I can sometimes feel disturbances. Sometimes I can pinpoint them. There's a disturbance around here somewhere and the closer I got to here, the more I felt it. It's moving down this alleyway though, so I don't have long to try and track it."

"Right. What did you say your ability was again?"

"I didn't," Gates said with a slight smile. "But this might not work since I'm not properly recovered from the banshee attack yesterday. I can try, but I can't guarantee that I can pick the disturbance."

Gates turned his gaze back to what was in front of him. He carefully put his left hand out in front of him and a clear, glass-like barrier flickered to life. Ash hadn't seen anything like it before, but it all made sense now as to why Matt had needed him and why everyone was still alive.

"How's that going to help?" Ash asked as Gates quickly checked the other side of the alleyway. Alex was still watching out for anyone who might look like they were going to come down the alley.

"Just give me one second," Gates said.

There were still a few cracks in the barrier from the amount of beating it had taken over night, but for the most part it was in one piece and not flickering. It had taken a bit longer than normal to stabilize but was working fine now.

Gates put his right hand on the ground, still crouching down. "Alright, here we go."

Ash turned her attention to the barrier, seeing it flicker, which caused Gates to swear to himself, trying again to stabilize it as he kept his right hand on the ground.

"You see it?" Gates asked giving his full attention to the barrier as it flickered again. "Sorry. Like I said, I'm still fucked."

"I'm not sure what I'm looking at," Ash said with a frown. She could see something, but she couldn't quite make out what it was.

"By the looks of it, it's Matt and Chris," Gates said, trying to see deeper. He was seeing it a lot clearer than Ash, but he was connected to it after all. "They're in the same area as us."

"But they're not here," Ash said, looking around as the barrier disappeared. "How can they be in the same area if they're not here?"

Gates linked his fingers together as he stayed crouched down but looking at her. Ash looked him over before returning her gaze to his face.

"You heard of alternate universes?" he asked, his voice still down. Ash shook her head. "Well, to keep it short, we're in a long line of parallel realities. I think Matt and Chris stepped into one when they stepped off the Road last night."

Alex looked over his shoulder, then returned his focus to the crowded marketplace.

"But how?" Ash asked. "Can we contact them?"

Gates shrugged.

"Matt's the one who knows about this kind of stuff. I've dug into it a bit, but I don't know how you know which one you'll end up in. It's a guessing game. You step through one portal, and you could end up anywhere. I don't know if we can get in contact with them or not. The problem is getting them back to this reality."

"So, how do we do that?"

Gates shrugged again.

"No idea, I think they'll have to figure that out for themselves. There could be a specific location they have to go to in order to get back here. Or they might end up in another place entirely if they go to the wrong place. As I said, it's a guessing game."

"Can we at least try to get in contact?" Ash asked. "You can see them. Can you try contacting them?"

"I can try, I guess," Gates said. "I can't guarantee they'll be able to hear me, but I can try. We're in the same area, so we might be alright. They've moved from here, though. The disturbance isn't in this alley anymore."

"Well, then, I guess we move to wherever they are?"

Gates shook his head. "If they're in the middle of the town square, I can't reach them. Too many people around and some people don't take too kindly to people using their abilities in public. Best to wait until they're out of the market area. Once we're in a more secluded area, I'll see what I can do."

Ash nodded and Gates pushed himself up to a standing position. He offered his hand to Ash and helped her to her feet.

"I guess we go find something you like while we wait," Ash said, making Gates smile as he let her hand go.

"I guess we do."

CHAPTER TWENTY

Communication

"Matt, I don't think this is a good idea," Chris said.

"Sure it is," Matt replied, watching people go past as they stayed out of sight in the alleyway. "We need money. What else are we going to do to get it? We don't know how long we're going to be here."

"Well, if we're here for much longer, we'll both have to get jobs to pay for a nice house and some food."

Matt rolled his eyes, before returning his attention to the people passing by. There were a lot of people around.

"Look, all you have to do is chat to a couple of people and I'll do the rest. There are enough people in the crowd that they won't know I've grabbed their cash," he said. "We just need enough to get a room for the night, that's all. No more and no less, got it?"

"How do we know when we have enough?" Chris asked. "We don't know what things cost here."

Matt sighed. "If it makes you feel better, I'll do it myself."

Matt disappeared, seeing that Chris didn't want to take part in the thieving. Chris shook his head and spotted Matt in one of the other alleyways, the one they'd previously made their way through.

He watched as Matt made his way into the crowd, disappearing into it within seconds. He was going about it the old-fashioned way.

Chris looked back down the alleyway he was in. A group of girls passed by and one of them shot him a bit of a smile, making him reluctantly smile back. Then, he went back to trying to find Matt in the crowd, but he was nowhere to be seen.

"You think four-sixty will do?"

Chris jumped, looking to his right to see Matt counting the money he'd managed to thieve.

"How the hell did you get that much in such a short time?" Chris asked as Matt pocketed the cash.

"You learn a lot when you don't have anyone around for a few years," Matt said, indicating for Chris to follow him to the Candlelight Inn which was just a few buildings down.

"I thought you had Zeke and Gates," Chris said with a frown as Matt knocked into someone and was suddenly holding a wallet.

Chris was slightly impressed that Matt knew how to walk and pickpocket at the same time.

Matt carelessly dropped the wallet on the ground outside the Inn, then went in first, not bothering to hold the door for Chris.

"You know, you haven't really spoken about yourself much," Chris continued as they went up to the front counter.

There was no one in sight.

"Because I have no need to," Matt said, hitting the small bell to signal someone was waiting. "You don't need to know about me, Chris."

Chris stayed quiet, wondering why Matt was so against telling anyone about himself. Surely, he had to have a reason. But was it good or bad?

A young woman appeared behind the counter, making Matt completely stop and gawk at her.

"Can I help you?" she asked.

Matt went to say something but suddenly couldn't speak. He looked like he'd seen a ghost.

Chris stepped in, not sure what his issue was. "We were wondering if you had any rooms left? We heard it's quite busy this time of the year."

Matt forced himself to look away from the woman.

"Let me have a quick look," she said, looking down at the reservations book in front of her.

Chris nudged Matt in the side, making him look at him. Chris raised his eyebrows and shrugged, making Matt shake his head and go back to looking anywhere else but at the woman.

"We do still have a few rooms left," the woman said, looking up with a smile. "Do you need separate beds or separate rooms?"

"Just the one room with separate beds would be fine," Chris said, returning her smile.

She nodded. "That will be one-fifty for the night. Are you only staying the one night?"

"So far. We may need to stay a bit longer, but we'll let you know tomorrow when we know for certain," Chris said. "Who do we ask for? Who deals with it all?"

"Oh, I do. My name's Vivian."

She extended her hand in a friendly manner and Chris shook it. Matt forced himself to look up and shake her hand too, looking extremely uncomfortable about it the entire time.

"Can I get your names for the register?"

"Chris and Matt," Chris said.

"Alright, well that'll be one-fifty for tonight," Vivian said, writing their names in the book.

Chris nudged Matt hard again in the ribs, miming paying her. Matt reluctantly handed the money over.

Vivian smiled at them again, then turned and grabbed two keys off the board at the back.

"You'll be in room four. It's just down the hallway and to your left," she explained, giving the keys to Chris. "Breakfast is included in the price, so feel free to come down and have something to eat whenever you're ready, as long as it's before ten."

Chris gave a nod of thanks, getting a smile in return before he headed off with Matt in tow.

"You alright?" Chris asked, handing one of the keys to Matt who took it without a word. "You kind of fell silent. Something up?"

"Everything's fine," Matt said quietly, his tone harsh though. "Just don't push it."

"She remind you of someone?"

"What did I just say?" Matt snapped, stopping outside room four. "It's not really any of your business, is it?"

"Well, Matt. In case you didn't know, we're kind of stuck here. Together," Chris snapped back, Matt shaking his head as he unlocked the door. "So, it kind of is my business."

"Yeah, well, we shouldn't be here."

"Well, that's too bad, because we are," Chris said, following Matt into the room and shutting the door after himself. "If you know her, she clearly didn't recognize you because she would've said something if she did."

Matt moved to the window, pulling the curtains open and looking out.

"Well, clearly I don't exist here!" Matt said, his voice raised as he turned to face Chris. Chris could see the sadness on his face as his anger died. "And honestly Chris, she's better off not knowing me. I don't want the same thing happening to her as it did to my Vivian."

"Did Marion do something to her?" Chris asked sadly, his voice down now as Matt switched his gaze to look out the window again.

"What Marion did isn't any of your business," Matt said harshly, glancing at Chris before going back to looking out the window. "Now, I'd appreciate it if you just forget about this conversation and don't say another word about Vivian."

"She was your girlfriend, wasn't she?"

"What did I just say, Chris?" Matt asked, sounding very tired and worn out. "Just drop it."

"Marion took her away from you, didn't she?"

"Chris," Matt warned. "You're seriously pushing your luck."

"She took her like she did Jamie with Abel, didn't she?"

"She fucking killed her!" Matt shouted. "She killed her, Chris. She fucking killed her. Happy? Now you know more about me, just like you wanted to. Marion killed my damn wife."

Chris fell silent, looking at Matt in shock. Matt went back to looking out the window, not saying another word.

"You never know when to stop, do you?" Matt said bitterly, arms crossed as he stared out the window. "Just for once, Chris, listen to me when I say I don't want to talk about myself. It's easier on both of us. Now get out, go wander the damn markets for a while or fuck off. I don't care which. I just want to be by myself."

Chris nodded, seeing that he'd pushed Matt too far for today. He was exhausted from the battle with the banshees and the sudden alternate reality jump, leaving him in quite the mood, especially now that he'd pushed him into revealing something about himself.

Chris walked out of the room, making sure he had his key with him as he shut the door. He thought he'd go back out to the markets to see what he could find, even if he didn't have any money with him.

"Come on, how can you not like this one?" Ash sighed.

Gates looked at the shirt with the same disapproval on his face as every other time.

"I mean ... it's just not you," Gates said, shrugging as Ash looked at him with no amusement on her face.

"I disagree," Alex spoke up, crossing his arms and making both of them look at him. "I think it looks very nice, and Ash should buy it."

"Oh, give it a rest, Alex," Ash scolded as she put the shirt back, continuing to browse. "We'll find something we can all like."

Gates smiled and Ash gave him a subtle smile back, hoping Alex wouldn't see it.

"There it is again," Gates suddenly said, looking off to his right this time. "Just give me a few minutes and I'll be back. Going to see if I can contact Matt or Chris. You find something you like, you buy it, yeah?"

"If you say so, as long as you promise not to disapprove later on once it's done," Ash called after him as he headed off into the crowd.

She smiled to herself as she went back to browsing. A bright green shirt got her attention.

"It won't work, you know," Alex said as he watched her.

"What won't?"

"Your very lame attempts at flirting with him," Alex said, watching as she picked up the green shirt, a hint of a smile on her face.

"I'm not trying to flirt with him. He's the one that came up to me," Ash said defensively.

"But you're flirting with him," Alex said disapprovingly. "He's not interested in you, and he probably never will be."

"You're just jealous because he's sexier than you," Ash said matter-of-factly.

Alex gasped. "You didn't just say that."

Ash shrugged. "It's true, though. He's hot, nothing more to it."

"So, what? You're going to flirt with him as long as he's around and then what?" Alex began. "You going to take it further? Maybe 'seduce' him into sleeping with you? I know you, Ash. I know how you work when you want a guy."

Ash stopped, finally looking at him.

"What's your problem with him?" she asked seriously. "He's never done anything to you, so why the sudden attitude? What's wrong with me just flirting with him, huh? As you said, he's clearly not interested."

"Ash..."

"No Alex, don't. You're my best friend but that doesn't mean you have a say in who I want to hook up with."

Alex sighed, watching as she dropped the shirt and went back to browsing.

"I didn't mean it like that. I'm just watching out for you," he said softly. "I don't want you getting hurt, Ash."

"It's fine, don't worry about it," Ash shrugged.

Another sigh from Alex. "Look, I just ... I thought you liked Chris."

"Well, Chris isn't around right now, is he?" Ash snapped, looking at him. "He clearly doesn't like me in the same way and, hell, at least I have a bit of a chance of getting with Gates at least once. Chris wouldn't even think about it."

"Just don't want you getting hurt," Alex said quietly.

"If I do, it'll be my own fault."

"Matt? Matt, you there?"

Matt frowned, looking away from the window. He'd seen Chris go past half an hour ago and hadn't seen him since. Not that he cared right now. He was far from in the mood to deal with Chris.

"Who's there?" Matt called out cautiously, looking around the room. "Hello?"

He moved further into the room, not seeing anyone. He could hear someone, but he couldn't pick where the voice was coming from.

"Stop moving. You're breaking the connection. Stand still."

"Gates?" Matt queried. He knew that voice.

"Yeah man, it's me. You OK?"

"How are you doing that?" Matt asked, looking around again but still not seeing anyone. "We're not even in the same reality."

"I know. It's hard to explain and I don't have much time but it's like an extension to my ability. Like I said, I don't have long because this is actually the first time I've managed to get through so I must be in the same area as you in our world. I'm going to have to make this quick. Is Chris with you?"

"I sent him out for a bit," Matt said. "Why?"

"You guys, OK?"

"For now. Until he pisses me off again, we'll both be fine."

"Do you know where exactly you are? Like, what reality?"

"You really think I know that?" Matt snapped, turning back to face the window. The street outside was still bustling with people. "Even if I knew that, there's no way we can just get back. We've got to find the right place and we don't know where that is or how to get there."

"So, no ideas on how to get back?"

"None," Matt sighed, moving back to the window. He crossed his arms and leaned on the windowsill. "We don't how we're going to get back, or even *if* we're going to get back."

"You'll get back. Did you move again?"

"Sorry. Anyway, you guys all OK? What happened after Chris and I disappeared?"

"Not much. We're at the City right now, so that's another reason this has to be finished up. Couple of people have been drifting past and the last thing I want is to get myself caught. You know how people are about public displays of abilities over here."

"Yeah, I know," Matt said, watching people walk past the window but taking no notice of him. He wondered if they could see in. "Look, just keep everything together. Do what you have to do, whether that's see the Wizard, kill Marion, whatever. Just do what needs to be done and Chris and I will work on a way back. Just hope it's not too late by the time we get there."

"Will do. I've seriously got to take off. I don't know if we'll be able to get back in contact again or not. The only reason I knew you were in the same area was that I felt the disturbance. If it happens again, I'll see if I can contact you or Chris again. Keep together, man."

"Be safe, Blaine."

"You too, Matt."

CHAPTER TWENTY-ONE

Dealing with the Law

"There you are. I wondered where you disappeared to."

Ash came to a halt in front of Gates who stood up straight, brushing himself down. Ash crossed her arms as Alex appeared, stopping just behind her.

"You get hold of either of them?" Alex asked, looking over Ash's shoulder directly at Gates, a slightly disapproving look on his face.

"Maybe," Gates said, returning Alex's disapproving look. "Maybe if you asked nicely, I'd answer properly. Stop looking at me like I've done something wrong."

Alex rolled his eyes, not saying anything but breaking eye contact.

"Did you manage to contact either Matt or Chris?" Ash asked.

"I got hold of Matt," he said, looking away from Alex.

Ash nodded as a group of people moved past them. Gates stayed quiet, not trusting people around here. Once the group was far enough away that they couldn't hear him, he spoke again.

"Chris wasn't with him at the time, but they're in the same place. So, at least we don't have to go searching for him. Had to cut the conversation short, though, because people were looking suspiciously at me as they went past. The last thing we need is for people to notice us."

"What do you mean?" Alex asked.

"People in Oz don't tend to like public displays of abilities," Gates said, his tone suggesting that Alex should have already known that. "The consequence if you're caught depends on how you're using it. That's why I'm over here, out of the way in the alley, because it's less likely someone will see me. But apparently some people use this alley as a way to get to other parts of the City."

"Do you think anyone really saw what you were doing?" Ash asked, a little worried now.

Gates shrugged, crossing his arms across his chest as he looked at her, ignoring the look Alex was still giving him.

"I hope not," he said. "Because I could get into some serious trouble if someone did."

"Well, let's just go about our business and hope no one saw anything."

Gates nodded, Ash smiling at him as he headed back out of the alleyway. Alex quickly hurried after them.

"You find anything to buy?" Gates asked as Ash caught up.

She shook her head, following Gates over to one of the stalls they hadn't looked at yet. She saw Abel was not far from them, still browsing as well.

"No, didn't find anything," she said, watching Alex wander off. It seemed he didn't want to be around Gates right now. "Maybe you can find me something."

Gates gave a bit of a laugh. "We'll see."

Ash smiled, heading over to another clothing stall. Gates followed and watched as she began picking up and putting down clothes.

"There, that's him," an accusing voice rang out.

Gates and Ash both looked up to see three men a few yards from where they were standing. One man stood in front of the other two and was pointing at Gates. The two men behind were clearly some kind of law enforcement officers.

Several people also paused to see what was going on.

"Sir, we've had an accusation made against you," one of the officers said to Gates. The accuser smirked and crossed his arms. "This man says you were using an ability a few alleyways over. Is this true?"

"No," Gates automatically responded, not moving or saying anything more.

"He's lying," the accuser said harshly. Gates just looked at him with his usual, unreadable expression. "I saw it, my wife saw it, and my children saw it. Even a few others that were with us saw it. He was using it, and he was communicating with someone. It's obvious he's working against the City."

"I'm not working against the damn City," Gates suddenly snapped. "You don't know me. You don't have any reason to be accusing me of such bullshit."

"We all saw you," the man snapped back.

"Really? Where's your evidence?" growled Gates with a shake of his head.

"Men, please," the officer said. "We can sort this out civilly. There's no need to be yelling back and forth."

They were starting to draw a small crowd now and Alex came back over and joined them.

"He did it! We saw him do it!" the accuser shouted, gesturing to the crowd to back him up. He looked back at Gates. "He has some... barrier or something."

"Now, that's just not true," Gates said, trying to get this man off his case any way he could. "You need to get your facts straight before you go accusing people."

"I can prove it."

"Really?" Gates scoffed, crossing his arms again. "How? How can you prove it?"

The man looked around before grabbing a bracelet off the closest stall. Without a word, he threw it hard at Gates who just stood there. The bracelet hit him on the shoulder and fell to the ground.

"Wow, that really proved your point."

The man glared and shook his head, looking around for something else to throw at Gates.

Ash looked at Gates, getting a glance in return. If this man managed to prove his point, there was going to be a bit of a problem.

Before any of them could do or say anything else, the man suddenly grabbed a kitchen knife off the closest stall.

"You're not serious," Ash said, appalled. "Just to prove a point?"

"If this is what I have to do to get this man locked away for his public display of abilities, then I'll do it," the man threatened, brandishing the knife at them.

He stared at Gates, who watched him carefully.

"So, what? You're gonna throw it at me? Make me use my ability again, if I even have an ability?" Gates asked seriously. He was over this. "You're really willing to possibly hurt or even kill someone to prove a point? You'll be in the same damn cell as me, buddy."

"We don't need this going any further," the officer said, holding out his hand and gesturing to the knife. "Put the knife down and we'll all go elsewhere to sort this out."

Gates shook his head as the man with the knife stayed where he was.

"You know, if it makes you happy and stops you doing something fucking stupid, I'll just show you. How about that?" he said, staring directly at the man.

The man looked taken aback for a moment but then nodded. "You need to be off the streets," he mumbled.

Gates glared at him, then indicated for Ash to move out of the way. She grabbed Alex and moved them both back.

Gates sighed and put both of his hands out in front of him. The barrier appeared with no hassles this time. He was clearly feeling a lot better physically, as last time it had flickered on, but this time it was strong and appeared straight away.

Gates looked at the man, lowered his hands, and the barrier disappeared.

"Happy? Now, get rid of the knife."

The man dropped it on the ground, then looked back at the two officers. "See, I told you! Didn't I tell you?"

Gates shook his head. The officer who had tried to defuse the situation moved forwards and stopped in front of Gates.

"Sir, can I see your ID, please?"

Gates rolled his eyes, pulled his ID out of his pocket, and held it out. The officer took it with a nod.

Gates glanced at Ash. She looked appalled at what he'd just done.

Abel and Zeke both headed over now, too. They had seen what was going on and they stopped next to Gates.

"Blaine Taylor from Wonderland, no occupation, and no reason to be in the Emerald City," the officer said.

"You don't know anything about my business for being here," Gates said with annoyance. "And maybe I should be asking you for your ID."

"Sir, if you wouldn't mind, please come with us," the officer said. He went to take a step towards Gates.

Gates moved back a step, automatically putting his barrier up so the man couldn't get to him.

Abel glanced at him before looking at the officer.

"Look, sir, we don't have time for this," Abel said, the man switching his gaze to him as Gates kept his barrier between them. "Whatever's happened, I'm sure it's all a misunderstanding."

"He was using his abilities in public," the first man whined. "Now, he's doing it again. This man needs to be arrested and off the streets of this City."

"Well, maybe you've just made him do it," Zeke snapped, indicating to Gates who hadn't moved. "You ever think threatening people with knives isn't the right way to go about shit? I don't know about you, but whatever he's doing now is clearly an act of self-defense."

"Well, it wasn't when I saw him before!"

"You want to know what it was before?" Gates snapped. Everyone looked at him and the barrier disappeared. "Yeah, I was talking to someone. A couple of our friends are in a bit of a bind, and we needed to make sure they were OK. That's what I was doing. Checking in with them to make sure they hadn't gotten into any trouble. Maybe if you stopped to think before you went ahead and accused me of being an enemy of the City, we wouldn't be having this problem."

"Sir, I still need you to come with us," the officer said.

"I'm not going anywhere," Gates said. "If you want me to go with you, you're going to have to force me and I'm not going to make it easy."

"We don't want any trouble." The officer took another cautious step forward, causing Gates to put his barrier back up. "We just need to get out of the markets, and we'll talk this over like civilized people."

"You really think I believe that?" Gates asked, backing up another step. "I'm not stupid. We stay here and sort this out now."

The officer moved forwards again. This time, Zeke stepped in his way.

"If I were you, I'd back off."

The officer looked at Zeke, not intimidated. "It's protocol. You can't step in the way of the law."

"Wanna bet?" Zeke said. "Also, I'll be taking that ID back."

Neither the officer nor Zeke moved, both refusing to back down.

"As I said, we don't have time for this," Abel repeated. "Deal with this now and we can be on our way. We've got other important stuff to do."

"Like what?" Ash scoffed, making Abel look at her as Zeke grabbed Gates's ID from the officer who just gave him a glare. "Go back and sit in the group room while we wait? Please, I'd rather stay out here all day."

"Why are you being like this?" Abel asked. "You don't want Matt and Chris back? Ever think maybe this is our way of getting them back from wherever they are?"

"Gates knows where they are. Didn't you know that?" she said in a demeaning tone.

Abel looked at Gates, who just returned the look from where he was standing next to Zeke, no barrier now.

"You know where they are?" Abel asked, crossing his arms in annoyance. "Care to share? You ever think we need Matt and Chris here?"

"That's what I was doing," Gates said, sounding offended. "Before this guy came up and tried to get me arrested. They stepped into an alternate reality, different universe. I managed to get in contact with Matt and they're stuck right now because they don't know how to get back."

"Matt really screwed up this time," Abel said with a shake of his head.

Gates glared at him. "What, so you'd prefer they both got taken back to Marion? Really, Abel? You really think that would be a good place for them to be? You know what Marion would do to Matt if she got her hands on him? Why do you think he's been avoiding her for years? Not to mention what she'd use Chris for. Matt's put his fucking life on the line for you guys, more than once."

"We never said he had to," Abel retorted. "He stepped in and helped. I never asked him to do anything."

"Well, maybe when they get back, I'll tell him that," Gates said. "Seeing as you clearly don't need him anymore. Without him, you would most likely be dead. He got you out of that damn castle. You guys had nothing to do with it. If he hadn't stepped in, you all would've been in the hands of Marion and probably dead. Then what? What would have happened if he hadn't stepped in? You treat him like a bad guy half the time, when all he's done is try and help you get rid of Marion. You're not the only one she's fucked over, you know. Just be glad you've still *got* Jamie."

Abel finally fell silent. Gates gave him a disapproving look before looking back to the problem in front of them.

"Are we done?" Zeke asked, looking directly at the officer. "Because as previously stated, we're not about to deal with this anywhere else. We have more important things to be doing, so if you'd be so kind as to step aside, we'll be on our way."

"I'm afraid we still need to sort this out," was the response.

"Then, we're gonna be here for a long time."

Gates sighed. "Look man, we just want this sorted. What's the consequence?"

The officer looked at Gates. "You've displayed your ability three times in public. That's usually a few days in the cells and a fine to accompany it."

Gates shook his head. "Well, I don't have a few days and I'm not paying a fine."

"It's the law."

"And the law's wrong!" Gates snapped. "Why the hell is there such a problem with ability displays? I haven't hurt anyone, have I? I'd understand it if I killed or severely injured someone, but I haven't. The only person who thinks he's been hurt is this prick who's accusing me."

The accuser shot him a glare and Gates glared right back.

The officer in front of Zeke looked at him. "Please move out of the way."

"Not gonna happen," Zeke said in response, reaching back and handing Gates his ID. "You're staying there and I'm staying here. You can talk to him, but you're not getting to him."

"I need to do what the law says."

"Well, you're not arresting me," Gates said. "So, too fucking bad. Go take your issues to someone else. I've done nothing wrong."

The accuser turned his glare on Zeke.

"People like you are the reason we don't feel safe around these streets!" he snapped. Several people in the watching crowd nodded in agreement. "We don't know how dangerous your ability is. We don't know what these others can do."

"You really wanna find out?" Zeke threatened. "Because, believe me, mine's a lot worse than his."

"You really want get fined and arrested too?" the man shot back.

"If it means shutting you the hell up, then sure."

"Everyone just stop!" Ash suddenly shouted, making Alex jump. "Just stop!"

Everyone looked at her. She shook her head, looking around at them all as she spoke again.

"Just stop," she repeated. "This has gone too far. No one is getting arrested or fined. It was a misunderstanding. He didn't know there was a problem with it."

"Actually, I did," Gates said as Ash looked at him in disbelief. "Oh, come on. I'm not about to lie, Ash. I told you about it too, so don't try and get me out of this by lying."

"So, you don't want any help? You want to get arrested?"

"This isn't really your problem," Gates snapped at her. "Just let us deal with this."

Ash shook her head and threw her hands up, turning away. "You're unbelievable."

The accuser turned to Zeke, who returned the look, not saying a word.

"Move out of the way so they can arrest him. He knew the consequences when he did it, so he deserves to be locked away!"

Zeke stared him down, clicking his fingers without a word. The closest stall was suddenly alight. Someone screamed and everyone quickly moved out of the way of the flames.

"Guess I deserve to be locked away, too."

"You do! You all do!" the man shouted.

It wasn't long before the stall was nearly completely engulfed in flames. Ash and Alex watched on in shock. Abel just looked confused about what had just happened.

"We don't like people like you around here!" the accuser screamed.

"People like us?" Zeke scoffed. "Oh my. You're serious, too. Ever think there are a lot more people like us around here than not? Nearly everyone gets a damn ability, so save it. Everyone's the same deep down. Some just don't realize how damn connected we all are. There are plenty more of 'us' than there are of 'you', please."

The man looked at the officer in front of Zeke as someone finally arrived with water to put the fire out. The other officer hadn't moved or said a word yet.

"You can't tolerate this! He could set this whole place on fire!"

"Don't tempt me," Zeke muttered to himself. "But really, you want us all arrested because of one incident that didn't hurt anyone? We've done nothing wrong, man. You're the one who should be arrested for threatening people with a knife."

"Get them out of here before they hurt someone," the accuser shouted.

Zeke shook his head in disbelief as more people in the crowd started agreeing.

"We're not going anywhere!" Gates shouted. "You'd better let us move out of here or we're going to have a serious problem."

Alex held on tight to Ash, and Abel shifted uncomfortably, not liking where this was going.

"Like what?" the accuser mocked. "You going to knock me over with your barrier?"

"Move," Gates warned, stepping forward to stand his ground next to Zeke. "We're not going to put up with this much longer. Don't make me tell you again."

The man shook his head, ducked down, and picked up the knife he'd previously dropped.

"You all need to be locked away for good," he said, pointing the knife at Gates. "We'll drive you down to the cells if we have to!"

The whole crowd gave a cheer of agreement.

Gates shook his head as Zeke looked around. Abel joined them, and Ash moved to stand with them too, dragging Alex with her.

"What are we going to do?" Abel asked, keeping his voice down.

The accuser started urging the crowd to chant and demand the arrest of these people.

"We've got to get over to the training arena. Either that or we get back to the castle," Gates said, looking around. "If we find Jacob we can stop this. He'll vouch for us. Problem is, we don't where he'll be: castle or training arena."

"You need to willingly come with us," the officer near Zeke said. "We don't want this to end badly with someone getting hurt."

"At this rate, someone *will* get hurt," Abel said, gesturing to the excited crowd. "You need to stop this, right now."

Before anyone could say anything more, the accuser suddenly threw the knife at them. Gates reacted quickly, putting the barrier up. The knife hit it hard, making Gates wince as it bounced off and fell to the ground. Ash gasped. If Gates hadn't put the barrier up so quickly, it would have hit her.

"Alright, we need to move," Gates said.

Zeke clicked his fingers again, and another stall whooshed up in flames, causing people to move backwards.

"We're heading over to the training arena," Gates continued. "Someone there might be able to help or even go and get Jacob if he's not there. We can't stay here any longer or we're going to be killed by the whole of the Emerald City."

Gates signaled for everyone to get behind him. He put his left hand out, creating a barrier around the group of them, not just in front.

"We don't even know where the arena is," Abel said.

"Well, I guess we're about to find out. Get going."

CHAPTER TWENTY-TWO

Market Riot

"Head down the alleyway, straight back," said Zeke.

"Then what?" Ash asked.

They pushed their way through the crowd that was growing bigger and louder as they moved. Gates tried hard to push people off with his barrier. Some of the people stumbled backwards, causing others behind them to move back as well, giving them a bit of space.

"I don't know," Zeke said, pushing Abel along as Gates winced again from someone throwing something hard against the barrier. "We're gonna have to just ... wing it."

Gates managed to push someone else back hard, which caused the barrier to flicker. It was already taking its toll on him, most likely because he wasn't completely healed from the banshee fight.

"Just keep moving," Gates said, shoving another person backwards. "Don't care where, just go. Split into two groups and get to the arena any way you can. Zeke, you go with Abel. I'll take the other two."

Zeke nodded, grabbing Abel as Gates put both his hands out in front of him. The barrier behind them disappeared as they turned down the alleyway. Gates stopped at the entrance, keeping the front barrier up and blocking the entrance way with it as he stayed behind it.

Zeke and Abel ran down the alleyway, reached the end, and turned left. Gates looked over his shoulder at Ash and Alex who had stopped halfway down.

"We're going to go right," Gates called, getting a nod from Ash. Alex was too freaked out to say anything. "I'll meet you at the end of the alleyway."

Ash gave another nod, grabbed Alex again, and ran to the end of the alleyway. Gates stayed where he was. There was a massive amount of people pushing against his barrier now.

"You should have just given up!" the original accuser shouted at him, right at the front of the crowd.

Gates readjusted his position as he began getting pushed back. There was a lot of force from the market people.

"You should have minded your own damn business!" Gates snapped back, wincing as people started pounding their fists against the barrier.

"Gates, let's go!" Ash called urgently.

Gates looked over his shoulder at her, feeling himself being pushed back a bit more. He suddenly turned and took off down the alleyway, the barrier disappearing as he did so.

People began to fall on top of each other as they lost their balance with the sudden disappearance of the barrier.

"Go!" Gates shouted, halfway down now.

Not needing to be told twice, Ash grabbed Alex by the wrist and took off to the right.

Gates nearly lost his footing as he reached the end and skidded around the corner.

Ash looked back to see him catching up to them with ease. She knocked into someone by accident, Alex quickly steadying her as the sound of the crowd, still in pursuit, got louder.

Ash stopped. There was a dead-end up ahead. Gates joined them, quickly looking around for somewhere they could go.

"What now?" Ash asked urgently.

Gates looked around, signaling to his left. There was a house. "In here."

He grabbed the door handle, luckily finding the house unlocked. He held the door for Ash as he watched the group behind starting to gain on them. Ash dragged Alex in with her.

Gates followed, shutting the door and locking it from the inside. Someone started pounding on the door as Gates backed up.

"How are we going to get out?" Alex asked. He was terrified and stayed close to Ash. "We're trapped in a house with no way out."

"There should be a back door. Most houses have a back door," Gates said, turning and heading further into the house.

Ash wasn't too far behind him, and she pulled Alex along with her.

"Then what? We won't know where we are if we get out the back," Ash said, following Gates past the dining room.

The house seemed to be empty, and Gates stopped and turned to look at her.

"I don't know!" he snapped. "This isn't exactly what I had in mind for today, OK? I know this is entirely my fault, but I promise that we'll get out of here and we'll find the arena and the others. I'm not about to give up."

He turned and continued through the house. Ash and Alex followed along as the pounding on the door got louder.

Gates went into one of the rooms, seeing a door at the back. He went over to it, unlocked it, and cautiously opened it.

"Alright, this is our way out," he said. "Go through and keep quiet. This has brought us to another alleyway. Don't draw any attention to yourself, got it?"

Both nodded, and Gates gestured for them to go out. Ash went through with Alex clinging onto her. Gates followed them out, quietly shutting the door as the commotion at the front of the house continued.

"Alright, go," Gates said in a whisper. "Go back the way we came and go the way Zeke and Abel went."

Ash moved to the end of the alley, looked to her left, and slipped around the corner. Gates wasn't far behind.

"That's them! Quick, before they get away!" someone suddenly shouted.

"Run!" Gate said urgently, not bothering to keep his voice down now. "Don't stop, just go!"

All three broke into a run. Gates made sure he stayed at the back in case something happened.

"Ash, I don't like this!" Alex exclaimed as Gates pushed past someone who tried to stop him. "We're not gonna make it!"

"We're fine!" Ash said with annoyance. "We're gonna be fine."

She dragged him along further, past the original alleyway. Gates looked back.

"You two keep going!" he called, sliding to a halt. "Just disappear and get to the arena however you can!"

"What? Where are you going?" Ash asked, pulling Alex to a stop.

"I'm going to keep them off you," Gates said. "I'll be there. Don't worry about me."

Ash shook her head, not bothering to argue. She grabbed Alex again and kept going, leaving Gates as he put his barrier up and backed his way up the alleyway they'd originally come from.

Zeke stayed quiet as he and Abel watched a group of people go past. Some of the original crowd had seen the two of them take off and had made a smaller group, which was now hunting them.

Once they'd been out of sight of the others, Zeke and Abel had quickly stopped at one of the houses, ducking around the back of it and keeping out of sight. Unfortunately, someone had seen them, and they'd had to keep moving. Now they had no idea of where they were or which direction the arena was.

"What are we going to do?" Abel asked in a whisper as someone went past, not even looking at the two men that were pressed against the wall of an off-street alleyway.

Zeke shook his head, still keeping watch on the street next to them. "I don't know," he said, his voice down as well. "But we've got to keep moving."

He moved down to the end of the alleyway, looking both ways before indicating to Abel that it was clear. Abel followed him out as Zeke tried to work out where they should go.

"We've got to get them off our trail," Abel said, looking around as well as someone else went past, also paying them no attention.

Zeke nodded, a thoughtful look on his face.

"I don't know what we can do," he said, beginning to walk. "We'll have to figure it out when we run into them again. We've just really got to get to the arena."

Abel nodded, walking alongside him now. Neither of them said a word as they walked, trying not to draw any attention to themselves as they made their way down the street the same way the other group had been going.

"Abel!" they suddenly heard, making them both frown and stop.

They turned to see Ash and Alex running towards them. Gates was nowhere to be seen.

Abel and Zeke exchanged looks before Zeke looked at Ash. "Please tell me they didn't get him."

Ash shook her head. "As far as we know, he's alright. He drew them away back into the marketplace. He told us to find you and said he'd find us at the arena."

Zeke nodded. It was obvious he wasn't overly impressed with Gates's decision.

"Alright, keep moving," he said, hearing the commotion of the group that was hunting them getting louder. "Back into the alley, quick."

Not waiting for anyone to move, Zeke pushed everyone into the closest alleyway. The four of them pressed against the wall in the hopes that they wouldn't be seen as the group started passing by. There were a lot more people now than they'd realized. They must have recruited more people as they'd searched.

Someone happened to look down the alleyway and see the four of them. They shouted and pointed them out, getting the attention of the rest.

"Goddamn it," Zeke said, quickly moving. A wall of flames appeared at the end of the alleyway, stopping the group in their tracks. "Go, go back."

They rushed down the alleyway as the flames died out. The stone of the streets meant the flames weren't able to last long.

"Oh God, we're back in the market!" Ash exclaimed. Alex continued to cling onto her, holding her arm tightly. "How? How did we get back here?"

"I don't know, but let's get to the other side and split again," Zeke said. "Gives us more of a chance."

Ash nodded, dragging Alex with her through the marketplace, Zeke and Abel not far behind. They all ran down the closest alleyway.

Someone suddenly grabbed Ash, pulling her and Alex back. Gates glanced at her as he backed up, the other group he'd been keeping at bay beginning to push them back.

"We stay together!" Gates said. "No one splits. We get there together unless we get cut off."

Everyone nodded, the barrier flickering as people pushed against it. Gates shouted and shoved them back hard into the crowd.

"Which way?" Abel asked as they reached the end of the alleyway.

"Just keep going straight, down the next one!" Gates called over his shoulder as a crack appeared in his barrier.

Abel nodded, and everyone rushed down the next alleyway. Gates stayed at the back, the barrier gone and the noise from the crowd getting louder.

Gates quickly caught up to them, and the five of them halted at the end of the next alleyway.

"We don't know where this arena is," Zeke said as the crowd made their way towards them. They started to slow as they realized the people they'd been pursuing had stopped. "We're kind of stuck."

Gates shook his head. "I know I said not to, but we're going to have to split again. Zeke, you take Abel and Alex this time. I'll take Ash and go to our right, you go left. You find the arena, you find someone to help, and we'll meet you there."

Zeke gave a nod of understanding as Alex shook his head.

"No, I'm not splitting from Ash," he said defensively.

"Alex, I can't keep this barrier up against these people!" Gates said urgently as the first part of the crowd halted, a few yards away from the others. "There are way too many of them and it's better if you're with Zeke. Ash won't get hurt, I promise."

"What if the barrier fails, though? Then what?" Alex continued to worry. "You'll both get hurt."

"We'll be fine," Ash reassured as Zeke kept a watch on the crowd, all of them having halted in the alleyway but hesitant to come any closer. "Gates can't keep all of us safe. Go with Abel and Zeke."

Alex looked at her with worry, reluctantly letting her go and getting a nod and a smile from her.

Gates looked at Zeke and nodded. Zeke grabbed Alex, taking off at a run to their left, Abel with them as Gates and Ash took off to their right.

"This is getting way out of hand," Ash said as the crowd protested and began pursuing again, splitting to go after both groups. "Where the hell is this damn arena?"

"I don't know, that's why we're running blind," Gates said, grabbing her wrist and picking up his pace, making sure she wasn't about to get left behind. "We've just got to lose these people and find it. Someone there will be able to help us."

"You sure?" Ash asked, trying to keep up with him as they passed more people. He was a lot faster than she was, but he still had a grip on her and was pulling her along.

"No."

Ash shook her head as they turned a corner. They could now hear the crowd but not see it.

Seeing something up ahead, Gates suddenly dragged Ash down the next closest side street.

Stopping halfway, Gates roughly pushed Ash up against the wall, staying close as he looked over his shoulder briefly.

"Careful there," Ash said, looking him over as he watched the entrance way to the side street. Some people went past but didn't look over.

Gates looked at her, Ash giving him a bit of a smile as he stayed close to her, more people going past. There were a lot more than had originally been after them.

"Sorry," he said, his voice down. "Just try to keep quiet, yeah?"

Ash gave him a bit of a smile as he went back to looking over his shoulder, still holding onto her wrist.

"How many are there?" she asked, her voice down too as she looked past him, able to see a few people but not a lot.

Gates looked back at her. "I thought you were going to be quiet for me. Don't particularly want to get caught out, do you?"

Ash rolled her eyes as Gates glanced over his shoulder, the final few people going past.

"Well, I am being quiet. I'm not speaking too loud, am I?" she asked, Gates turning his focus back to her now. "By the way, you've still got hold of my wrist."

"I know. I can't have you disappearing on me, can I?" Gates said with a bit of a smile.

"I'm not like that, I'm not about to disappear. You really think I can fend for myself against such a big group of people?"

"Matt seems to think you're rather untrustworthy," Gates remarked.

Ash shifted a bit as she looked at him. "Matt has issues with everyone."

Someone came down the side street and they both became silent until the person had walked past.

"That's because he's been wronged by too many people," said Gates as he looked her over briefly before looking back at her face. "I know for a fact that he doesn't trust you one bit."

"Well, Matt's not here, so his opinion of me doesn't really matter, does it?"

"I guess not."

Ash looked him over again, Gates just watching as she did so, not saying a word.

"What about you?" she asked, looking back to his face. "Do you trust me?"

Gates gave her a bit of an amused smile, holding up her wrist and making her look at it. He still had hold of her.

"If I trusted you, would I still be holding onto you?"

Ash smiled as Gates lowered her wrist, still not letting her go.

"You never know," Ash said, putting her free hand on his shoulder. "For all I know, you're into that kind of thing."

"I can guarantee you that I'm not."

"Well, I don't know that. I don't know you."

Gates gave a bit of a laugh, clearly amused at her attempts at flirting.

"Well, I don't know you, either," he said to her, watching her run her hand down his arm. "For all I know, you could literally be playing me right now and I'd have no idea."

Ash smiled at him, getting a brief shake of the head in return.

"Just so you know, I'm not just going to up and leave," Ash said, putting her hand back on his shoulder as someone else came down the side street. "I know Matt doesn't trust me, but that doesn't mean you can't."

Gates looked at her for a few seconds before turning his attention to the end of the side street. The coast seemed pretty well clear.

"We should keep moving," he said, moving back a bit and getting a disappointed look from Ash. "Oh, come on, we're in public."

He let go of her wrist and started walking.

"Doesn't mean we can't have a bit of fun," Ash called after him as he checked both ways to make sure they were in the clear.

She stopped just behind him, making him look at her.

"Ashley, public indecency isn't really my kind of thing," Gates said, turning and heading off back down the side street, planning on going whichever way it took them.

"Well, I don't know that," Ash said as she caught up to him, walking alongside him now. "Like I said, I don't really know you, so how am I meant to know what you like?"

"Now's not really the time," Gates said seriously as they neared the end of the side street.

"Then when is?"

Gates sighed, coming to a halt and making Ash halt too.

"If you hadn't noticed, we're kind of in the middle of being hunted down by an angry mob," he said. "This seriously isn't the time to be asking me about this kind of stuff. Anyway, it's none of your business what I'm into, is it?"

Ash rolled her eyes as Gates began walking again, forcing her to start walking again so that she wasn't left behind.

"Just trying to get to know you a bit more, seeing as we're kind of in this together," she called, hearing Gates sigh even though he was a few paces in front of her. "If you hadn't noticed, Gates, even once we find this arena, we're still in a group that wants Marion gone. No matter what you do, you can't avoid me forever."

"I never said I was going to," Gates said, halting in the middle of the street to allow Ash to catch up. "I was just saying that now's really not the time, OK? You really want to get to know me, you come find me once this is done and we're back in the castle, got it?"

A sly smile crossed Ash's face as she stopped in front of him, making sure she stood rather close, looking him straight in the eyes as she spoke.

"Sounds like a good idea to me," she said as someone passed by, heading down the street they'd just come down.

"I know what you're trying to do, and it's not going to work," Gates said before grabbing her wrist again, turning, and walking down the main street again.

Ash sighed, but smiled to herself, as he dragged her along.

Gates just wanted to get to the arena and fix the current mess they were in.

CHAPTER TWENTY-THREE

Dark Pasts and Grim Presents

"I'm really sorry about this morning," Matt said quietly.

Chris looked up from where he was sitting at the small table in their room at the Inn.

Matt was sitting on the edge of the bed closest to the window, a sad look on his face as he looked at Chris.

"It's fine, Matt. I shouldn't have pushed it," Chris said, still feeling bad about what had happened. "I should've left it alone like you asked."

Matt nodded and sat there, linking his fingers together as he looked down. Chris stayed quiet too. He had nothing to say to him.

It was late afternoon, and he was certainly feeling it from the long night and day. It made him wonder how everyone else was coping, wherever they were.

"I'd known Vivian since we were kids," Matt suddenly said, making Chris look over at him. Matt didn't look up. "We met through a mutual friend."

Chris nodded, not sure what to say in return.

Matt sighed, shifted his position, and looked out the window. "Marion killed her. That woman has never shown mercy or empathy in anything she's done. I know Abel thinks she hasn't been corrupt for long, but she was always like that, even before he got there. She never cared about how the things she did affected anyone, never cared about anyone but herself."

"How long ago did Vivian die?" Chris asked sadly.

"Five years ago," Matt said quietly. Chris was sure he saw a tear run down his face. "She's been gone for five years."

"Why didn't you do anything about Marion at the time?"

Matt shook his head, looking down again as more tears ran down his face. It was making Chris uncomfortable, but he could see Matt wanted to get this out.

"There was nothing I could do," Matt said with another shake of his head, back to looking out the window. "You really think some low-life peasant could get in Marion's way? Make her stop? No, I couldn't do anything."

"Why did she kill Vivian?" Chris asked, hoping it wasn't the wrong thing to ask.

Matt finally looked over at him, having wiped away his tears. "You know, Chris. after all this time, I still don't know."

"She didn't have a reason?"

Matt shrugged. "No idea. One minute she was there, the next she was gone. Marion did it herself. She wonders why people hate her, not that she really cares. She took the life of an innocent woman and now look. Look where she's ended up. Abel's just lucky Jamie's still alive. I don't get that kind of luxury."

"Matt, I'm really sorry," Chris said truthfully, the sadness on his face reflecting the look on Matt's.

"Yeah, well. Nothing I can do about it now, is there?" Matt said bitterly. He sighed and went back to looking out the window. "Just wish I'd gotten out of there before it was too late."

Chris nodded, not saying anything else as Matt stared vacantly out the window.

"Hey," Chris said after a bit of silence, making Matt look at him. "How did you learn to use your ability?"

"Still wondering about that, hey?" Matt said with a bit of a laugh.

Chris gave him a sad smile and a small shrug.

Matt shrugged too, looking down briefly before looking back at him.

"I don't know. I kind of found out about it by accident. Sometimes people need certain things to trigger their abilities. After Viv died, part of me did too. I guess that was the trigger for me. One day, I was just sitting there in my place—the underground place you saw—and it was dark. I must've been thinking about a certain place in the castle, because I stood up in the dark and next thing I knew, I was in the castle dungeons with no idea how I got there."

"I think mine only works in self-defense," Chris said, making Matt laugh a bit.

He seemed to be cheering up slightly. Not a lot, but a bit. Chris smiled at him.

"You'll get the hang of it, eventually," Matt said. "There's a training arena at the Emerald City. They have instructors to help people with getting a grip on their abilities. Funny, Gates first used his in self-defense too."

"Really? Against what?"

Matt shook his head and chuckled softly. "We were in the town square at the castle in Wonderland and someone tried to accuse him of stealing something. The guy went to hit him, and Gates automatically put his hands out to stop the guy. Next thing, this barrier appeared, completely stopped the guy. He couldn't get to either of us. We took off pretty quick after that, stolen items and all."

Chris laughed while Matt smiled at the memory.

"So, how did you guys get a grip on them?" he asked.

"It was just trial and error really, and time," Matt said. "When I was getting the hang of it, I used to just try and move from one room to the next. Couldn't figure out why it only worked when there were shadows around. It wasn't until later that I figured out it was shadow-stepping. I could only use the shadows to move myself to different places."

Chris nodded again. "Must've been really weird the first few times."

"I remember that nearly every time I stepped from one room to another, my head would spin, and I'd be dazed for a few minutes. The more I did it and got the hang of it, the dizzy minutes went to seconds and then the seconds went to never," he explained, Chris nodding in interest. "Just ... that damn banshee place completely messed me up. Whenever I was down there or up above, the energy around there screwed it all up again. I got back up after the dagger was gone and I was on my damn knees, completely drained with my head spinning. That hasn't happened since I was learning to get a grip on it. Tell you what, Chris, I absolutely hate that."

"I can imagine."

"Just wish I'd known how to shadow-step before everything happened," he said, sadly. "Viv would most likely still be around if I could. She and I'd be back home if I could."

"Where are you actually from?" Chris asked curiously.

"California," Matt said with a laugh, causing Chris to smile a bit. "You know, I can't even remember how I got down here in the first place. I've been here too long. Seven years total. Can't even tell you what my home looks like back up top, I've been gone that long. Don't even know if it's still there."

"Wow..."

Matt nodded. "Yeah, don't get caught down here for too long, Chris. It'll kill you eventually. I'm pretty well dead inside."

"Come on, Matt. Don't be like that."

"It's true," Matt said. "Any part of me that wasn't dead inside, died with Viv. I can never forgive Marion for what she did, but I'm not going to be the one to kill her. Abel feels wronged by her enough that he'll be the one to do it."

"Haven't you ever wanted to kill her?" Chris asked.

"I've always wanted to kill Marion, ever since she took Viv from me," Matt admitted. "But killing another human isn't that easy. Believe me, I know."

Chris stayed silent, not knowing what he was supposed to say in response to that statement.

Matt sighed.

"I was the one to kill three out of four of Marion's elite guards about three years back, just before Abel got here," he explained. "Marion had an informant who was telling her about the people developing abilities. This guy could tell you who had what. His ability was to read other people's abilities. He'd informed her that I'd gotten quite the hang of mine and was too dangerous not to be stopped."

"Marion has an elite guard?"

"Not anymore," Matt said before continuing with his story. "She sent her top four guards after me, managed to track me down to one of the domains I never used to reside in. I'd been in and out of the castle the entire time they'd been discussing it, so I knew they were coming for me. The fourth one that I left alive was later killed by Hunter at the tournament. Just wish it hadn't had to go down that way."

Chris nodded, seeing Matt wasn't about to say anything more about it. He glanced out the window and saw a few streetlights coming on, even though it wasn't night yet.

"How did Zeke find out about his ability?" he asked.

A bit of a smile appeared on Matt's face at that memory.

"Once again, complete accident," he explained. "Blaine said something to him that really pissed him off. He said something like he'd be able to beat him in a fight with ease or something. Zeke was all like 'I could beat you like that' and clicked his fingers. Next thing we knew, a vase of flowers was on fire."

Chris laughed out loud at the image, Matt laughing a bit too.

"After that we set up an area for us in an empty house in the same domain," Matt continued. "Making sure there wasn't anything Zeke could accidentally set on fire if he got frustrated with himself. We all worked on it and now here we are. Top of our game and knowing what we can do with our abilities."

Chris nodded, while Matt shrugged and went back to watching people outside walk by the window.

"So ... are you OK?" Chris asked, making Matt return his gaze to him. "You're a bit torn up from the banshee."

"Nothing I can't deal with," Matt said with a shrug.

It was then that Chris noticed the bloodstain on the thigh of Matt's jeans.

"What about that?" he asked, pointing to it and making Matt look down.

"Tore the stitching, that's all. Nothing I can't deal with. That's what happens when you go against the entities of the dark and you sacrifice your life for the better."

"Any ideas on what happened to the girl in the coffin?"

Matt shook his head. "Honestly, no. My best guess is that she's now free-roaming, coming out during the night to take unsuspecting victims back to the burrow and feeding herself and the other banshees. When we opened the coffin, we most likely broke the binding. You never know what can happen with dark magic."

Chris nodded and Matt said no more.

"Matt, are we ever going to get back home?" Chris asked after a few minutes of silence.

"Right now, Chris, I'm not counting on it."

CHAPTER TWENTY-FOUR

Trial by Combat

Gates checked both ways down the street, making sure no one was coming from either way. He looked back at Ash and gave a nod, indicating for her to go out first.

For now, it seemed as though they had lost the crowd that had been following them. Gates hoped the others had lost theirs, too.

"Alright, there's the arena," Gates said pointing. "We're going to get to it and go inside. The others will have to find us in there. We can't afford to get stuck waiting outside."

The arena was still a few streets over, but it was like a stadium, and they could see it over the top of the houses from where they were standing.

Ash was very glad to see it and didn't mind that Gates still had a firm grip on her wrist.

Gates picked up his pace, dragging Ash with him between several houses, the arena getting closer.

"Hey, Blaine! Stop!"

Gates stopped upon hearing his name, pulling Ash to a stop, too.

Zeke gestured for them to come over to where he was, off to the side of someone's house.

"Why are you over here?" Gates asked, quickly moving over to him. Zeke was by himself. "Where are the other two?"

Zeke shook his head, looking around the corner to make sure no one was around.

"No idea, I turned around and they were gone," he said, crouching down and forcing Gates and Ash to do the same.

Gates let go of Ash's wrist.

"We were a couple streets over and I stopped briefly to keep a couple of people back. I turned and they were gone. I don't think they realized I'd stopped, but I hope they might be close to the arena by now. We could see it when we got split."

"Well, we don't really have time to hang around and find out," Gates said. "We'll sort this out once we get there. Let's go."

The three of them stood up, quickly checking to make sure they weren't being followed, before moving back out and moving in between more houses.

"Oh, can this day get any worse?"

They slowed their pace as they approached the arena. The entire crowd was blocking their way into it. There was no way around.

Abel suddenly appeared from a side street, accompanied by a small blue cat.

"Well, glad to know you're still alive," Zeke said.

"Sorry, we didn't realize you'd stopped until you were gone."

"I figured."

"What are we going to do? We have to get into that arena," Ash said as the small cat rushed over to her. She picked him up, glad to see that Alex was alright.

"We're going to have to go through them," Gates said, clearly not liking the idea of it. There were a lot of people in their way, and it looked impossible. "We have no other choice."

"You can't get through all of us!" said the man who had tried to get Gates arrested to begin with. Of course, he was at the front of the crowd.

Gates shook his head. "You're wrong. We're not about to give up."

"You're all going to get locked away," the man said, triumph in his voice. "You should just give up now and save yourselves the hassles of trying to weasel your way out of it."

"None of us are getting locked away," Gates shouted at him, slowly closing the distance between himself and the crowd. He glanced over his shoulder at the others. "Get behind me."

Zeke, Abel, and Ash didn't need to be told twice. Ash made sure she kept hold of the little blue cat so he wouldn't get crushed or lost in the crowd.

Gates's barrier suddenly appeared in front of them and some of the people in the crowd started to look a bit wary.

"I'm going to give you one warning: move out of our way and this doesn't have to go any further," Gates called.

Ash hoped that they'd listen to him and move aside.

"We're not going anywhere," the man said. "You don't belong here. None of you do. You're not even from this county!"

"Screw it, I warned him," Gates said, more to himself than to anyone else.

He started moving, keeping the barrier in front of him as the others trailed behind. Just before they reached the crowd, Gates moved one of his hands back and the barrier appeared around the sides and the back of his small group.

"I'm going to move quick, so keep up," he said.

He picked up his pace, everyone else doing the same. Once they reached the crowd, Gates pushed hard against everyone in his way, knocking the first man straight back into the people behind him. The people in the crowd kept trying to push them all back, but Gates used all his strength to push against them.

"This is ridiculous!" Zeke commented as they pushed through the final lot of people.

Gates turned around. He kept his back to the others, so the barrier in front was the only one there now. The crowd was not giving up, though, as they desperately started trying to break through again.

"Get into the arena!" Gates shouted.

More and more people were now shoving and banging hard against the barrier, making Gates wince from the force.

Ash, carrying the cat, went first through the arena gates, followed by Abel and Zeke. Gates wasn't far behind, still trying to keep the crowd at bay.

The arena was huge. It was a lot like the tournament grounds in Wonderland, except larger and more modern. It had a dirt floor and a lot of areas up the back that were obviously used to train different people and their abilities.

Jacob was in there with a few people. He looked to be explaining something to one of them, and he looked over with a frown as the small group rushed in.

Gates still had his barrier up and was being pushed further and further into the arena. Zeke, Ash, and Abel could see how strained he was becoming from the constant force.

"What the hell is going on?" Jacob shouted, abandoning his post with the people he'd been training.

"We ran into a bit of a problem and were hoping you could help us out," Abel tried as Jacob broke into a jog to clear the space between them.

"Everyone stop!" Jacob shouted, slowing his pace and holding his hands out to try and force everyone to calm down as they continued to push Gates further back. "Stop now!"

When no one stopped or listened to what he said, Jacob stopped a few paces away and flicked his hands straight down. The bright light they remembered from the previous night suddenly burst into sight, causing everyone in the arena to stop and shield their eyes.

"Everyone stops when I say stop!" Jacob snapped as the light slowly died down. "What the hell is going on?"

People blinked and rubbed their eyes, trying to see again as their eyes refocused.

"These people need to be locked up!" the original accuser shouted from somewhere in the middle of the crowd. "Public displays of abilities are punishable!"

Jacob strode forward to stand next to Abel.

"What have you done?" he asked, not caring who answered him. No one spoke up. "Someone had better answer me!"

"I was trying to get hold of Matt and Chris," Gates finally spoke up. "I moved out of the way, someone saw me, and now here we are, being chased down by an angry mob of market goers!'

"Hey, watch it!" someone in the crowd shouted, while several others jeered.

The accusing man finally moved to the front of the crowd.

Gates looked at him with disapproval as he stepped away from him, wanting his space back.

"This one," the man said, pointing at Zeke who just flipped him off. "Set two whole stalls on fire and tried to burn people too!"

"You were hunting us down!" Zeke snapped. "I was trying to get you all to back off! I was not trying to burn anyone."

"You didn't have to burn the stalls!"

"You didn't have to be a complete psycho and hunt us!"

"Everyone shut up!" Jacob yelled. He walked over and stood in between Gates and the crowd. "We need to all shut up and figure out what we're doing about it."

"I'm not getting locked away for days," Gates said. "And these pricks won't take anything else as a consequence."

"It's the law!" the man shouted.

"Stop," Jacob warned, looking between the two of them. "We're going to sort this out. No more yelling or getting defensive. Now, what does everyone want?"

"For him to be locked up!"

"Trial by combat!"

"Kill him!"

"Fight to the death!"

Gates shook his head, looking over at his companions. Abel shrugged. Ash looked back at Gates with worry and started stroking the small cat, trying to calm herself and Alex down.

"Alright!" Jacob shouted, raising his arms and trying to get everyone back on track. "Everyone who wants him locked up, put your say in now."

The crowd started shouting about it.

"Alright, trial by combat? We're not going to kill him or make him fight to the death. It's not punishable by death."

The entire crowd this time shouted, even the ones who'd wanted to see Gates locked away.

Jacob looked at Gates and shrugged. "Crowd's voted. Sorry, Gates."

—◦❖◦—

"Well, we've really done it this time. Why couldn't we just get here, see the Wizard, find Marion, and kill her?" Abel said.

They were sitting in a room under the arena, out of sight from the still angry crowd outside.

"Nothing's ever easy," Gates said. He was the only one standing. His arms were crossed, and he leaned back against the wall. "Hopefully the Wizard will be back tonight, and we can get in to see him."

Ash was sitting next to Abel, with Zeke on her other side. She continuously patted the little cat on her lap. Alex was clearly enjoying it but still seemed worried.

"You don't even seem worried about this," she stated.

Gates shrugged. "No reason to be. What happens, happens."

Ash shook her head as the cat lowered his head onto his paws, trying to relax.

Everyone looked over as Jacob gave a brief knock on the open door and came into the room.

"How are you all doing down here?" he asked, stopping a few paces in. He sighed as everyone shrugged. "Look, I know this seems bad, but just know you haven't really done anything wrong. Yes, public ability displays are an issue, but you didn't know that and, even if you did, you shouldn't have been hunted down like that."

"Damn right we shouldn't have," Zeke said. "All we wanted was to know that Matt and Chris were OK and now look, Gates has to go and fight some prick."

"That's what I came down to tell you about," Jacob said, switching his gaze to Gates. "I assume you don't know how this works?"

Gates shrugged. "I've heard about them but surprisingly never seen nor taken part in one."

Jacob gave him an unamused look before explaining.

"The rules are simple. You can use your ability, but you can't have any form of weapon apart from that. You can't kill your opponent. You have to get them to the point of either knock-out or submission. Everything else is pretty well legal. Understand?"

Gates nodded, ignoring the look of worry on Ash's face.

"Why is this even happening?" Abel asked, standing up. "Can't you just let us go and we'll stay in the castle?"

"Rules are rules, Abel," Jacob said. "The crowd voted. Sorry, there's nothing I can do about it. Just like abilities, working for the Wizard also has its downsides. We've got to go by the rules and keep the peace."

Abel shook his head, not bothering to sit down again.

"We have trained people for this kind of thing," Jacob said, looking back at Gates.

Gates sighed. "Great, just what I need. What happens if I lose?"

"You get locked away for a couple days," Jacob said. Gates shook his head. "You win and you get to go without consequence. Best to keep out of everyone's way for a few days. You should be OK, though. You seem to have a pretty good handle on your ability."

"Yeah, but I'm not recovered from the attack last night!" Gates finally snapped. "And I'm hurting more now because of those idiots out there. Every time they shoved themselves into the barrier, I felt it. Every little damn impact. I'm not recovered enough to fight a professional. The bruises are spreading up my damn arms already from the impacts I've taken today!"

He held both his arms out so everyone could see the damage. There were a few slashes on his right arm, and the bandages on his wrists no longer covered the purple bruising that was now spreading up his arms. Gates pointed to it.

"That's literally all from today," he continued. "Marks and all. I've taken too much over the past twenty-four hours and now I've got to fight someone? Those cuts are from the things people threw at me today. Do you know how much pain I'm in right now? Do you even care?"

"You'll be fine," Jacob reassured as Gates crossed his arms again. "Once this is done, we'll get all of you back to the castle and we'll deal with it."

"Yeah, sure you will."

Jacob sighed. The crowd outside suddenly started cheering.

"What are they cheering about?" Ash asked cautiously. Alex was also looking alert now, staring out at the open door.

"It means the fighter is out," Jacob said as everyone exchanged looks. He looked at Gates. "Nearly the entire City's here. You've had an hour's rest and now it's time to get out there and get this done."

Gates shook his head, finally pushing himself off the wall. "Fine. Let's get this over with."

Jacob nodded, indicating for him to follow as he left the room. Gates followed him out and everyone else stood up.

Ash picked Alex up and he meowed at her.

"Yeah, I know," was all she said in return as they all followed Jacob and Gates.

Jacob jogged up the steps, hearing the crowd get a lot louder. Gates shielded his eyes from the light, as they got to the top, and stepped out into the arena.

"This is a joke," Abel said as they halted behind Jacob and Gates.

"Just be grateful none of you have to be in this, too," Jacob said over the sound of the crowd.

"This is way more people than Wonderland ever got. This looks like the entire City's turned out for some entertainment," Abel remarked as he looked around.

"I assume that's the guy he's fighting," Abel continued, pointing at a tough-looking guy standing in the middle of the arena, looking their way.

"You assume correctly," Jacob said, turning to look at them all before looking directly at Gates. "Good luck. Remember, you can use your ability. These fighters, though, are trained by the best in the county. They have no abilities of their own but are taught how to get around everyone else's."

"Oh, so now you tell me?" Gates said disapprovingly. "A head's up would have been nice!"

"Sorry," Jacob shrugged.

Gates shook his head and walked away from them, heading further into the arena.

Ash watched him walk away. She held Alex even tighter as he was looking very freaked out as the crowd got even louder.

"You really get this many people out to see this kind of thing?" Ash asked.

Jacob nodded as he crossed his arms but didn't move. They were obviously watching from where they were standing.

"You should see when we have fights to the death when something goes seriously wrong."

Ash shook her head, keeping a tight hold on the cat. Abel and Zeke exchanged looks before going back to watching Gates.

Gates halted a few paces away from his opponent. The man smiled and cracked his knuckles, making Gates wince.

"You ready to get pounded?" the man said loudly, causing the crowd cheer and stamp their feet.

"They'll cheer for anything, won't they?" Gates remarked, shifting his position. He heard the crowd start to protest against him.

The man suddenly rushed at him, but Gates put his barrier straight up. The impact of the man bouncing off it sent Gates stumbling back a few paces. He shook his hands out.

His opponent was very muscular. He put Matt to shame, and made Gates look a lot smaller than he actually was. The man gave a laugh as he stayed where he'd stopped, just watching Gates.

"You're weak!" he called. Gates could only just hear him because of the cheering and jeering of the crowd. "You should just give up now before I seriously hurt you!"

"I'm not going anywhere," Gates snapped back, putting his barrier back up and making the man laugh again.

"You really think that's going to stop me? Me?"

"Never said this would."

Gates suddenly pushed his right hand out hard and a new piece of the barrier suddenly spun off, heading towards the man. It hit him hard in the chest as Gates kept his main barrier up. The man stumbled backwards, caught off guard.

"I didn't know he could do that," Abel said to Zeke as they watched Gates do it again, pushing the man back another few steps.

"You'd be surprised at what Blaine has taught himself to do," Zeke said, crossing his arms as he watched on. "Helps lessen the impact on his barrier. Even though he still feels it, it's less than when someone goes against his main one. He used to try and get different uses for hours to stop himself getting so hurt. He's got more than that in his arsenal, believe me."

Abel gave a brief, unsure nod as he went back to watching Gates, who continued to stand his ground.

His opponent was mad now. "You won't win this! You'll be locked away before you know it!"

"You want to bet? Bring it on!" Gates shouted back at him, far from intimidated, and keeping the same stance.

The man growled and suddenly sprinted towards Gates who looked ready to take the hard impact.

The man smashed into the barrier, knocking Gates onto his back. He quickly rolled out of the way as the man went to punch him but hit the dirt ground hard instead.

Gates had his barrier straight back up. He pushed it forward and a piece knocked hard into the man, making him stumble backwards.

The crowd had gone silent. This was not what they'd expected to see.

Gates stepped back and put his left hand out. A barrier appeared on the right side of the man as he tried to regain his balance.

Next thing he knew, Gates had him stuck within the confines of a barrier on each side of him. He started pounding against it, Gates flinching with every hit.

"You can't keep me in here forever!" the man shouted, hitting the barrier and causing a crack to appear. An amused smile appeared on his face as he saw Gates flinch, realizing he was feeling it. "You're going straight to the dungeons!"

The man kicked the middle of the barrier as hard as he could. Gates shouted in annoyance and doubled over in pain, which caused the barrier to disappear.

Not waiting a moment, the man rushed towards him again. Gates held his side as he used his right hand to put up his barrier again. The man pushed against it hard, making Gates strain to keep it up.

The barrier flickered a bit, giving the man the slight advantage he needed. He'd figured out Gates's weakness.

The barrier disappeared and he grabbed Gates by the front of the shirt.

"This is over. Just give up and I won't hurt you."

Gates shot him a glare, putting his hand up right between the two of them. The barrier flickered to life, catching the man's hand half in it. He shouted in pain as Gates pushed back against him.

"*You're* not going to hurt *me*?" Gates mused. The man's hand was still trapped within the barrier, clearly causing him a lot of pain. "You feel it yet? Any longer and it'll lose circulation. A bit longer than that and it'll die and need to be amputated. Give in yet?"

"No!" the man shouted.

Gates glared at him and pushed more, making the man shout again.

"One word and I'll let you go," Gates said, turning his hand to the side a bit, twisting the barrier to his right and forcing the man to his knees. "Believe me, this is just the start of what I can do."

"Alright, alright!" the man shouted, submitting. "It's over. I quit!"

The barrier disappeared and the man held his hand against his chest, glaring at Gates.

The crowd began protesting as Gates moved back a couple of paces. He collapsed to his knees.

Zeke ran over to him. Abel and Ash exchanged looks before joining him.

"Alright, let's get you up," Zeke said, helping Gates to his feet. "Let's get out of here before they decide you cheated and come after us again."

CHAPTER TWENTY-FIVE

Beginning of the Iron Army

"I don't know what we're going to do about those intruders!" Carmen said, pacing back and forth.

Marion sat back, watching her. Hunter looked disinterested as he sat next Marion. His dog was dozing at his feet, clearly happy with where he was.

"Where did Shade and Chris end up?" Marion asked, looking at Heather who was sitting a few chairs away.

Carmen stopped pacing and also looked at Heather.

"They stepped off the Road in the dark," Heather said. "Which means they're long gone. There's no way of reaching them now."

"Vincent might be able to," Carmen said, drawing everyone's attention back to her. "He's powerful enough that he might be able to reach them and pull them back or at least guide them in the right direction."

"How's he going to even find them, Carmen? They're in a completely different reality!" Heather exclaimed, far from happy with the current circumstances.

Carmen shot her a glare before looking at Marion. "We'll get them back and we'll get them here. They can't stay under the City's protection forever and since they're after you, they'll come along soon enough. All of them will."

Marion's lips twisted into an unamused smile. Hunter shifted his position as he listened in but didn't contribute to the conversation.

"By the way, we have something to show you," Carmen informed Marion. Heather's face lit up with a grin and she jumped up out of her chair as Carmen looked at the open doorway. "Vivian! Get in here!"

Vivian appeared at the doorway, looking at the floor as she stayed silent.

"Help Marion up and bring her with us down to the dungeons," ordered Carmen. "There's something we need to show her that we think she'll enjoy seeing."

Vivian nodded, staying silent as she went over to Marion and helped her out of the chair. Marion nodded at her and signaled that she could do the rest herself.

Hunter got to his feet as well, his dog sitting up automatically as he heard Hunter stand.

"This way!" Heather said, rushing out of the room.

Carmen glared at Vivian. "Get back to work."

Vivian left the room and Carmen indicated for Marion and Hunter to follow her as she headed out after Heather.

"Heather came up with an idea a few months back," Carmen explained as they followed her to the dungeons. "She's very proud of it too."

They continued through some empty rooms and down a few stairs until they reached the dungeon doors which were currently open.

These dungeons were a lot smaller, and quieter, than the ones in Marion's castle back in Wonderland. This was a smaller castle, though, and they didn't have any prisoners as of now.

A few candles lit parts of the dungeons, and Heather gestured impatiently to Marion to join her in the dim dark outside one of the cells.

"What have we got?" Marion asked.

Hunter stopped just behind her, and he crossed his arms as he waited. His dog sat obediently at his feet, also waiting.

Heather went into the cell and came back holding something in her hands.

"I came up with the idea," she said, handing Marion a pair of shackles.

"Wow, shackles..." said Marion, disappointed.

"Not just *any* shackles," Carmen said.

Heather nodded enthusiastically as Marion looked them over again, still unimpressed.

"We started experimenting," continued Carmen. "We were trying to figure out if we could block people's abilities."

Marion raised her eyebrows, her interest piqued now. "You have my interest."

Carmen smiled, while Heather looked very excited about showing her invention off. Hunter and Marion both looked over the shackles as Carmen explained.

"We managed to infuse it with magic blocking spells, using ingredients that can dampen abilities. We did a lot of research and experimenting and we think we've finally done it."

"So, how does it work?" Marion asked, intrigued at the idea.

Heather pointed to the inside of the shackles, to the thin metallic spikes inside.

"It turns out that abilities are born in the bloodstream, that's why they're unique to each person," she said. "But different things trigger them in the brain somehow. We're still not exactly sure how or why. This metal spike goes into the top of the wrist and straight in. Everything it's infused with goes directly into the person's bloodstream and stops the ability from working. There's also a magic chemical I didn't find until yesterday to put into it. But now it should work perfectly."

"Well, now," Marion said, looking at Hunter who also was looking very interested.

Marion looked back at Carmen and Heather. Heather had a wicked smile on her face, clearly proud of her work.

"At least now if we manage to get someone, we have something to hold them with. Is this the only pair?" Marion asked.

Carmen nodded. "We haven't had the chance to make another one yet. That's next on the list. Now, there's also something else I want to show you. This way."

She walked out, heading back up the stairs as Heather went back into the cell to put the shackles back in their place. Marion and Hunter followed Carmen back up the stairs, Hunter's dog trotting along behind.

"So, if we manage to get one of them," Marion mused as she reached the top of the staircase. "Is there any way we can stop them from using their abilities so we can get them into the shackles?"

Carmen glanced back at her as they headed outside. Heather had caught up with them now and walked just behind Hunter. The red dust of the barren land kicked up behind them as they walked.

"We've been working on that," Carmen said as the bright sunlight hit them all. "Our best bet is to get the shackles on quickly, but we're hoping to have a spell or something to at least weaken them and then get them into the shackles because I doubt they'll be put in them willingly."

"You think?" Hunter scoffed as they descended a hill, seeing an abandoned castle a little way down. "Where are we going?"

"I told you; I have something else to show you."

Heather laughed and picked up her pace so she could walk with Marion. She linked her arm with Marion's, ignoring the look Marion gave her.

"You are going to love this," Heather said. "Been working on it for a while now and we think it'll come in handy for you to try and take down Vincent and your friends."

"Once again, they're not my friends."

Heather laughed again.

Carmen was ahead of them, and she pushed the doors open and entered the abandoned castle. The others followed. Hunter's dog started growling and trying to hang back the closer they got to the doorway.

Heather looked back at it. "Quit it, dog."

The dog stopped fussing and reluctantly slunk along behind Hunter as they all went into the castle.

Carmen looked at them from where she was standing near the back of the room. There were several lines of figures in the dark near her.

Heather let go of Marion's arm and Marion stopped near Carmen.

"This is the Iron Army," Carmen said. "We've been working on them for a while now. We're going to get our land back and we need an army to do so. This is it, or the start of it. Have a look."

Marion cautiously walked over to the first line of figures. They were humanoid, at least six-foot-seven high, all wearing some form of silver and black armor.

"What are they made out of?" she asked, putting her hand against one of them and feeling how cold it was. She could hear what sounded like a heartbeat when she moved closer to it.

"It's a magic material. We've combined the strongest metals from around Oz, all magically infused," Carmen explained. "We couldn't recreate the shackles' binding ability though, so the soldiers will have to deal with people's abilities by themselves until we can figure it out. At this rate, though, they'll just have to deal with it anyway."

Heather skipped over, stopping beside the soldier next to the one Marion was inspecting.

"Aren't they pretty?" Heather said, putting her arms around the still soldier. "They'll take over Oz in no time once we have a few more, a lot more…"

Heather held onto the soldier for a few minutes, before reluctantly letting go and giving it a quick, undeserving kiss.

"They're certainly impressive," Marion said, moving back and admiring the motionless soldier in front of her. "Did I hear a heartbeat?"

Carmen nodded. "Their hearts are made of steel. We're trying to make them impenetrable, but that's what keeps them alive. Believe me, Marion, this is how you kill those travelers and take over Wonderland *and* Oz."

"Wonderland's already mine," Marion said, narrowing her eyes as she looked back at Carmen. She held her side, wincing at a sudden sharp pain. "But I'll help you with Oz once I've gotten rid of the ones who followed me here. How did you say Shade and Chris might get back?"

"Vincent might be powerful enough to locate them and pull them back. It'll take a lot of power though and will leave him defenseless for a good few days," Carmen said as Heather joined her.

Marion looked at the soldier in front of her. Its eyes were closed, and it looked like it was sleeping.

"Why do you need those two?" asked Carmen.

"I have my reasons," Marion said, a bit of a smile forming on her lips. "And they won't know what hit them until it's too late."

CHAPTER TWENTY-SIX

The Wizard

"Hey, you doing OK?" Alex asked, looking at Gates from the infirmary doorway, hands in pockets as he watched him.

Gates looked up from where he was sitting on the edge of a bed. A nurse was in the middle of bandaging up his wrists again, extending them further up his arms this time.

"I'm fine, really," Gates said, the tiredness showing in his voice.

Alex nodded awkwardly. "Just ... thought I should come by and see..."

Gates nodded, noticing Alex's slight smile, before turning his attention back to the nurse. He just watched as she finished up with his left wrist and half his arm.

"I want to apologize for earlier, in the markets," Alex said.

Gates glanced at him before going back to watching the nurse begin on his right, starting with the slashes on his arm.

"Nothing to apologize for," Gates said, flinching as the nurse cleaned the slashes with something that stung. "Jesus Christ, that hurts."

"What happened exactly?" Alex asked, coming in and standing in front of him.

Nixx appeared at the doorway and wandered over to them, too.

"I don't know. It's always happened, though," Gates sighed as the nurse started bandaging his right wrist and arm. "Ever since I first started learning how to control it. The more damage the barrier takes, the more damage I get. It's never been this bad, though. First time I've had cuts because of it. Also, first time it nearly shattered last night with the banshees. Never taken such a beating like that yesterday or today in my whole life."

"It's rare but some people do get physical effects from their abilities," Nixx said. "I heard you lot got yourselves into a bit of trouble with the law today."

"It was a misunderstanding," Gates said. "Nothing more."

"I also heard you got hold of Matt," Nixx continued.

"News certainly travels fast around here, doesn't it?"

"When you talk to the right people, yes it does."

Gates sighed, going back to watching the nurse as she finished up.

"You should get some rest," Nixx said, looking at Gates as the nurse left the room. "You're exhausted again."

"It's been a long day," Gates said, pushing himself off the bed and groaning as he did so. "And I somehow forgot just how much I currently hurt."

"Ash was worried about you," Alex spoke up.

Gates glanced at him as he shook his hands out. "Sure. Look guys, if you don't mind, I think I'm going to go lie down for a few hours."

"We don't mind at all," Nixx said as Gates passed him, giving him a thumbs up as he headed to the door. "The Wizard is due back at eight, so we should be in not long after that."

"Yep, come find me," Gates said as he disappeared out the door.

Nixx shook his head and looked at Alex. He indicated for him to come with him. Alex nodded and did as he was told.

Abel looked up at the knock on the door. Nixx and Alex were standing there, looking in.

"How's she doing?" Nixx asked as he came in, his voice down.

Alex followed him in, shutting the door quietly behind himself.

Abel shrugged, looking at Jamie asleep in the bed on his left.

"She's OK. Exhausted, but OK," he said, his voice down too. "Going to take her a bit to get back on her feet but she should be OK. I'm just glad she's alright."

"Has she been awake yet?" Nixx asked.

Abel nodded, still watching Jamie. "She woke up briefly for few minutes after I got here. She was still half asleep, though. I don't think she knows where she is at the moment."

"That's good. We thought we'd stop by and check in," Nixx said. "We were told that the Wizard should be back by about eight. Did you want one of us to come by and get you, or do you want to stay here?"

"I think I'm going to stay here, just in case."

Nixx nodded again, going back over to the door with Alex in tow. Abel didn't move as they left and shut the door.

"Think she's going to be alright?" Alex asked as they began walking down the hallway.

"She should be," Nixx said. "You got her here just in time. Don't know what would have happened if you two hadn't made it."

Alex shrugged and stopped as Nixx turned and faced him.

"Did Gates say where Chris and Matt ended up?" Nixx asked. "It seems like a lot of people don't quite know what's going on."

"He said something about alternate realities," Alex said as Nixx nodded with interest. "And apparently, he somehow contacted Matt and got through to him. They seem to be OK, but that was what caused the issue with the law today."

"Right, public ability displays."

"Even you know about that?"

"You'd be surprised," Nixx said, beginning to walk again, Alex hurrying after him. "I've spent the majority of the day in the library, and you learn a thing or two when you find the Oz Law section."

"If you wouldn't mind, please come this way and mind your step."

Everyone got up from where they were sitting, following the woman down the hallway. There was a door at the end, and she stopped in front of it.

She opened the door, gesturing for them all to go inside. One by one they all went in, Nixx first, followed by Gates and Zeke, with Ash and Alex last. Alex was once again clinging onto Ash.

The room was quite large. There were several doors around the room, leading to other areas of the castle. The bottom half of the walls were red, the top white. There were lamps and light fittings around the entire room, as well a lot of decorative items on shelves and small tables. A long wooden dining table, set for dinner, sat in the middle with a lot of chairs stationed around it.

"Reminds me a bit of home," Nixx remarked as the door closed behind them.

"Please take a seat at the table. Dinner will be served shortly," the woman said, indicating for everyone to sit down.

They all exchanged looks. Weren't they here to see the Wizard? Hesitantly, everyone went over to the table, cautiously looking it over.

"Guess we do as asked?" Alex said, inspecting the plates on the table. "I *am* hungry."

"You can sit down, you know. It won't hurt you."

They all looked over to see a young woman enter the room, walk over, and stop at the table near Nixx.

"I'm Dorothy," she introduced herself. "I take care of a lot of the Wizard's affairs. Please, take a seat. He shouldn't be much longer."

"At this rate, we'll get dinner before we get the Wizard," Gates muttered, Zeke smiling in amusement as they all took a place at the table.

Alex made sure he was next to Ash. Gates sat across from her with Zeke next to him, facing Alex. Nixx took the seat closest to the head of the table on the same side as Gates and Zeke.

Dorothy smiled as she went to the opposite end of the table, taking the head of the table position at that end.

No one said a word as waiters came out carrying plates of food.

Gates shook his head as they placed the trays and plates in the middle of the table near them. "Called it."

Zeke shook his head this time, amusement on his face which caused Alex and Ash to both smile as well. Nixx was the only one not amused.

"Shame Matt and Chris aren't here," Alex said as more plates of different types of food were brought out. "Matt really wanted to meet this guy."

Everyone else shrugged, not game to say a word.

"Hey, sorry I took so long. Business to attend to, you know?"

A man bustled into the room, taking the seat at the head of the table opposite Dorothy. He mustn't have been any taller than five-foot-six and had a neatly trimmed beard and long brown hair that came down to his shoulders.

"I'm Vincent," he said, smiling at everyone around the table. "Some people refer to me as 'the Wizard' but, you know, I'm still just a guy." He paused, looking around at the group. "Wait, shouldn't there be eight of you? Jamie's out of action so she doesn't count right now, but there's only five of you. I was told you were a travelling group of nine, including Jamie."

"Abel's with Jamie at the moment," Nixx explained, figuring he was the only one who was going to speak unless spoken to directly. "We're currently two people down."

"OK," Vincent said, trying to make sure he understood correctly. "So, where are your other two people?"

"Alternate reality," Gates said, watching as someone brought out another plate of food. It never ended. "We don't know how we're going to get them back."

"Riiight," Vincent said slowly, dragging the word out. "How did they get into this alternate reality?"

"Stepped off the Yellow Brick Road in the dark," Zeke said, frowning as even more food came out. He exchanged looks with Gates who just shrugged at him.

"OK," Vincent said. "And, why did they step off the Road?"

"We got blocked by some stupid bitch and Marion's champion, Hunter," Ash spoke up. Alex nudged her side to try and get her to be quiet. "They wanted both of them, so Matt grabbed Chris, they stepped off the road and are gone."

"Uh-huh," was Vincent's next response. "And how do we know which reality they're in?"

"We don't," Nixx said. "Gates managed to get in contact with Matt. They're OK but they can't get back. We're hoping that maybe you could help us out with that."

"Some realities are harder to reach than others," Dorothy said, everyone looking down the table to her. "He might be able to reach them but there's also a chance that he won't be able to."

"Sorry, who did you say you were again?" Gates asked, looking directly at her. "Because I'm pretty sure he can speak for himself?"

"Dorothy takes care of my affairs," Vincent said, everyone looking back to him. "I get that you guys and gals are all stressed and probably tired out from the day and everything that's happened, but there's really no need to be rude about things."

"I'm not tired. I have no idea what you're talking about," Gates said, with a frown. "I'm absolutely exhausted and I'm not sitting here, listening to this. Can you, or can you not, get Matt and Chris back?"

"I'm going to assume you're the one who contacted them," Vincent said, choosing to ignore Gates's snide remarks. "If I can find them, then yes, I can get them back. If not, then no. There can be consequences too, if we're not careful."

"Always with the damn consequences," Gates muttered.

"Would you just calm down?" Nixx scolded, Gates shooting him a glare. "I could have left you up in your room, but you insisted on coming down here. If you don't want to be here, go back to your room and stop being such a downer. Hear the man out."

Gates rolled his eyes.

"Alright, so what else can I help you with, besides getting your group members back?"

"They're friends," Gates said defensively. "Not just people in the group. One of them is family."

Vincent nodded and smiled. "And I understand that. Family will do anything for family. I promise I will do all I can to get them back for you."

Gates nodded, deciding to fall silent now.

Vincent looked at Nixx, seeing he had something he wanted to say to him.

"We wanted to start by saying thank you for helping Jamie," Nixx began, Alex nodding to confirm the statement. "We don't know what we would have done if you hadn't done that."

Vincent waved a hand, dismissing it, that smile there the whole time. He was certainly cheerful, and it didn't sit right with Gates.

"It was nothing. I'm here to help," Vincent said. "Alex over there was the reason she got here. It's very good to know you guys are a team and work well together. You all made it, so that's a plus, right? Well ... nearly all of you."

Gates rolled his eyes, choosing not to comment on that.

"Either way, all of us, especially Abel, are very grateful," Nixx continued, Vincent nodding again and still smiling. "We were also hoping you'd be able to help us out with another issue."

"Which is what?" Vincent asked. "By the way, put something on your plates! Eat something! There's more than enough to go around. I don't know why they cooked so much when they knew there wasn't going to be a lot of us."

"Are you aware of what's been happening over in Wonderland?" Nixx asked, watching Vincent begin putting food on his plate.

Alex took that as the cue to help himself to food as well. Ash also started loading her plate up.

"Oh, Marion's still at it?" Vincent sighed. "She'll never learn."

"Well, you see, she's not there now," Nixx said. "We came from there, followed her here, and she disappeared into Oz. That's why we're really here, besides Jamie of course."

Vincent stopped loading his plate and looked at him. "She's in Oz? She must be hanging out with Carmen and Heather."

"Didn't we already mention that?" Gates asked, not moving to get anything to eat. It seemed he wasn't hungry or, if he was, he wasn't showing it. "I'm pretty sure someone said that."

"For Christ's sake, Gates, give it a damn rest. Can't you even go five minutes?" Nixx scolded.

"I went five fucking minutes," Gates snapped back. "He's not listening."

"Just shut up and calm down."

"You gonna make me?"

"If I have to!"

"Please, I'd appreciate it if you didn't use your abilities here. Keep it for the arena," Vincent said. "We're a clean city, you know."

"What's the deal with the abilities law anyway?" Gates asked as Nixx sighed. "I nearly got arrested today after I contacted Matt out of sight. We got hunted down because of it. What's the deal with that?"

"It's a protection for the City," Vincent said, finally sounding annoyed about Gates's tone. "We've had incidents in the past where people would use them against city dwellers and we had to put a stop to it, a law against it. It works and it keeps the peace."

Gates gave an unamused smile, not saying anything more.

Vincent switched his gaze back to Nixx, indicating for him to continue from where he'd left off.

"We were having problems with Marion in Wonderland," Nixx continued. "We almost got her, but she escaped through a manufactured door and into Oz. She's after Matt and Chris for some reason, which is why they stepped off the Road. We need to get to her before she gets to us because she's going to bring a war."

"Hmm," Vincent mused, picking something up off his plate and examining it before biting into it and chewing slowly. "We certainly don't want another war. If she's hiding out with Carmen and Heather, there's not a lot I can really do. That's their domain. We don't venture out that far and it's wise not to go near it. It's warded like you'd never believe. It's not somewhere you want to be."

"Is there anything we can do?" Zeke asked, as Vincent switched his gaze to him.

"For now, we need to pretty well just gear up, I think," Vincent said after a couple of seconds. "We can't really do anything until they come to us. We have alerts around Oz so when they reach certain areas, we'll know. Carmen and Heather will play a big part in this, if it happens. They've been building an army for years and it won't be long before it's ready for them to use. We can't do much for the moment. I'm not starting a war."

"What should we be doing in the meantime?" Nixx asked.

Vincent shook his head. "I'd suggest you all go down to the arena and get yourselves trained up, not just with your abilities. There's always potential to unlock with abilities, it can be endless, really. Go find Jacob tomorrow and he can help you out. He's the best I've got. I know you've already met with him a few times."

Everyone nodded, Vincent giving a nod as well.

"Well, then," he continued. "Everyone enjoy something to eat and then you should all go and get some rest. A few of you look exhausted and it'll be a long day tomorrow if you do decide to go down to the arena."

"I think I'll be giving that a miss," Gates said, pushing his chair back. "And I'll be giving this a miss. Thanks, but I think I'm going to go sit in the quiet for a while."

Vincent gave an understanding nod, Gates giving a nod back as he headed to the door and left the room.

"He's not normally that rude," Zeke said. "He's had a hard day. We all have."

"It's fine," Vincent said. "Anyway, like I said, have something to eat and get some rest. I'll see about your friends tomorrow."

CHAPTER TWENTY-SEVEN

The Return of Alice

"Didn't take you as the type to be down here," Ash said from the doorway.

Gates looked over at her. He'd been in the library for the last hour or so.

"You'd be surprised," he said, looking back down at what he'd been reading. "It's quiet down here with not many annoying people."

Ash smiled and wandered in. Gates paid her no attention as she came over. When she sat next to him on the sofa, he glanced at her before looking back to his book.

"What are you reading?" she asked, trying to see the cover of the book he was holding.

"Nixx pointed me towards the law section," Gates said with a bit of a smile, showing her the cover. "Just trying to catch up on what not to do."

Ash gave a bit of a laugh. Gates smiled as he went back to reading.

"Look, I just wanted to thank you again," Ash said, but Gates didn't take his focus off the book. "If you hadn't stepped in, that knife probably would've hit me."

"You've thanked me once today already. You don't need to again."

"That was different," Ash said. Gates sighed and looked at her. "That was on behalf of the others. This time, it's directly from me."

Gates looked her over as he thought, before returning his gaze back to her face. Ash shifted a bit.

"You didn't come down here just to say thank you," he stated. "Why are you really down here with me, Ash?"

Ash looked at him for a minute before deciding to answer.

"You said to come find you after we'd dealt with everything for the day," she said. "And I wanted to make sure you were alright. I was worried about you."

"So I've been told," Gates said with a sigh. He put the book down on the coffee table in front of them, before looking at Ash again. "Why do you suddenly care so much? You don't even know me."

"That's why I'm here now, isn't it?"

"Ash, look," Gates began. "I get that you supposedly want to check in with me and now apparently want get to know me, but I want you to know that you don't need to constantly keep tabs on me. What do you want to know about me?"

Ash looked at him in surprise, caught off guard by the fact that he was saying he'd tell her something if she asked. Gates sat back, watching her and waiting for some sort of question or response.

"I guess we could start with ... your interests?"

"Not getting myself arrested in some foreign county."

Ash rolled her eyes, getting a slightly amused smile in return.

"So, you're just going to be a jerk about it whenever I ask a personal question?" she said, not very impressed.

Gates shrugged. "Never said I couldn't answer sarcastically."

Ash glared at him, Gates still smiling as he shifted his position.

"What happened to the other one?" he asked, pointing to the necklace she was wearing and making her look down. "The first one?"

"It's in my room," Ash said, getting a nod as she looked back up at him. "Didn't want to break it by carrying it around. Why do you ask?"

Gates shrugged again. "No reason, just wondering. I think it looked nicer than the one you're wearing. Also, where the hell did you get that shirt?"

This time, Ash smiled.

"Found it before I came back here," she said. It didn't look like Gates was disapproving of it. "You guys had already come back so I ducked out to get something. You like it?"

"Ah, well," Gates said, still looking her over a bit. "It's ... well ... interesting. Certainly doesn't leave much to the imagination."

"That's the point," Ash said with a laugh, Gates looking back at her face. "I like it."

"Well, as long as you're happy with it."

Ash rolled her eyes again, shifting and moving a bit closer to him. Gates didn't move or comment on how close she was.

"Are you ever happy?" she asked. "Seriously, does anything actually make you happy?"

Gates looked at her for a few seconds while deciding how to answer.

"I'm just tired," he said, the look on Ash's face showing she didn't believe him. "The past two days have been full on, that's all."

"So, when you're not tired, you're actually happy?" Ash asked. "If you're supposedly tired, then why are you down here and not asleep in your room?"

"Because it's not that late, I don't sleep early, and I have nothing else to do."

"It's nearly ten o'clock."

"Exactly."

Ash looked him over as he stayed where he was.

"Well, I mean..." she began, avoiding eye contact. "There's always something else to do if you want to go up to your room..."

"Let me guess," Gates said, catching onto her hint as she looked up. "This 'something' involves you going with me?"

"I'm just throwing ideas around here," Ash said, holding her hands up in her defense as Gates shook his head and looked away. "And I can already see you considering it."

"How would you know?" Gates asked, glancing at her but not looking at her directly. He was aware of how she worked. "You don't know what I think about."

Ash put one of her hands on the side of his face, forcing him to look at her.

"You'd be surprised," she said quietly, keeping her hand where it was. "I know how people work."

"Ash, I know what you're doing," Gates said, his voice equally as quiet. "And I'd appreciate it if you stopped. I don't want this going any further. This isn't going to happen."

Ash looked at him in annoyance, as Gates just looked back at her without a word.

"You need to lighten up and have a bit of fun," Ash said, clearly not about to take no for an answer.

Gates rolled his eyes in response, but still didn't say anything. Ash shook her head and moved so she was sitting in his lap. She put her hands on his shoulders.

"Ash, get off me," Gates said sternly. "I said no, and I'm not about to change my mind."

"I wouldn't count on that," Ash said, annoyed at being denied. It didn't happen very often, and she didn't like it when it happened.

Ash leaned forward and kissed him. Gates pushed her back.

"Don't."

Ash glared at him. Gates was starting to look angry with her for not listening to him. Ash increased her grip on his shoulders, making him shake his head.

"One thing you'll learn very quickly, is that I nearly always get what I want," Ash said.

She looked at him, making sure she kept direct eye contact now. It seemed like this was the only way this was going to work.

"One thing you'll learn about me is that when I say no, I mean it," Gates growled in response.

Ash smiled and leaned forward a bit more, making Gates look away.

"Come on, don't do that," Ash pouted, putting her hand on his face and forcing him to look at her again. "You make my job a lot harder if you look away."

"Don't you dare," Gates warned, knowing exactly what she was trying to do. She knew how to use her ability too well, and he knew that's what she was doing right now. "I'm seriously done with this, Ash. Get off me."

"Now, where's the fun in that?" she asked, making sure she kept eye contact again. "Why don't you want to have some fun?"

Gates didn't say anything, the glare on his face said it all. Ash smiled, seeing that her ability was slowing bringing him around. It was very rare that it didn't work.

"I hope you know this is far from OK," Gates said as Ash put her hand back on his shoulder, still not breaking eye contact. "And I'm not a willing participant in tonight's list of activities. Also, I'm very mad at you right now."

Ash shrugged. "How else could we have some fun if you keep saying no? You'll be willing in a few minutes. You'll forget you're mad at me."

"Yeah, maybe until the morning," Gates said back bitterly. "When this shit wears off. How long does it last?"

"Depends on how long I need it to last."

"I hate you right now."

Ash smiled. "You won't hate me in a few minutes, handsome."

"Hey Matt, you awake?" whispered Chris.

"Does it look like I'm awake?" Matt said, clearly in a bit of a mood again this morning. "No Chris, I'm still asleep. Of course I'm awake!"

Matt sat up in bed, then moved over to sit on the edge of it. A couple of the blankets had ended up on the floor overnight, accompanied by one of the pillows.

"What time is it?" Matt asked.

Chris was sitting at the table, having been awake for a good half-hour at least. He shrugged, getting out his phone which was now fully charged due to the fabulous electricity and free chargers provided by the Inn.

"About nine," Chris said, putting his phone away. "So, what's the plan?"

Matt shrugged, looking around on the floor for his shirt. He hadn't slept with it on and now couldn't remember where he'd left it.

"Don't know just yet," Matt said, getting off the bed and moving around to the other side of the bed. "Just got out of bed. Give me time to think."

Chris could see the marks on the back of Matt's shoulder, and they looked painful. There were four individual wounds, with bad bruising around all of them. When Matt moved to push a couple of blankets aside in the search for his shirt, Chris could see the damage extended to both the front and back of his shoulder.

"Is your shoulder alright?" Chris asked. "It's not looking great."

"It's fine. Like I said, nothing I can't handle."

Matt stood up and pulled his shirt over his head, having found it in among the blankets. He looked down at himself, not happy with what he was seeing.

"Give me a second."

He disappeared, leaving Chris in the room by himself. Moments later, he was back, wearing a jacket over his shirt.

"Where did you get that?" Chris asked as Matt adjusted it a bit.

"Punk kid next door. He won't miss it," Matt said. "Figured it'd be best not to walk around with a torn shirt. People might start asking questions."

Chris nodded, not planning on saying anything more on the matter. He knew Matt always had reasons to do what he did.

"I was thinking that maybe we go and see if we can find a library or bookstore," Matt said, having made up his mind on what to do. "See if we can find out a bit more about how we can get back. Surely someone around here would know or know of someone who can help us."

Chris nodded. "Sounds like a plan to me."

Matt gave him a brief smile, walked past, and headed for the door.

Chris got up, making sure he had his room key with him, and followed Matt out. He double-checked the door was locked before quickly hurrying after him. It wasn't like they had anything in that room worth stealing, but he didn't want anyone else in their space.

"Go pay for another night," Matt said, handing Chris some cash. "I'll wait for you outside."

Before Chris could say anything, Matt disappeared. Chris sighed, knowing it was probably best not to ask Matt to be with him at the Inn, especially around the front desk. It all made a bit more sense to him now why Matt was like he was.

Chris waited at the front desk, ringing the bell a couple of times when no one appeared.

"Anyone around?" Chris called, looking over the desk and trying to see if anyone was indeed around. "Hello?"

When no one answered him, he sighed. He quickly checked that no one was watching and went around to the other side of the desk.

He opened the register book and leafed through it. Finding where their names had been written down, he double-checked that there was still no one around or about to appear, and picked up the closest pen.

He added them down for another night and left the money in the book, shutting it and putting the pen back. He went back around to the right side of the desk before heading outside.

Matt looked up as the door closed behind Chris.

"Any idea of where we should start?" Chris asked, standing next to Matt who readjusted his snapback. Chris was sure he hadn't had that on when they'd left the room.

"If this layout is more like the Wonderland layout, I might be able to get us to a bookstore," Matt said, looking around as someone passed by them. "Wonderland never had a library in their main town. Some of the side towns did and the castle did, but never a public one."

"What about Oz?"

Matt shrugged, watching a group of girls walking down the street near them, chatting about something.

"There was one in the Oz castle, too," he explained, never once looking at Chris which struck him as a bit odd. "Like a real massive library. Nixx would be at home in it, Zeke too actually. That kid's always loved books..."

"Kind of going off track here," Chris said.

"Right, sorry," Matt apologized, shaking his head and finally looking at him, even if it was only for a few seconds before he went back to looking across the town square. "There were a couple bookstores halfway across the City. I think there was a library near the arena. Don't quote me on that, though."

"Well, where do we start then? Wonderland or Oz?" Chris asked.

"I think we go Wonderland," Matt said, looking at Chris again, holding the stare for a few more seconds. "But, if this is a mix of both, we could have more than one bookstore and a library."

"Let's stop thinking logically and go find the closest bookstore. Lead the way."

Matt nodded and walked off. Chris turned around and followed him, picking up his pace as Matt left the town square.

"What are we looking for in this bookstore or library exactly?" Chris asked as they walked.

"We're mostly looking up about parallel, or alternate universes," Matt explained. "We need to see if there's any real way of getting back and, if so, where we need to go to find the way back to our time and place."

"And if we don't find that?"

"We're fucked."

Chris didn't say anything more as they continued to walk. Without warning, Matt turned down a side street. Chris nearly missed it and quickly changed course.

Someone grabbed Matt by the arm, forcefully pulling him off the side street and into an alleyway.

"The fuck?" was all Matt had time to say before he was pushed up against the wall, a knife at his throat. A slight amused smile crossed his face as he saw who it was in front of him. "Well, if it isn't my favorite little misfit."

Chris stayed at the entrance to the alleyway.

Alice glared at Matt, pressing the knife against his neck a bit more.

"What are you doing here?" she snarled, her full focus on Matt who still seemed rather amused. "How did you get here?"

"I could ask you the same question, darlin'."

There was that cocky attitude making itself known once more. It had been a while since Chris had heard that from Matt, but Alice brought it out.

"How did you find me?" Alice snapped.

Chris and Matt exchanged looks.

"It looks like you found us," Chris said, getting a glare from Alice before she looked back at Matt who was smiling. "We didn't find you at all."

"Is he still after me?" Alice asked, pushing up closer against Matt, causing him to shift uncomfortably as she pressed against his hurt shoulder. "Does he know I'm here?"

"Sweetheart, no one knows you're here. We didn't even know you were here until you pulled me off the street," Matt said. "How long have you been watching us?"

"Since you got here yesterday," Alice said, looking Matt over, not releasing him or moving the knife. "Where are we?"

"Shouldn't you already know that?" Matt scoffed. "How long have you been here?"

"Since he started hunting me," Alice said, pushing the knife against his throat a bit more. "Found the door in Marion's basement and now here we are. Well, after I stepped off that stupid yellow road!"

Matt smirked at her, gaining a growl from Alice in return.

"What a coincidence we've ended up in the same reality then."

Alice narrowed her eyes at him. "What do you mean?"

Matt rolled his eyes, glancing at Chris who still stayed where he was, not daring to move in case Alice did something drastic.

"You step off the Yellow Brick Road in the dark and you end up in an alternate reality, a parallel universe with slight differences from the one you know," Matt explained, really wishing she would put knife away. "Out of all the universes, we happen to get stuck in one with you? How charming."

"You'd better quit it. Don't talk to me like I'm an idiot, Matthew," Alice snapped, making Matt roll his eyes again. Alice narrowed her eyes again, pointing at the cuts on Matt's face. "What happened?"

"Had a fight with the girlfriend," Matt responded sarcastically. "It's none of your business, Alice. Put the knife away."

"And let you disappear and leave me here? I don't think so," Alice snarled. She looked at Chris, making sure the knife didn't move. "Where's the rest of your stupid crew?"

"They're back in our reality," Chris said, not taking his eyes off Alice. "We're trying to get back there and finish what we started."

"You really think you can kill Marion?" Alice asked with a bit of a laugh. "You're all as good as dead." She looked back at Matt. "Maybe not you, though. I might keep you alive. I like you."

"Well, I don't much like you," Matt said with a shrug. "Sorry."

Alice growled again as Matt gave her that smile again. He suddenly moved, catching her off guard. Before she knew it, they'd switched places. Now Matt had her pushed up against the wall. He knocked the knife out of her hand, causing her to shriek. He turned her around, held her hands behind her back, and pushed her face against the wall.

"Now," he began as Alice struggled against him. "We're more than happy to help you get out of here and back to our proper place and time, but you've got to trust us. We know what we're doing, and you clearly don't."

Alice struggled again and Matt leaned against her to stop her moving as much.

"Trust you? As if! You don't trust me so why should I trust you?" she said. "Get off me!"

"Not going to happen," Matt said, in the same tone. "You going to cooperate? I'm not going to let you go until you promise us you won't try and kill us at any point in time while we're here. When we get back, I will happily let you go. You can come find us when it suits you and you can go back to trying to kill us then. Sound like a deal?"

"Never," Alice sneered, struggling against him again.

"We can easily leave you here with no way of getting back home," Matt said. He leaned in a bit closer, and Alice stopped moving. "And honey, I can easily tell Hunter where you are."

"You wouldn't."

"Wanna try me? Believe me, if we can get here and back, so can the man hunting you."

Chris watched as Alice's face twitched, seeing she had no other choice but to help them to get back to her real home.

"Fine," she spat.

Matt moved back a bit. He gestured for Chris to pick up the knife from where it was on the ground out of Alice's reach.

"You promise not to try and hurt us in any way while we're here?" Matt confirmed.

"Yes," Alice said bitterly, watching Chris pick up the knife and tuck it into his belt before moving his shirt over it so it couldn't be seen.

"Say it," Matt ordered, applying a bit more pressure to her wrists and making her shriek again.

"I promise!"

"You promise what?"

"I promise not to hurt either you or the freak while we're in this time!" Alice snapped.

Matt finally took the pressure off. "Good."

CHAPTER TWENTY-EIGHT

Problem Solving

"Where are we going?" Alice asked, her tone full of irritation as she dragged her feet, following Matt and Chris down the stone street.

"We're going to the bookstore," Matt said, not bothering to glance back at her.

"Why? I can't even read."

Matt looked at Chris. "Why doesn't that surprise me?"

Alice hissed from behind them both, making them look at her. She continued to drag her feet while glaring at the two of them, not saying a word.

Matt shook his head, going back to watching where he was going as he turned down a street.

"Should be down here somewhere," he said, slowing his pace and looking at the stores on his right, Chris doing the same.

"What's the name of the place?" Chris asked, looking at the stores they were passing. Interestingly, one was an alchemy store.

"Evelyn's Books," Matt said. "Just hoping it's here and has the same name. It'll be just our luck for it not to exist here."

"Why are we looking at books?" Alice spoke up, still sounding mad at the two of them.

"Because shut it, that's why," was Matt's response. "Here we are. This is the one."

Without waiting for his two companions, Matt trotted up the few steps and entered the store through the open doorway. Chris followed, with Alice mumbling something to herself as she trailed behind.

"Where do we start?" Chris asked, seeing Matt already looking around the small bookstore.

"Anywhere. Just find anything you think might help."

"No Gates this morning?" Nixx asked, looking at Zeke as he browsed one of the sections over the other side of the library.

"Haven't seen him since last night," Zeke said. "Why?"

"No reason," Nixx said, watching Zeke pull a book off the shelf just above him. "You planning on going down to the arena today?"

Zeke shrugged, flicking through the book. "Not sure yet. Was thinking I might, but then I was thinking I might not. Depends what everyone else does today, I guess. Don't think I really want to go out in public today due to the incident yesterday. Doubt that Blaine would want to either."

Nixx nodded. "That's fair enough."

Vincent suddenly appeared in the doorway, with a slightly disapproving look on his face.

"I need to see everyone in the group room in five minutes," Vincent ordered before he moved on.

Zeke and Nixx exchanged looks.

"Wonder what that's about," Zeke said, putting the book back in the place he'd found it.

"Don't know, but we should probably go see what he wants. He didn't look overly impressed about something," Nixx said with a shrug.

Zeke and Nixx walked in silence down to the room where they'd originally come into the castle. Alex and Abel both looked over as they appeared, Ash not paying them any attention.

"Anyone know what's going on?" Alex asked as Nixx and Zeke took a seat. Everyone shook their heads. "Also, where's Gates?"

"No idea, haven't seen him today," Zeke said as Vincent came into the room.

Everyone stopped talking as Vincent took a seat opposite Alex, Abel, and Ash.

"Look, I'm sorry for pulling you all away from whatever you were doing, but there's something I've got to make clear," Vincent began, not waiting for anyone else it seemed. "I received a report this morning that one of you, I won't name who it was, was using their ability last night. I'll be having a word with who it was, privately."

Everyone looked at each other, no one game enough to say anything.

"I want to make sure it's absolutely clear that while you're in this castle, you do not use your abilities," he continued, looking around at everyone. "If you do, word will get back to me. You have three strikes before I kick you out, no matter what. I don't care if you're trying to overthrow Marion. You'll be straight out of here, out of the City if need be. Is that clear?"

Everyone nodded, still no one saying anything. Vincent nodded, looking around at everyone again before smiling.

"Well then, glad we got that settled," he said. "Now, as I stated last night, you'd all probably benefit from going down to see Jacob. Abel, I've been told you're one of the main ones who needs a bit of help with your ability. Jacob's the best I've got, so go have a chat with him and he'll be more than happy to help you out."

Abel nodded as Vincent stood up and headed back out of the room. There was silence for a few minutes, still no one game enough to speak.

"So, who did it?" Zeke finally asked, looking around at everyone. "Which one of us used our ability? I know it wasn't me."

"Does it really matter?" Ash asked, making everyone look at her. "I'm sure whoever did it had their reasons."

Zeke gave her a slightly suspicious look, which she chose to ignore.

Alex looked at her, crossing his arms as he leaned back a bit. "You wouldn't happen to know where Gates is this morning, would you Ash?"

"Why would you think I'd know?" she looked down at the table, avoiding eye contact with any of them.

"You seemed to be kind of hanging off him a bit yesterday," Abel remarked, making her glance at him. "One has to assume..."

"Assume what?" Ash snapped, looking around at everyone. "You really think I'm the one who did it? Please."

She shook her head, got up, and stalked out of the room.

Zeke looked at Alex once she was gone. "Did she?"

Alex shrugged. "Don't know."

Alex stood up and headed out after Ash. He sighed to himself, seeing Ash up ahead, just leaning on the wall. She looked at him as he stopped near her.

"What now?" she sighed, going back to looking at something over the other side of the hallway.

Alex shrugged, putting his hands in his pockets as he followed her gaze. No one else had come out of the room yet.

"What are we going to do today?" he asked, looking back at her.

He saw Gates heading down the hallway towards them and he didn't look impressed.

"Also, what did you do to piss him off?"

Ash frowned, turning her gaze to see where he was looking.

"Shit."

Gates grabbed her, pushing her against the wall, the look on his face enough to make Alex worried.

"What the hell is your problem?" Gates shouted at her, making her cringe as the others came out of the room to see what was going on.

"Gates, what's going on?" Nixx asked, the three of them coming to a halt just behind Alex.

Gates continued to look at Ash who looked over at Alex, clearly wanting a bit of help to get out of the current situation.

"You look at me when I'm fucking talking to you," Gates growled, and Ash reluctantly looked at him. "You really think I'd let this slide, Ash? Really? What did I say?"

"Come on, calm down," Alex tried, going to move forward a bit.

Gates put his hand out and the barrier appeared, stopping Alex right in his tracks.

"You stay the fuck back. This is between us."

Alex looked at Ash who just shrugged. Gates still held her against the wall with his other hand.

Nixx sighed, moving to stand with Alex near the barrier. "Whatever's happened, we can sort it out," he said. "Just get rid of the barrier and we can talk this over."

Gates was back to looking at Ash, not paying attention to Nixx or the others.

Gates shook his head. "This isn't your problem. Everyone needs to back the fuck up."

Nixx held his hands up in his defense, moving back as asked. Alex also moved back, not saying a word.

The barrier disappeared when they were far enough back. Gates glanced over at them again before looking back at Ash who hadn't even tried to move.

"You want to explain something to me?" he asked harshly, keeping his voice down. "Why, when I clearly said no, did you continue to push yourself onto me? Why did this happen when I was being clear about what I wanted and didn't want?"

"Look, Blaine..."

"No, don't you fucking dare!" Gates shouted, taking a step back and letting her go. "You have no damn right to call me that! You've no right to use my real name!"

Ash stayed quiet.

"I want you out of my damn sight," he said, shaking his head and pointing at her. "You stay the hell away from me. Don't talk to me, don't look at me, don't even look in my direction. You're a selfish bitch and none of us want you here. You've done nothing to help out. I saved your damn life yesterday when that prick threw that knife, and this is how you repay me? By manipulating me against my will? You knew exactly what you were doing too. You're absolutely heartless. Don't you ever come near me again."

Gates stalked off, not saying another word as he went back down the hallway, most likely going back to his room to get away from everyone.

Alex looked at Ash sadly and Zeke crossed his arms, looking at her with annoyance and disgust.

"Well, guess we all know who it was now," was all he said before walking off down the corridor, most likely to go and find Gates. "Disgraceful."

Alex continued to look at Ash sadly as Abel and Nixx also headed off, seeing this wasn't any of their business. Abel was going to go and sit with Jamie and Nixx was headed back to the library for an hour or two before going off to the arena to seek out Jacob.

"Why?" Alex asked once everyone was out of sight. "I thought you were better than that now, Ash."

Ash crossed her arms as she looked at him, and he saw the sadness on her face.

"I don't know Alex," she sighed, looking down at the floor. "I just ... sometimes I can't help it, OK? It just happens."

"Sure," Alex said, the disappointment in his voice. "Whatever."

He walked off, leaving Ash standing alone in the middle of the hallway. Ash watched him turn a corner and he was gone.

"Find anything?" Chris asked.

Matt shook his head as he continued to look at a few books. Alice occupied herself by occasionally taking the books he'd gotten out and putting them back on the shelves in the wrong places just to get on his nerves.

"Nothing," Matt said, reaching for another book, only to find it not there. He looked at Alice who was kicking the floor beneath her feet. "Could you stop being an irritant and stop putting books away? I got them out for a reason, Alice. Go and look at the kids' books."

Alice ignored him, watching a man come into the bookstore. She was instantly alert and started to follow him around the shop. When all he did was browse the shelves like they were doing, she decided he was no threat and came back to find another way to annoy Matt.

Matt shook his head and put the book he had back, before trying to find the other one he'd had.

"What are we going to do if we can't get back home?" Chris asked, watching Matt grab the book he'd been after.

"We'll get back," was all he said before beginning to flick through the book.

"Matt, I'm serious," Chris said. "Right now, there isn't much chance of us getting back, is there? How long do we keep looking before we give in? How long do we wait?"

Matt sighed and lowered the book to look at him. Chris watched Matt's expression sadden ever so slightly. Alice stopped what she was doing to look at him as well.

"I don't know, Chris. I honestly don't know," Matt said, putting the book away. "Right now, I'm really not counting on getting back, honest to God. You guys keep searching and I'll be back in a flash."

He stepped back into the dark shadow in the corner of the room and disappeared.

A glare crossed Alice's face. "Why does he do that?"

Chris looked back at the book he had in his hand. They were at the back of the store, so it was unlikely they'd be seen using their abilities if they had to.

"Why does he just up and disappear?" Chris asked, not taking his focus off the book. Alice nodded, making him shrug. "He has his reasons. He clearly needed to go somewhere."

"And leave us here? In this horrible, small paper shop?" Alice said disapprovingly, looking around in disgust. "I hate these places."

Chris shook his head, not bothering to say anything. He wondered where Matt had gone.

About ten minutes passed, and Matt was still not back.

"He's not coming back," Alice said, walking over to one of the shelves as Chris grabbed another book, the one he'd been reading having nothing of value.

"He will."

Alice rolled her eyes, browsing the books, even if she had no idea of what the words said.

"There's a library across town," Matt said, making Chris jump.

Chris frowned as he watched Matt remove his sunglasses.

"When did you get those?" he asked, watching Matt hook them onto the front of his shirt.

"Some guy was selling them near the library. Needed a new pair anyway."

Chris shook his head, putting the book he had away. "So, we going to the library?"

Matt nodded, heading out of the store, followed closely by Chris and Alice.

"We'll probably have more luck there than here," Matt said as he walked down the steps and onto the street. He put his new sunglasses back on as he looked around. "More chance there'll be a proper section on it in a library. We need to find out soon how we can get home. I don't about you guys, but I'm kind of sick of this reality already."

Chris gave a nod of agreement as he walked alongside him down the street. Alice trailed behind again, grumbling and dragging her feet like before.

"You think the others might have a way of getting us back yet?" Chris asked as Matt turned down a street.

Matt had told Chris earlier about how Gates had managed to get in contact. Chris was hoping they could do it again and, between them, find a way back.

"No idea," Matt said. "We mustn't be in the same area as Blaine. He would've gotten through again if we were. We need to try and figure out where they'll be so we can get through to him."

"How are we going to do that?"

"I don't know," Matt admitted, turning down another street. "It's literally a guessing game. He could be anywhere, and he was the one who found *us*. I have no way of getting into contact with him. He has to make the initial communication attempt."

"So, we've got no way of knowing where he is, and he has no way of knowing where we are."

"That's certainly how it seems right now," Matt sighed, continuing straight down the street. "I really don't know. Time difference is a factor here as well. When we stepped off the road it was night, and when we got here it was day. Who knows what they're all doing right at this moment."

Chris didn't say anything as he walked alongside Matt. As they approached what looked like the library up ahead, he pointed to the building next to it.

"What's that building?"

Matt shrugged as Alice quickly caught up.

"Not sure," Matt said, stopping outside the library, but still focusing on the building next to it. "In Oz, that would've been where the training arena was. Don't know if there was anything like it in Wonderland."

Chris nodded slowly, looking at Matt and seeing the thoughtful look on his face.

"What?"

Matt shook his head, still thinking.

"Depending on the time difference," he began, crossing his arms and still looking at the building. "We might be able to get hold of

Blaine, or vice versa. I'd be very surprised if none of them went down to the arena to get a bit of control practice in."

"So, what do we do?" Chris asked.

"We're going to be here a while, put it that way."

CHAPTER TWENTY-NINE

Training

"How's Jamie doing?" Nixx asked.

Abel walked alongside him, and the small blue cat ran along with them.

The arena was not far ahead. As they walked, people moved out of their way, remembering that Abel had been part of the group involved in the previous day's incident.

"She's alright," Abel said. "It'll take her a bit to get back on her feet, but she'll get there eventually."

Nixx nodded and Abel gave him a slight smile as they entered the arena. There weren't many people around at this time and they wondered how many they usually got here. Zeke and Gates were already here, up the back, talking about something.

"Zeke!" Abel called, making the two of them look over as the cat ran to them. "Do you know where Jacob is?"

Zeke shook his head as they reached them. "Nah, sorry. He was here when we arrived about an hour ago, but I don't know where he's gone. I'm sure he'll be back though."

Gates crossed his arms as Alex sat down in front of him. Gates eyed him off while Alex stared him down.

"What?" Gates said to Alex. Alex meowed at him.

"Don't worry about him," Nixx said, waving his hand to dismiss it. "Alex isn't very happy with Ash at the moment. None of us are."

"Really," Gates stated. "Because I somehow doubt you guys are as mad at her as I currently am."

"You have every right to be mad at her," Abel said. "Ash doesn't know when to stop. She's always been like that."

Gates gave him an unamused smile. "Kinda figured."

"She doesn't know how to control herself," Nixx said. "Really, she needs to learn some self-control."

"Doesn't mean I can't be mad at her," Gates said, shifting his position. "Because, believe me, I don't particularly enjoy being manipulated into anything, let alone sleeping with someone!"

"We get that, really, we do," Abel said. "One of us will have a word with her. She can't just go around doing that kind of thing. I'm sure she'll listen to Alex."

They all looked at the small blue cat who remained silent, still watching Gates.

"Either way, I don't care," Gates said, tearing his gaze away from Alex and looking at Abel. "From now on, what that bitch does, doesn't concern me. I want nothing to do with her and I think I made that pretty clear this morning. And, if it wasn't clear, then she's an idiot."

No one said anything more as Gates uncrossed his arms and looked at Zeke.

"Wanna do something?" Zeke asked. Gates nodded. "You sure? You're still pretty beaten up."

"I'm fine," Gates said, as far from a good mood this morning as he could be. "I'm not going to stand around here all day when we could be doing something. So, let's do something."

"Can I stop you for just a second?" Nixx spoke up.

Gates and Zeke both looked at him, while Nixx looked at Gates. Alex finally moved and went and sat next to Abel.

"Your barrier, does it only stop physical attacks?" asked Nixx

"What do you mean?" Gates frowned, crossing his arms again.

"Well," Nixx began. "You can block physical attacks with your ability. Can you stop other, non-physical attacks? So, for example, can I get past it?"

Gates exchanged looks with Zeke before they both looked back at Nixx, the interest clear on both of their faces.

"Guess there's only one way to find out," Gates said, Nixx nodding in agreement. "Honestly, it's never once crossed my mind. I've only ever dealt with physical attacks."

"Well, are you up for seeing if it works?" Nixx asked.

"Yeah, why not?" Gates said. "Not going to know unless we try."

Jacob walked across the arena and stopped next to Abel, with Alex stationed in between them.

"Hey guys," Jacob said, looking at Abel and Nixx. "Sorry, had to step out for a bit. Good to see you all here. You're also missing someone."

"She's busy," Gates said bitterly. Jacob raised his eyebrows at him. "You don't want to know."

Not pushing it any further, Jacob gave a nod of understanding, looking around at the group.

"So," he said. "Anything I can help you with?"

"We were just going to try something out," Nixx said. "Gates and I were just discussing whether or not he could only block physical attacks."

That piqued Jacob's interest, and he nodded slowly and looked at Gates. "That's a very good question. I assume you don't know whether you can or not."

"No idea," said Gates.

"Well, there's only one way to find out, hey?" Jacob said with a bit of a smile. "Go ahead, I'm not going to stop you."

He motioned for everyone except Nixx and Gates to take a step back.

Nixx looked at Gates, giving him a nod. Gates put his hands out, the barrier appearing as he did so.

"Should I be worried about what you're going to try?" he asked, seeing the thoughtful look on Nixx's face.

Nixx shook his head. "Just going to see what I can do, if I can get through to you."

"How, may I ask? What are you going to do to me exactly?"

"Going to see if I can calm you down. You're still pretty worked up," Nixx said as Gates rolled his eyes. "Seriously, I can feel it. Well, I can only *just* feel it now since you put that up."

He indicated to the barrier.

"What does that mean?" Gates said with a frown. "Does that mean you can't get through it?"

Nixx shrugged. "Not sure yet. I can still feel it, but not as much as when you don't have it up. Alright, just do whatever you normally do, and I'll see if I can get through."

Gates gave a nod, the others all staying back and watching. Gates shifted his position a bit, steadying himself as Nixx stayed where he was.

"You're worried, aren't you?" Nixx said with a bit of amusement. Gates shrugged, trying to make it look like he didn't care. Nixx smiled. "I felt that slight change."

"Whatever you've got to do, just do it," Gates said impatiently.

Nixx rolled his eyes, looking directly at him before flicking his wrist to the side. Gates flinched slightly.

"I felt that, only just though," he said, Nixx nodding in interest. "Went straight through the barrier."

"Hmm, there's not much change, you're still mad inside," Nixx said, flicking his wrist again. Gates pushed back a bit this time with the barrier. "How about that time?"

"Nothing. I think I pushed it back," Gates said. "What about you? Any change?"

"Nothing, still feeling the same as before. Seriously, you actually need to calm down."

"Believe me, man, I'm calm," Gates said with a bit of an unamused laugh. "Go again, I want to see what happens if I don't try and deflect it."

Nixx nodded, still watching him as he pushed his hand out a bit. Gates flinched once more, before nodding again. Nixx did the same thing again, but this time, Gates pushed back a second or two later, not flinching.

"How did that go?" Nixx asked.

Gates shook his head, lowered his hands, and the barrier disappeared.

"First time with no deflection, I definitely felt it. It hit me a lot harder than the first time," he said.

"That's because I made sure it was a harder hit," Nixx said, Gates nodding.

"Yeah, well the second time I felt nothing when I pushed back," Gates said, Nixx nodding this time. "By the looks of it, it's like a timing thing. I can deflect it if I time it right, otherwise it gets through."

Nixx nodded, a thoughtful look on his face as Gates crossed his arms again.

Nixx looked at Jacob. "Do you know of anyone else who has non-physical abilities?" he asked. "I'm wondering if it's just me who can get through or if other people can too."

"That's a very good question," Jacob said. "I do know someone. I think he was here earlier on. We've been working on getting him a bit more advanced with his ability. It's only a mind-reading thing, though. Will that do?"

Nixx nodded. "Anyone at any skill level."

"Maybe the less advanced, the harder it would be to get through," Gates suggested as Jacob and Nixx both nodded. "I mean, it'd make sense, right? You've developed yours for years. This kid probably can't do much at all."

"He's getting there," Jacob said with a shrug. "I'll go find him and see if he'd like to help us out. You guys go back to whatever you were doing. If you need any help ability-wise after we've done this, let me know and I'm more than happy to help."

Everyone nodded as Jacob headed off to find his mind-reader.

"Well, this is going to be interesting," Gates said. He suddenly frowned, looking to his right. "You guys feel that?"

Everyone exchanged looks, shaking their heads as Gates moved a couple of paces over before crouching down. He put his right hand on the ground, his left out, and the barrier appeared.

Nixx moved over beside Zeke and Gates's barrier flickered.

"What's he doing?" Abel asked quietly.

"No idea," said Zeke.

"Matt, that you?"

Matt paused, looking around as he put down the book he was holding. Chris and Alice both stopped what they were doing, too. For the past half hour, Chris had been looking through books, while Alice just tapped the table in boredom.

"Where the hell have you been?" Matt snapped. "Jesus Christ, Blaine, we've been hanging out here all damn day. It's nearly dark outside!"

Chris and Alice exchanged glances, then Chris leaned back in his chair and crossed his arms.

"Oh, well, so fucking sorry I didn't know. You think I'm a damn psychic and know where you are at every damn moment? Please, give it a rest. Wait, did you say it's nearly dark? Man, it's like, not even afternoon here. What time zone are you in?"

"Yeah, it's nearly dark here," Matt said. "We're in a different zone to you. Hell, it's Tuesday here."

"Oh, it's Friday here."

"Figured."

Chris looked at Matt. "Can anyone else but us hear this?"

Matt shrugged.

"You found a way for us to get back yet?" Matt asked Gates.

"Could ask you the same question. By the way, is there someone else there with you?"

"Chris is here, why?" Matt said with a frown, looking at Chris who shrugged.

"No, not that. There are three of you. Just can't quite pick who the third is."

"Oh, it's Alice."

There was a pause.

"As in, the psychotic bitch you let out of the dungeons?"

Alice growled and Matt smiled as he looked over at her.

"That's her."

"Alright, I'm not going to question it. Anyway, we might have a way back for you. We met with the Wizard, and he was saying he may be able to pull you back. No guarantees, but he seemed fairly positive he might be able to get you back here. He said there might be consequences though."

"Like what?" Matt asked, frowning now.

"We don't know, he never actually said. We're at the arena at the moment, so it'll be a little bit before we can go talk to him about it. But just be ready for if he can do it, yeah?"

"Sounds like a plan. You guys keep up whatever you're doing. Keep in contact."

"No promises."

It was suddenly quiet in the library again.

"Well, looks like we might be getting home after all." Matt said to Chris.

CHAPTER THIRTY

Stepping Back

"What did you just do?" Abel asked as Gates stood up and looked at the rest of them who were staring at him.

"Oh," Gates said. "Matt and Chris are in the same area. I was just getting hold of them to make sure everything was OK."

"Right," Abel said. "We could only hear your side of the conversation."

Gates nodded, not saying anything as he watched Jacob and a young man walk across the arena and stop when they reached the small group. The man gave them a nervous smile.

"This is Don," Jacob said. "He's the guy I told you about. He says he's happy to help out."

Gates nodded, looking Don over. He looked like he was no more than about sixteen at the most.

"Alright, kid, what can you do?" Gates asked, looking him over again before resting his gaze on his face.

Don shrugged, looking intimidated by Gates.

"Not much," he admitted, avoiding Gates's gaze. "Just a couple of things. We've been working on a bit more, but at the moment I can really only tell you what you're thinking."

"Awesome," Gates said with no enthusiasm. "Just what I need, someone telling me what I'm thinking."

"Come on, you said you wanted someone else to see if they could get through your barrier," Abel said as Don shifted uncomfortably. "So, you know, this is as good as you're going to get for now."

Gates sighed, crossing his arms and looking back at Don. "Alright, fine. Go for it."

Don frowned, finally making himself look at Gates and meet his unimpressed gaze.

"Shouldn't you be doing something too...?"

"Not yet. Got to make sure you can do it first."

Don gave a small nod, while Gates stayed where he was.

"Um, well," Don said, clearing his throat as he forced himself keep Gates's gaze. "Right now, you've got a lot going on in your mind. Lots going on up there."

"Wow, you're real great at this," Gates said, the sarcasm as clear as day. "I already know that. All of us do. Care to elaborate?"

Don shifted uncomfortably, dropping his gaze for a moment before looking at Gates again.

"OK, um ... well, there are a couple of things you're mainly thinking about," he said as Gates sighed. "The main one, besides the little amount of faith you have in me, is something to do with a girl named Ash. And, now that I've said that you've tried to stop thinking about it. Dwelling on it won't help."

"I know," Gates said bitterly. "Alright, fine then. I'll give you the benefit of the doubt. Let's get this done."

Don frowned, watching Gates move back a pace and put his hands out. The barrier appeared,

"What am I doing exactly?" Don asked.

"Try again, same thing you just did."

Don gave a nod, not saying anything as he stared at Gates, frowning a bit. He shook his head.

"Nothing," he said. "I've got no idea what you were just thinking of."

Gates lowered his hands and the barrier was gone.

"Hmm, probably a good thing," Gates said, more to himself than anyone else. He looked over at Nixx who returned the look. "Guess that answers that. The lower the skill, the less likely they'll get through. I could barely feel him touch the barrier."

Nixx nodded, the interest once again on his face. He looked at Zeke as Gates glanced at Don.

"What about you?" Nixx asked, Zeke frowning now. "Is there any way you're able to stop non-physical attacks?"

"I doubt it. I don't have barriers," Zeke said, glancing at Gates. "Mine's completely different to his. Like, completely."

"Why are you suddenly so interested in whether or not people can stop this stuff?" Abel spoke up. "Why all of a sudden?"

"Well, you never know what Marion's going to throw at us to try to stop us," Nixx explained. "We've got to be as prepared as we can be for this. We don't know what tricks she'll have up her sleeves. For all we know she may have physical and non-physical attacks. We have to be prepared for anything."

"Fair enough," said Abel, nodding his head. "I hadn't thought of that."

"Which means we have to get everyone knowing their abilities and limitations inside and out," Nixx continued, Jacob nodding in agreement. "We've got to make sure we all know exactly what we can do, no matter how long we've known about our abilities."

"What do you suggest?" Zeke asked. "Gates and I pretty well know our limits. What more can we do?"

"We all need to know what each other can do as well," Nixx suggested. "You never know what might come in useful. Some of our abilities might work well combined."

Jacob just watched and listened. Don stayed quiet.

"That never even crossed my mind," Abel said. "How would we figure that out?"

"Trial and error is really the only way," Nixx said with a shrug. "Once we get Matt and Chris back, we'll get everyone down here, Ash included, and work through what we can and can't do."

"Why? How is Ash going to be able to help?" Gates asked seriously. He would be mad at her for some time at this rate. "Seriously Nixx, there is nothing useful about that woman."

"Well, now you never know," Jacob spoke up, everyone looking at him now. "Some people, like yourself, Gates, have extensions to their abilities. Some even have more than one ability. We don't know why it happens to some people and not others, but that's the way it is."

"You think Ash might have more than her currently active ability?" Gates asked, sounding skeptical. "Great, just what we need with her. More bullshit."

Jacob shrugged. "The only way we'll know is if she comes down here once your other two friends are back."

"Hey, come on through."

Vincent held the door open, ushering everyone inside before shutting it again once they were all in. The room was dimly lit, giving it an eerie feel.

"Take a seat, take a seat," Vincent urged, going over to the closest chair and sitting down next to Dorothy. Everyone else sat down as well. "Alright, once again, sorry for dragging you all away from whatever you were doing. It's good to see you in the arena, though. Probably an idea to just chill down there for a few days, get to know your abilities, and stay out of the city folks' way for a bit."

A couple of them nodded, everyone else choosing to stay quiet. Vincent cleared his throat awkwardly, before continuing.

"OK, so," he said, linking his fingers together as he looked at everyone. "By the looks of it, I can get your friends back. It seems possible, and I think I can do it."

"There are three of them now," Gates spoke up, everyone looking to him. "Matt and Chris are still there, but Alice is now with them."

"Wait, Alice?" Abel said. Gates nodded. "How?"

Gates shrugged. "Just telling what I'm seeing. I don't know the details and I don't want to know. I don't ask. Matt and Chris are our main priority, and I don't care if Alice gets back or not."

"Hang on," Dorothy spoke up. "Do you mean Alice, as in the girl who went down to Wonderland? Down-the-rabbit-hole Alice?"

"Yeah, why?" Gates responded.

"I didn't think she was still around," Dorothy said.

"You know her or something?" Nixx asked.

"I might," she said. "If she's the Alice I think she is."

"Dorothy's sister, Alice, went missing about a year before Dorothy ended up down here," Vincent said, filling in the blanks.

"Your sister?" Gates said. "Man, she's seriously messed up in the head. Sorry you're related to that."

"She wasn't like that when she disappeared," Dorothy said in her defense. "Whatever happened to her in Wonderland has messed her up if she's like you say she is. I haven't seen her in years."

"Oh, she's completely nuts," Zeke input. "As in, stab you whenever she can, nuts."

Dorothy shot him a glare as Gates nodded in agreement with Zeke's statement.

Vincent cleared his throat again, getting everyone back onto the main topic at hand.

"I'll make sure I get her back here as well then, seeing as you think she's with them."

"She is, no doubt," Gates said with a shake of his head, choosing to ignore the fact that Ash was looking at him as he spoke. "Matt said she was, and I could tell she was there too. The power doesn't lie."

"Well, OK, I was just saying that I'll do what I can," Vincent said, sounding offended as Gates leaned back in his chair. "But as I said before, I'm pretty sure I can get them back. It might take a bit, but they should be OK when they get back into their real time here."

"What if it doesn't work?" Nixx asked, thinking of the possibilities that could occur. "If this doesn't work, then what do we do?"

Vincent shrugged. "I don't know. I haven't had to do this very often and it depends on the people as well. Some people just aren't able to get back."

"What usually stops them?" Abel asked.

Vincent shrugged again. "Could be anything. From the person just being unable to physically get back, to the point where I can't reach them. It differs with each person."

"So, in other words, you might be able to get Chris, but not Matt," Nixx said, Vincent nodding. "Or vice versa."

"Either way, you're bringing Matt back," Gates said sternly, Zeke agreeing with him. "You're not giving up on this until he's back."

"Chris is part of this too," Ash said with annoyance as Gates shot her a glare. "We need them both, not just one. And if it's only one, it's not going to be Matt."

"Did anyone ask for your opinion?" Gates snarled.

"Well, too bad if you didn't, because I'm part of this too."

"Yeah, well you shouldn't be."

"Alright, just stop," Vincent sighed, putting his hands up. "I don't have time for this. I'll do everything I can to get everyone back here safely. Just keep it cool and we'll get this done. Everyone needs to shut up now and let me do my thing."

"Did you hear that?" Chris asked.

Matt stopped, turning to look at Chris who had come to a halt a few paces back. Alice stopped as well when she saw they weren't moving.

"Hear what?" Matt asked.

The sun had disappeared, so he took his sunglasses off and hooked them on the front of his shirt.

Chris held his hand up to signal Matt to be quiet and the three of them listened. A sudden, loud crash of thunder made Alice jump in surprise and Matt look up.

"I heard it that time," he said. "Is it just me or has it gotten real dark all of a sudden?"

Chris followed his gaze, seeing the dark clouds that had come overhead. A flash of lightning lit up the sky as another crash of thunder sounded.

"It's getting closer," Matt said, as a breeze picked up.

"Should we be worried?"

"I don't know."

"What's happening?" Alice asked, moving to stand next to Matt and looking up at the sky like he was.

Matt shook his head as the breeze grew stronger. A few people rushed past trying to get back into their homes and out of the sudden weather change.

The thunder sounded again, a lot closer and even shaking the ground this time.

"No idea. I'm just kind of hoping it's not something bad," Matt said. "I'm also kind of hoping maybe this is our way out."

"Why would it be?" Chris asked. "We don't even know what happens to get us back. Gates never specified."

The breeze was now a strong wind and Matt held onto his snapback as he looked at Chris.

"Because he didn't know!" Matt shouted over the wind and thunder as the ground shook again.

A sudden lightning strike hit the ground close by and they all stepped back slightly. Matt looked back at Chris as Alice looked around, a nervous look on her face.

"We don't know what happens, Chris," yelled Matt. "But we've got no other choice."

"So, what? We just stand here and hope we don't get struck by lightning?" Chris called back.

Lightning struck the chimney of a house a few yards away with a massive crash, causing bricks to tumble onto the street.

"Well, I don't think I'm about to give up this chance," Matt called back. "We've just got to wing it. We might get killed here and now, or we might get back home. We have no idea!"

Chris looked at him and Matt shrugged, making him sigh. He gave a reluctant nod and Matt nodded back as the thunder shook the ground once more.

"If we die, Matt, I'm gonna haunt you forever. I just want you to know that!"

Matt smiled. "We'll both be dead. You can't haunt the dead, Chris."

Chris shook his head as a close flash of lightning lit up the entire surrounding area, the three of them shielding their eyes against it as the ground shook again.

"Maybe we should get inside," Alice suggested.

Another flash lit up the area making them shield their eyes again. It was very bright.

"We're not moving!" Matt said firmly. "We stay here until it passes, just to be sure."

Once more, the ground shook, thunder roared, and lightning flashed. The three of them stayed where they were, shielding their eyes as the light grew brighter and brighter. The ground continued to shake with every peal of thunder.

A few minutes passed before the light started to die and the ground slowly stopped shaking.

Matt was the first one to look around, trying to get his eyes to refocus. Someone appeared in front of him.

Chris and Alice were both rubbing their eyes and blinking, trying to get their sight back as the light finally faded and the ground became steady again.

"What just happened?" Chris asked, still trying to see.

Matt's sight was back, and he looked at the man in front of him. He didn't know who he was.

"Where are we?" he asked.

The man in front of Matt gave him a cheerful smile. Chris looked at him now as well, not knowing whether or not this was where he thought it was.

"Welcome back."

CHAPTER THIRTY-ONE

Test of Ability

"Jeez man, so good to see you back," Gates said, pulling Matt into a hug while Zeke just stood back smiling.

"Careful of the shoulder," Matt said, half-hugging him back as he sat on the bed in the infirmary.

"Sorry," Gates apologized. "Are you guys OK? You gave us all a scare when you disappeared."

Matt nodded as one of the nurses came over to tend to his shoulder.

"Yeah, we're fine," he said, taking his shirt off. He winced as the nurse started cleaning his shoulder. "Tell you what, I don't think I'm ever going to go stepping into another reality again."

Gates and Zeke both laughed, while Matt smiled tiredly at them.

"How's everything coming along?" Matt asked, flinching as the nurse began dabbing something on his wounds. "Anything I missed or should know about?"

Gates shook his head as Chris appeared at the doorway. Matt gave him a nod of greeting as he came in.

"Nothing really," Gates said, frowning as Ash followed Chris in. She'd latched onto him again now that he was back. "We were going to spend the next however long down at the arena during the day, working on our abilities. Gives us something to do."

Matt nodded, trying not to say anything as he watched the nurse begin stitching him up.

"You doing OK?" Chris asked.

"Getting there," Matt said, flinching. "This hurts like a bitch. I think I'm gonna get some sleep after I'm done here. I'll go down to the arena a bit later, maybe when no one else will be in the way."

"You look tired," Zeke noted, stating the obvious.

"Yeah," said Matt with a nod.

"Well," Gates said, all of them looking to him now. "Nixx was thinking earlier that maybe we could all work on a few things together. He thinks maybe some of our abilities will work well with each other."

Matt nodded again. "Wouldn't surprise me if we could work better together at times. It just depends on what everyone can do and how to make it work to someone else's ability."

Gates nodded, shifting his position as Ash glanced at him, not saying anything. Gates reluctantly looked in her direction. He crossed his arms as he looked just in front of her, not looking at her directly

"Jacob wants you down there with us," he informed her. "So, you're expected to be there too when we all go down later, once Matt's feeling up to it."

"You don't have to wait for me," Matt said as the nurse finally finished up and started to bandage his shoulder. He looked at her. "Think you could fix the stitching in my leg too, while you're at it?"

The nurse nodded. "I'll see what I can do once I'm done here."

Matt gave a grateful nod back.

"Alright, then," Gates sighed. "Get some rest and we'll head down to the arena. You know where to find us."

"So, this is the arena, huh?" Chris looked around.

It was beginning to get dark, but the floodlights surrounding the arena were on, making it look impressive from where he was standing.

Abel nodded. Zeke, Gates, and Nixx were up the back, talking something over. Matt wasn't around yet but he would most likely appear sooner or later, as he'd been out for a few hours now.

Ash looked at Abel as the small blue cat sat down next to her. Alex wasn't in the mood to try anything new today and was happy with just being a cat for a while.

"Why did Jacob want me down here?" she asked. "I really can't do anything useful."

"He thinks otherwise," Abel said, beginning to walk over to the others. "Thinks you might have a hidden ability."

Ash frowned, exchanging looks with Chris who just shrugged and followed Abel.

"Hey guys," Nixx said. "Chris, good to see you back in one piece."

Gates nodded at them, while Zeke stayed silent, not bothering to greet any of them.

Chris gave a brief smile, not saying anything. A man came over to them, trailed by a younger kid.

"You must be Chris," he said with a smile. "I'm Jacob. I help train people here."

He extended his hand in a friendly manner and Chris shook it with a brief smile.

"I've been told you and Abel both need a bit of help with learning how to use your abilities. Correct me if I'm wrong?"

"No, you're not wrong," Chris said with a bit of a laugh.

"Well, we can work on that a bit later," Jacob said, before looking at Ash. "Now, you, I've been told you've been getting up to no good."

"Who told you that?" Ash asked, automatically shooting Gates a glare. He returned the look without a word.

"I've also been told you aren't much help right now," Jacob continued, not bothering to comment on her snide remark and the way she looked at Gates.

"What can I do besides seduce people?" Ash asked. "I don't see how that's going to useful against Marion."

Gates shook his head.

Ash glared at him again. "Oh, get over it, Blaine."

"Don't call me that," Gates snapped. "You lost that right."

"She never had it to start with," Zeke commented, mirroring Gates's position as he looked at Ash. "She's also violating the 'don't look at you' rule."

Ash rolled her eyes, looking back at Jacob. Chris looked at Abel in confusion, but Abel just shook his head. Jacob sighed, choosing to once again ignore the childish behavior.

"You're all adults, you'll get over it eventually," Jacob sighed. "Not everyone uses their ability for good and some need to learn to control themselves."

"I don't think Ash is ever going to learn to control herself," Gates said, looking Ash over disapprovingly. "She's too much of a whore to ever do that."

"Excuse me?" Ash exclaimed, rather offended now. "How dare you."

"Hey, this is your own fault," Gates said with annoyance. "If you'd listened for once in your life and learned how to take rejection, then none of this shit would have happened."

"Alright, stop arguing like children," Jacob stepped in. "Yes, Ash screwed up. It's happened and there's no way either of you can change it. One thing you all have to learn about people with Ash's kind of ability, is that sometimes it gets the better of them and they can't help what they do."

"Hang on," Gates stated, holding up a hand. "Back up a step. You're saying that because her current ability is to seduce people, that she can't physically control herself when it gets to a certain point. That's got to be bullshit."

Jacob shook his head. "Look it up. There are books about abilities in the castle library."

Gates shook his head. "I refuse to believe that Ash couldn't control what she was doing. She knew exactly what was happening the entire time she came onto me. She also knew I was saying no. Case settled."

Ash rolled her eyes again, deciding to stay silent as Jacob sighed.

"Whether she was aware of it or not, this kind of thing happens with seductresses," he informed. "Whatever the case, let's drop the subject and do what we're here to do."

Gates glared at Ash. "You still need to stay away from me."

"Oh, grow up," she said.

Jacob shook his head.

"Alright, that's enough. We're not here to argue. We're here to train and get some more insight into our abilities. The more you argue, the more time you're wasting. I don't know about you lot, but I won't be here all night. I have a family to go home to and I don't plan on being out here all hours."

"Yeah, well some of us aren't lucky enough to be able to go home to our families."

Matt came up behind them and stopped next to Zeke. For the few hours of rest he'd had, he still looked spent.

"You must be Matt," Jacob said, Matt giving a non-caring shrug. "I'm Jacob, head trainer here. Oh, and this is Don."

Don gave them all a wave, but he stayed just off to Jacob's side, trying not to get in the way. Matt, Chris, and Ash were the only ones who hadn't been previously introduced to him.

"What are you doing back?" Gates asked, turning his gaze to Don.

Don shrugged, avoiding his gaze again. "Just wanted to hang around for a bit. Maybe see what you guys can do."

Gates gave a slight shake of his head, not speaking.

There were still a few people in the arena but not many. It looked like one or two other trainers were still working, even though the light was fading, but it wasn't fully dark yet.

"Well, then," Jacob said with a clap of his hands. "As well as reading minds, Don can also read other people's abilities, something I never mentioned this morning. He's not the best at it yet, but he can figure out the basics of what everyone can do."

Everyone nodded, except Ash who was still eyeing off Gates who was ignoring her.

Jacob indicated to Don to say something. He shifted awkwardly, then looked at Chris.

"Um, OK, well," he began, concentration on his face as he stared at Chris. "Yours is like a ... stopping ability. Stopping people where they are until something touches them."

Chris nodded to confirm it. "Yeah, that's right. I just don't know how to work it at the moment. Only ever done it once."

Don looked around. He'd only seen Gates demonstrate his ability and hadn't been told what anyone else's abilities were. He probably didn't even know that Alex wasn't really a cat.

He turned his gaze to Zeke. "Yours is fire."

Zeke nodded as Matt put his hands in his pockets, looking rather bored.

Don looked at Matt, a frown on his face as he tried to read him. "You, I don't know ... I can't read yours."

Matt raised his eyebrows in interest as he looked the kid over.

"Hmm, well, then," he said with a smirk as Don continued to stare at him with concentration on his face the whole time. "Guess you're not as good as you thought, hey kid?"

Don looked away from him, making Matt smile in amusement.

"He's still learning," Jacob said. "What *is* your ability?"

"Shadow-stepping," Matt said proudly. "One minute I'm here, the next I'm gone."

Upon saying that, he stepped backwards and was gone. Don looked around but Matt was nowhere to be seen. Jacob shook his head, not impressed.

Don next looked at Abel, and he jumped when he saw Matt standing next to him. Matt shot him a cocky smile and adjusted his snapback, not saying anything as Don tried to figure out what Abel's ability was.

"Yours is kind of complicated," he said. "It's hard to explain. It's like a mix of a few things. Depending on what you're feeling can trigger certain reactions. Like, the weather will change, or you can use the darkness to your advantage. It's hard to explain."

Abel nodded and Matt disappeared again.

"I wish he wouldn't do that all the time," Chris sighed. "It gets really annoying sometimes."

"Got sick of standing with Abel," Matt said from his position over with Gates, making Don and a few of them jump. "Anyway, I love Gates more."

He put both his arms around Gates who smiled and put his arm around him in return.

"Jealous?" Gates asked Ash who was glaring at him, but she chose not to speak.

Matt and Gates let each other go and shifted so they were leaning against each other as they watched.

Don looked at Nixx, getting back to what he was doing. Nixx watched Don with interest.

"Yours is a little complicated too," he said. Nixx nodded. He already knew that. "You can change how people feel, but there's something else there, too. Something I can't quite pinpoint. It's like ... I don't know. I can't reach it."

"It's complicated," Nixx said, not bothering to explain. He already knew what he could do and wasn't about to tell some kid if he couldn't figure it out.

Don looked at Gates.

"Yours is the barriers," he said, making Gates roll his eyes.

Don looked at the cat and frowned. "Wait, you're not a cat."

Alex said nothing and stayed where he was sitting next to Ash. He stared at Don who shifted uncomfortably before looking at Ash.

"Yours is the seducing," he said as Ash looked unimpressed. "But there's something else there too. A second one you haven't managed to trigger yet."

Ash frowned. "Like what? How do I trigger it?"

Don shrugged. "I don't how you can trigger it. It's like an ... ice thing. You're pretty cold, actually."

Gates suddenly laughed, unable to help himself due to Don's word choice. Ash shot him a death-glare.

"You shut it," she warned, pointing at him.

"Or what? You gonna freeze me?" Gates remarked, laughing again. "See, I knew you were cold-hearted."

The glare remained on her face as she stared him down. Gates and Matt were both thoroughly amused but didn't say anything else.

Jacob looked around at everyone. He sighed as Ash continued to glare at Gates.

"Look, can we cut this out? If you really want to fight this out, then I'm not going to stop you."

"Oh, I'll happily fight this out and teach her a lesson," Gates said as Matt let him go. "Maybe get her mad enough to trigger her second ability. I want to see what she can do."

"You're an asshole," Ash said in response.

"I'm far more delightful than you."

"Alright, that's it," Jacob said with irritation. "Gates, back it up. You and Ash are first up. Show me what you can do, and we'll see where we can go with it."

Everyone, except Gates and Ash, moved back to where Jacob was standing so they wouldn't be in the way. Matt suddenly appeared next to Don with his arm draped over his shoulder, startling him and giving him a smile.

"She can't do anything," Gates scoffed, moving back a couple of paces. "She's going to get knocked flat."

"Like to see you try," Ash snapped back. "I could knock you down easy, once I get the hang of my supposed new ability."

"Bring it."

Ash growled as Gates put his hands out. The barrier appeared in front of him, and he smiled at her, edging her on.

Ash looked over at Jacob. "How am I meant to trigger this?"

Gates pretended to check his non-existent watch. "Ain't got all day. Come on, teach me a lesson. Hit me."

Ash rolled her eyes and put her hands on her hips. She looked at Jacob again.

"Depends," Jacob said.

Matt smiled as Gates sat down where he was, the barrier now surrounding him entirely.

"Think I might've trapped myself," Gates remarked, looking around the small confines of the barrier. "Nah, I can get out if I want to."

Ash glared at him. "Would you give it a rest for a minute?"

She looked back at Jacob.

"The main things that trigger abilities are usually anger or self-defense," Jacob said.

Gates nodded and got to his feet, the barrier disappearing when he put his hands down.

"That's how I figured out mine: self-defense," he said. He brushed himself down. "Let's see if that's how we get yours going."

Before Ash could say anything, Gates pushed his hand out, the barrier appeared and knocked her to the ground.

"What is your problem?" Ash snapped as Gates laughed, the barrier no longer there.

Matt was trying not to laugh as well.

"Self-defense," Gates said with a shrug. "Gotta learn how to defend yourself any way you can, against anything and anyone at any time."

Ash just sat and glared at him.

"There you go," Jacob said, pointing to the ground beneath her. They all saw the light sparkle of a small piece of ice there. "You've got it going. Looked like it was the anger factor. See if you can hit him with it."

Gates smirked at her as she got to her feet, a sudden chill in the air. "Yeah, see if you can hit me."

Ash growled in annoyance again, this time stomping her foot on the ground in anger. Within seconds, a wall of ice was headed Gates's way.

He quickly put his barrier up and the ice smashed into it, making him flinch as it pushed him back a bit before disappearing back into the ground.

"Wow, got a bit of an anger issue there," Gates remarked. "You mad at me or something?"

"Alright, Gates, don't edge her on," Jacob said as Gates smirked. "She needs to get the hang of it before you do that. We don't want something going wrong before she can control it."

Gates rolled his eyes, the barrier disappearing as he stayed where he was.

Jacob looked at Ash, indicating for her to move out of the way. It looked like he wanted Gates as the main person everyone went against. He could defend himself better than the others.

"I'm not going anywhere," Ash said, still glaring at Gates. "I want to get the hang of this so I can put him in his damn place."

"Oh, put me in my place?" Gates said with a laugh. "I've already put you in your place. Who ended up on the ground? Oh, that's right, it was you."

"Gates," Jacob warned.

Ash pushed her hands forwards, hoping to get some kind of reaction happening. The chill in the air returned as Gates suddenly put the barrier back up, shielding him from the small, sharp shards of ice that appeared.

Gates didn't say a word as Ash did the same thing again. More shards smashed into his barrier, making him either flinch or wince with every hit.

"Alright Ash, that's enough," Jacob said as Ash did it for a third time. Gates pushed back as hard as he could to try to lessen the impact. "You've proven your point, step back."

"Not so tough now, are we?" Ash said smugly as the barrier disappeared and Gates looked at her.

"Look who's talking," he said in response, moving slightly and wincing at the pain.

Ash flipped him off before walking over to where Jacob and the others were. She stopped next to Chris who just glanced at her, getting a slight smile in return.

Jacob looked at the group as Gates shook out his hands, wincing again.

"Alright, who's next?"

CHAPTER THIRTY-TWO

Advances

"So, you slept with Ash?"

Gates rolled his eyes as Matt sat on his bed, an amused smile on his face.

"Not willingly," Gates said as he looked at himself in the mirror. He touched a series of cuts on his left side. "Shit, she left a damn mark."

"That she did. Must have been the ice shards," Matt remarked, watching Gates sigh and shake his head before putting his shirt back on. "What happened with you two? Did she, ah, seduce you?"

"What do you think happened?" Gates asked, crossing his arms as he looked at him with no amusement. "Really, what's your best guess?"

"I don't have a guess," Matt said with a shrug. "All I know about Ashley is that she gets people when they're caught off guard. So? What did she do to you?"

"Exactly what you think," Gates said, sighing and heading to the door. Matt jumped to his feet and followed him out. "She found me in the library and tried to come onto me. I said no and next thing you know, she was using her ability against me."

"Did you at least try to get away from it?"

"The fuck do you think?" Gates snapped, stopping halfway down the hallway. "Do you know how hard it is to get away from her when she uses her ability? Either way, I won't be sleeping with her again ... ever."

"I hope not," Matt laughed as they continued on their way. "Hey, can I ask you something?"

They turned into a kitchen and Gates glanced at Matt before looking for something to eat in one of the cupboards.

"Sure, what's up?"

Matt shrugged as he sat down at the table.

"Do you ... do you ever regret coming down here?"

Gates frowned, stopping what he was doing, and turning to look at Matt. He leaned against the kitchen counter as he crossed his arms.

"Why do you ask that?" he asked quietly.

"You ever wanna go home?"

Gates sighed, looking down.

"Honestly, I haven't thought about that in years," he said, a hint of sadness in his voice. "Even if I wanted to, I can't. You really think Skye would have waited seven years for me to turn up? Matt, the four of us, back home? We're all missing, Viv included."

Matt nodded and Gates sighed again, looking at him.

"What about you?" he asked. "You ever wanna go home?"

"I don't have anything to go back to," Matt said quietly. He looked away and rested his arms on the table. "Even if I wanted to, it's too late for me now."

"It's never too late, Matt," Gates said sadly. Matt looked up and met his gaze. "If you really want to go home, then go home. You don't have to stay down here. You don't have to be a part of this anymore."

"There's no point in me going home, Blaine," Matt said sadly. "Viv was the main thing I had back home, and she's gone. I literally have no reason to go back, whereas you do. Skye's still up there."

Gates shook his head. "I doubt that. It's been seven, nearly eight years. We're all probably presumed dead by now. Can you imagine the look on her face if I just suddenly showed up? Like, oh, hey Skye, so sorry I've been gone seven years, how are you doing? She's probably moved on by now anyway."

Matt shrugged as Gates fell silent. "Just a thought."

Gates shook his head. "It's fine, Matt. I completely understand. Let's just deal with Marion and then we'll see where it goes from there."

"Honestly, I'm probably going to go back to Wonderland," Matt said, Gates nodding in understanding. "Like I said, I don't have any reason to go back home, back up top. Probably better off with me staying down here for the rest of eternity."

Carmen looked over as Marion came into the room, Hunter not far behind with his dog.

Marion took a seat, while Hunter stood near the door, leaning on the doorframe, his dog at his feet.

"The two you were after are back," Carmen said, glancing up from the new concoction she was making. "Vincent managed to get them back."

"Well, good. Now, I just need the two of them," Marion said with a sigh.

Carmen stopped what she was doing and looked at her. "Why do you need those two in particular? And how do you plan on getting them?"

"I need Shade because he's been a pain in my side for years. He just won't die, and he won't stand still long enough for me to get him," Marion said as Heather waltzed into the room, a smile on her face. "Chris is very important to me. He can help me out once he has a grip on his ability. I don't have a way of getting either of them at the moment. Shade is the one I need first, though. Chris can wait a bit longer."

Carmen nodded, a thoughtful look on her face as she tried to figure out the best way to catch the man who was uncatchable.

"I have an idea," Heather said.

"What might that idea be?" Marion asked, linking her fingers together as she leaned back in the chair. Her side was healing but the pain was still there.

"You need to get a hold of Shade, no?" she began. Marion stayed silent, hearing her out. "We also need to get the Iron Army out for a test run. Why not use one of them to grab him. Keep him out in broad daylight if you can't knock him out, bring him back here, throw him in the dungeons with our fabulous binding shackles so he can't get out, and he's yours."

Marion nodded slowly, thinking through what Heather had just said.

"What about Chris?" she asked, looking at Heather. "He won't come willingly."

"Oh, neither will Shade," Heather said, coming over and sitting on the chair next to Marion. "We'll make something up for you so you can trap this Chris fellow. Shade might be hard to lure out, though."

"We need to get both of them out in the open," Marion said, thinking as she spoke. "Maybe we take a few soldiers from the army out and set off a couple of alerts. Surely Shade would be one of the main people that Vincent would send out with his enforcers. He knows his ability well enough that he'd be valuable in the field. Chris, I'm not so sure about."

"Why don't we focus on getting one of them first, then worry about the others later," Carmen said. She leaned back as smoke rose from the bowl in front of her. "Get rid of the main threat and then get the next person."

Marion nodded, liking the idea. It would be a lot easier to get one person to begin with and then figure out a way to get the others.

"When did you want to try out the Iron Army?"

"We'll just send a few of them, maybe six or seven to start with," Heather said, Carmen nodding. "Just so they don't all get wiped out at once. Carmen can work on the next half of the army while those few are out seeking your special man."

"Hmm, yes, Shade won't know what hit him when he runs into them. That's the only way we can get him. Once he's out of my way, we'll have one less person to worry about."

"What did he actually do to you?" Carmen asked, more smoke rising from the bowl as she put another ingredient into it.

Marion shrugged. "He's been avoiding me for years, been off my radar for the past few. He skipped out of his fight with Hunter not that long ago. That would have been my way to kill him off once and for all. Just never been able to get my hands on the bastard. He's always avoiding my patrols, and I just don't like him. He needs to be contained because otherwise he'll be my downfall."

"Not Abel? He seemed pretty adamant on killing you," Heather said.

Marion waved a hand dismissively. "Abel's got nothing on me. He's not someone I have to worry about."

"Matt, hey," called Nixx.

Matt looked up and Nixx stopped just in front of him outside the castle. Matt looked him over, summing him up before speaking.

"What?"

Nixx looked around before looking back at him, making sure there was no one around who might interrupt them.

"I have something for you, something I need you to keep away from everyone," he said, keeping his voice down.

"You have something for me?" Matt said in disbelief. He scoffed. "Wow, and it's not even my birthday."

Nixx gave him an unamused look before holding out a dark, leather-bound journal. Matt frowned but reluctantly took it.

"I need you to keep hold of it and don't tell anyone you have it," Nixx said, putting his hands behind his back.

Matt turned it over in his hands.

"What is it?" he asked cautiously, not daring to open it.

"It's one of the doctor's journals," Nixx said. "This stays between us. No one, no matter how much you trust them, can know you have it. It holds vital information that if it gets into the wrong hands, will ruin a lot of people."

Matt switched his gaze back to Nixx.

"Why are you giving this to me?" he asked seriously.

Nixx waited, watching someone walk past, before returning his gaze to Matt, a bit of a smile on his face.

"Because I know I can trust you with it," he said. "I'm only telling you and no one else. I have one, Abel has one, and Chris has one. Under no circumstances can anyone find out you have the fourth one. It's safer that way. If no one knows, then they won't know who might need to be killed for it when it comes down to it."

Matt gave him an unamused smile. "Charming."

"Just hold onto it, store it somewhere while we're here," Nixx said. "And remember, don't tell a soul you have it."

CHAPTER THIRTY-THREE

Catching a Shadow

"**A**lright so, here's the deal. I'll happily help you guys out with what you need, but as I stated last night, we won't be down here all hours," Jacob said, looking around at everyone in front of him. "I get that you want to take down Marion, but this kind of thing doesn't happen in a day. You've got to put in the effort, and you'll get the results. Sound good?"

Everyone nodded.

"So," Jacob continued. "I know some of you have good control of your abilities and I won't need to work with you as much, so if you want to do your own thing for a bit while I take Ash, Abel, and Chris, then be my guest. Just don't seriously hurt each other, OK?"

Jacob indicated for Ash, Abel, and Chris to follow him as he headed towards the back of the arena.

The others went about their own thing, including Alex who stayed behind, having decided not to be a cat today.

"Alright, so I'm going to have to work individually with each of you, but even if you're watching what we're doing that's fine. Think about how you can maybe make your abilities work together," Jacob said. He looked at Abel. "For example, you might be able to use yours together with Zeke. Just think about how they can work together to create more devastation."

"Because that's really what we want," Ash stated, everyone looking to her. "More devastation than we already have."

Jacob shrugged. "You never know. It might be the only way to ensure you take down Marion. It's not going to be easy."

Ash rolled her eyes, crossing her arms and not saying anything more.

Jacob looked at Abel. "May as well start with you, seeing as Ash has a bit of a grip on hers anyway, and, for Chris, we'll have to do a bit more work."

Dorothy walked quickly across the arena and stopped next to Jacob, who waited for her to speak. The rest of the group saw her and also came over.

"One of our alerts has gone off," Dorothy said, a sense of urgency in her voice. "It looks like Heather's out with a few people."

Jacob nodded. "What do you want us to do about it?"

Dorothy looked around at everyone before returning her gaze to Jacob.

"Vincent wants to send a couple of these guys out with the security patrol," she said. "But only the ones who know what they're doing. No novices. Whoever you think is field ready."

Jacob nodded again, looking around at everyone.

"Any volunteers?" he asked, looking at Matt, Gates, and Zeke who were all standing together. "You three, besides Nixx, are the most experienced with what you can do. Are you OK to go? I'm guessing you can all defend yourselves without abilities too, correct?"

"Yeah, we'll go," Matt said.

"Are you sure you should be going?" Chris asked Matt. "Marion was after you as well. If Heather's out, then it could go very wrong. What if that's the reason they're out doing whatever they're doing."

Matt shrugged, a non-caring look on his face.

"If I get caught, I get caught," he said. "If I don't come back, at least you'll know where to find me if you decide to look."

"Matt, you're part of the team too," Abel said. "Believe it or not, we need you here as much as anyone. You're the main reason we got here."

Matt just looked at him, thinking but not saying anything. After a minute or two, he looked away from Abel and at Dorothy.

"When do we leave?"

"Why did we agree to do this?" Gates asked with a sigh as they followed a group of people through the castle. "We don't know what Heather can do, what she wants to do."

They were part of the security patrol Vincent was sending out to push Heather back to where she was meant to be.

"Doesn't matter what she wants to do," Matt said, the three of them stopping as the group halted near a closed door. "We're going to do what we've been asked to do, then come back here and continue on with whatever we have to do."

Gates rolled his eyes as they followed the group into a small room, none of them saying anything. The door closed once everyone was in.

"Well, this is gonna be fun," Gates muttered to himself as a bright light appeared, making him sigh.

Next thing they knew, they were outside, and the Emerald City was nowhere in sight. The group leader looked at everyone, Matt shifting his weight as he crossed his arms and looked back, unimpressed.

"Alright," the group leader said. "We need to approach this carefully. We all know Heather is dangerous, and we don't know who she has with her. Our alerts said there are eight including her, so everyone be on your guard and we'll push her back."

Everyone, apart from Gates, Matt, and Zeke, nodded. The leader looked at the back of the group where the three of them were standing.

"We were informed that you three can help us out in a different way," he continued. Matt shrugged and Zeke put his hands in his pockets. "Which one of you has the barrier?"

Gates reluctantly raised his hand slightly, looking as impressed and motivated as Matt. The leader nodded as Gates lowered his hand.

"We'll need you up the front of the group with me," he ordered. Gates didn't look happy with this decision. "We've also been informed that the shadow-stepper needs to be watched closely. Heather's apparently after him."

"The shadow-stepper has a name, you know," Matt said with irritation as the leader looked at him. "And he can easily take care of himself. He doesn't need you."

"We have our orders," the man said before switching his gaze to Zeke. "So that makes you the fire one."

"Same as him, I have a name," Zeke said with annoyance. "Maybe this would work better if you took a few seconds to ask who we actually are?"

"We don't have time for introductions. We're here to do our job."

"Yet you have time to stop here and chat," Zeke remarked, mirroring Matt's position. He looked at Matt. "Doesn't make much sense to me."

The leader shot him a glare before indicating for Gates to make his way to the front of the group. Gates sighed, pushing past a few people as he did.

"Alright, let's do this," the leader said, beginning to walk.

Gates walked next to him, while the rest of the group followed.

"This is stupid," Zeke said to Matt, his voice down as they trailed along behind. "You'd think they'd already know what was going on, you know? Maybe we should've stayed back at the City."

Matt shrugged. "I don't know, man. I just want to do something and get out for a bit, you know? There's only so much I can do back at the City."

Zeke nodded in understanding as they continued their way towards a forest. Both of them assumed these guys knew where they were going and what they were doing.

The leader signaled for them all to halt on the edge of the forest.

"Aw, not coming in to join us?" Heather appeared, leaning against the closest tree. "We're having so much fun."

"Heather, you know you're not allowed out here," the leader said. "You need to leave, or we'll force you out. You know how this goes."

Heather rolled her eyes as a strange, very tall, figure stepped up next to her. Zeke frowned, exchanging looks with Matt who shrugged.

Heather pouted at them all, the figure not moving. It looked like a person but seemed metallic and had what looked like black armor shielding it.

"Where's the fun in leaving willingly?" she asked. She laughed a bit before settling her gaze on Matt, a smile lighting up her face. "Well, hey there, handsome. I was told you were back from your little ... trip."

Matt gave her an unamused smile back. "Couldn't keep away."

Heather laughed again and clicked her fingers. Another six tall, metallic figures appeared, surrounding the whole group.

Gates put his hands out, the barrier up instantly, locking the group within it.

"You think that's going to keep them out? Really?" Heather said with a smile. She pushed off the tree and wandered towards them.

She stopped in front of Gates on the other side of the barrier, giving him a smile. "Nice try, but don't believe this is going to stop them."

Gates narrowed his eyes at her. "Care to elaborate?"

"Nope," Heather said in response, the smile never leaving her face.

She turned her gaze to look at the closest metallic soldier, clicking her fingers again. All at once, the seven soldiers started hitting the barrier as hard as they could. Gates flinched with every hit.

Heather smiled as she watched. "They can do more, you know. This is just to see how much you can handle."

Gates pushed back as hard as he could, managing to make one of the soldiers step back.

Heather pouted at him. "Why would you do that?"

"Because I'm not going to stand here and let them break through," Gates said through his teeth as a crack appeared in the barrier. He was still beaten up from earlier in the week and wasn't back to his full strength yet. "Going to have to try harder than that."

Heather sighed. It sounded like a chore to her. "Well, if you insist."

She clicked her fingers again and the soldiers stopped hitting Gates's barrier.

A second later, a high-pitched sound started. The entire group, including Gates, Matt, and Zeke, all automatically put their hands to their ears, trying to block it out.

"What?" Heather said, pretending to be confused as the barrier disappeared. "You hearing something I'm not?"

She looked around, shrugging before clicking her fingers once more. The noise stopped. "See, told you it wouldn't work."

"What do you want?" the group leader asked as Heather pretended to look at the paint on her nails.

"Oh, I was just taking my beautiful new men out for a wander," Heather said. She switched her gaze and winked at Matt who was still standing with Zeke at the back of the group. "And to see my favorite shadow-stepper."

Matt gave her an unamused smile, Heather returning it.

"Why is Marion after me and Chris?" Matt asked. "What have we done? I would have thought the bitch would be after Abel more than us."

"What she wants with you two isn't my business," Heather said with a shrug. "Never asked. But she's very insistent on getting her hands on you."

"Well, I don't think that's going to be happening any time soon."

Heather laughed. "Oh, I wouldn't put my money on it."

She clicked her fingers, a bit sharper this time. Without warning, one of the soldiers at the back grabbed Matt, pulling him backwards. Matt shot Heather a glare as the other soldiers closed in on the group.

"See, this was just too easy," Heather said, that smile still on her face. She looked at Matt as he tried to break out of the soldier's iron grip. "No use struggling. He won't let you go."

"What are you going to do now?" Matt asked, giving up on trying to break the grip. "You know as soon as there's a shadow, I'm out."

"That's why we're out here in the open!" Heather said, spreading her arms out to her sides.

There wasn't any form of shadow in sight.

She laughed, not saying anything more as she looked at the group. None of them had moved, seeing there was nothing they could do now. She sighed, looking back at Matt.

"Well, we'll be on our way," she said, walking past the group and stopping next to the soldier that had Matt completely trapped. "I do hope this hasn't inconvenienced too many of you. Now you know what you're up against. Go tell Vincent that he's going down a road he won't be coming back from."

With that, Heather clicked her fingers one last time and disappeared with the soldier and Matt.

Gates put his barrier back up to keep the remaining six soldiers at bay.

"What now?" Gates asked, looking at the group leader.

Zeke stayed at the back of the group, knowing he was about to be needed.

The group leader shook his head. He was obviously out of his depth and useless at his job.

Gates growled in annoyance and looked over his shoulder at Zeke. "You all good to help take care of this?"

Zeke nodded and Gates nodded back before looking back at the leader of the group.

"You and your guys are going to move out of the way. Get clear," he instructed. "I've got your backs for a good distance. We'll deal with this."

CHAPTER THIRTY-FOUR

Preparations

"Are you alright?"

Gates and Zeke both looked exhausted as everyone appeared in the doorway of the infirmary. Abel and Nixx moved aside to let Chris, Alex, and Ash in.

"We're fine," Gates said, wincing as the nurse continued to tend to him again. He was getting a bit tired of the amount of time he was spending in here.

"Where's Matt?" Nixx asked, noticing his absence.

Gates shook his head, wincing as the nurse cleaned a cut on his face. Nixx looked at Zeke who sighed and just returned the look.

"Heather got him," Zeke said, watching Nixx's expression fall.

"It was all an elaborate plan to get him out there and show us what we're up against," Gates finally input. "They knew Matt would go out with the group and they set it up so they could grab him. Now he's gone."

"Where would they take him?" Abel asked. "He can shadow-step. They won't be able to keep him long, wherever he is."

Gates shook his head, Zeke speaking this time.

"It's not that simple," he said as Vincent appeared at the door. "Heather knew exactly what she was doing. They've clearly got some plan that's going to stop him from leaving."

"They can't keep him out of the dark all the time."

"Well, they've obviously got some way of keeping him."

Vincent moved into the room and everyone looked at him.

"I'm just going to go ahead and say I'm very sorry that Heather got her hands on Matt," he said straight out. "I didn't know that was why Heather was out there. But we'll get him back."

Gates scoffed, everyone looking at him as the nurse finally finished up with him, moving onto cleaning up Zeke.

"Man, you weren't out there. You didn't see those … metallic soldiers we were up against," he said with a shake of his head. "Seriously, just six of them nearly killed us. By the way, your damn security group is useless. Get a new team."

Vincent looked at him with a hint of annoyance. "They don't deal with the witches very often. A lot of them were new on the job, so cut them some slack."

"How long has that damn leader been going out on patrol?" Gates asked seriously. "He knew nothing, couldn't make a decision. Yeah, it was a new threat, but he was useless."

Vincent stayed quiet, having nothing to say. Gates shook his head and looked away.

"So, what do we do?" Chris asked.

Vincent shook his head. "Until they physically make it known that they're going to attack us, we can't do anything. Best just to get healed up and back into training. We all need to be prepared as much as we can be for when it finally happens."

"You need to have regular scouting groups," Zeke suggested. "From today alone, we're gonna need a lot more monitoring on what's happening."

Vincent agreed with his idea. "I'll see to it."

"How did it go?" Marion asked as Heather came into the room, a smile on her face.

"Well, the army works fine," she said, sitting on the chair opposite her. "They're very good. It will take a lot to get past them, let me tell you. I think we have quite the chance of getting this land back. I really don't think Vincent will be able to defeat all of them, especially when we're at full strength."

Marion gave her an unamused look; that wasn't what she was really asking.

Heather looked at her, realization on her face. "Oh, he's in the dungeons. He won't be going anywhere for a while, I don't think."

"Good," Marion nodded.

Carmen looked over. "What are you going to do with him? You can't keep him down there forever, you know."

Marion shrugged. "Give him a few days down there, then I'll go see him. He won't be leaving any time soon."

Carmen shook her head, going back to what she was doing.

"So far, the binding on the shackles seems to have worked," Heather said. "He's been sitting in the dark for the past hour or so and he's still there. I don't think he's getting out. Then again, I don't know how conscious he is, the shackles seemed to really drain him."

"Well, it's taken me this long to get him, so I don't expect him to be getting out," Marion said, no amusement in her voice.

"He didn't put up much of a fight," Heather noted, leaning back in her chair. "It was a bit disappointing, actually. Had more trouble putting him in the shackles than getting him here."

"I somehow doubt he was ever going into those shackles willingly," Carmen remarked. "They're not the most comfortable things."

Heather shook her head, looking back at Marion with a bit of a smile.

"We're getting closer with the spell to get you Chris," she informed her. "By the looks of things, the group that followed you here won't be much use against the Iron Army. That stupid barrier guy wasn't very good. The other one never even stepped in until we were gone."

"Really," Marion stated, Heather nodding. "Because I've seen Gates do quite impressive things."

"Well, he didn't seem to be in the best shape when we surrounded their little party today."

Marion shrugged, not even caring now. The easier they went down, the better.

"Just let me know when you have everything ready, and we'll head out with a few more of your army to test them out. I want to see it for myself."

"What do you think Marion's going to do to Matt?" Abel asked as he and Chris stood back, watching Gates and Zeke going back and forth in the arena.

Gates was refusing to go and rest. He deflected one of Zeke's attacks, making Zeke quickly step out of the way.

The two of them looked rather mad, most likely because of Matt's capture, which was why they were at the arena now.

Chris shook his head and sighed, crossing his arms as he watched them. "No idea. If she's smart, she'll kill him. You think Gates gets burnt from that?"

Abel shrugged. "Who knows? He gets hurt from everything else, so it would make sense that he gets burnt from Zeke's attacks. Wonder if Zeke feels it at all."

Chris shrugged this time and they both looked at Jacob who'd just joined them.

"You guys going to do anything today?" he asked. "I know we already worked on a couple of things, but maybe you want to try by yourselves. Maybe even against one another like those two?"

"They know what they're doing," Abel said, shaking his head as he watched Gates push Zeke back, wincing as he did so. "We don't know what we're doing."

"Come on over and we'll work on it, then," Jacob said, indicating for them to follow as he headed over to one of the areas up the back.

"How are we going to learn how to control this anyway?" Abel asked as he and Chris stopped next to Jacob.

"It's just practice," Jacob said with a shrug. "From what I saw earlier today, yours seems to mostly work when you get worked up, mad or upset. If you can figure out how to control that, you should be able to control your ability."

"That's well and good for me, but what about Chris?" Abel asked, glancing at Chris who nodded in agreement. "How's he going to get his to work?"

"Once again, practice," Jacob said in response.

He indicated to Zeke and Gates. Gates managed to knock Zeke to the ground. Zeke quickly moved out of the way and got back to his feet within seconds.

"You see, they literally just worked on theirs. It's all practice," Jacob continued. "They've taught themselves how to use their abilities to their advantage. Some are harder to get a grip on, like yours, Abel, but in the end, you just have to put the effort and the time in, and you'll get the hang of it."

Chris and Abel looked back at Jacob who gave them an encouraging smile.

"I've only managed to use mine once and it was in self-defense," Chris stated. "I literally have no idea how it works."

"Alright, we'll work on yours for a while," Jacob said, nodding as he thought. Abel went back to watching Gates and Zeke. "Once you have a brief hang of it, we'll go from there."

CHAPTER THIRTY-FIVE

Passing Time

"Please, take a seat," Vincent said, gesturing for everyone to sit down.

Time had gone by rather fast. It had already been three months since Heather had shown up with her soldiers and taken Matt. It had been very quiet since then, which was setting people on edge. Something should have happened by now.

The seven of them did as asked, sitting around the table as Vincent took his usual place at the head of the table. He looked around at everyone.

"I just want to start off by saying you've all been doing very well with your training in the arena," he began as Dorothy came in and sat at the other end of the table. "Also, there have been no alerts going off at all."

Everyone nodded, while Gates glared down the table at Vincent.

"Matt's been gone for months," he stated. "We're also none the wiser about what they're planning. We can't afford to keep sitting around and doing nothing. Training isn't going to cut it against those damn soldiers."

Vincent nodded again. "I know it's been a few months. But there's nothing we can do. I've already told you this. We can't go into their territory. We have to wait for them to bring the fight to us."

"So, what? We're going to leave Matt there until we kill the rest of them?" Zeke asked, sounding as unimpressed as Gates looked. "We don't know what Marion and those witches have done to Matt these past few months. He could already be dead for all we know."

"And if that's the case, then yes, it's a sad thing," Vincent said, Gates shaking his head. "We can't do anything if he's already dead. We have to go about this carefully and not rush into things."

"It's been three months," Gates said sternly. "All we've done is train down at the damn arena. You haven't even seen this ... Iron Army they have going. You've no idea what you're up against. Even with us all knowing what we're doing, none of us are getting out of that alive."

"We've got more than just the seven of you," Vincent said. "We've got my people as well. Jacob's in it with us. A few of my people are coming with us, including Dorothy."

"There were six of them and we only just made it out," Zeke said. "Even with your people, against an entire army? Man, we're fucked."

"Look, we'll deal with it, and no one is dying," Vincent said seriously. Gates was shaking his head again. "We'll come back to that topic a bit later. Abel, how's Jamie doing?"

Abel nodded. "She's OK. She's moving around more but still spends most of her time in her room. You know how it gets for her at the moment."

Vincent nodded. "It's good to hear she's up and about. Just make sure she takes it easy because of the baby and everything. Dorothy, how's Alice?"

Dorothy shrugged. "She still won't say anything. Still goes to attack anyone when they come near. She still doesn't seem to recognize me."

"Alright, well, I'll see what I can do to help the girl," Vincent said. "She's been rabid for so long, though. She might be too far gone."

"Wouldn't surprise me," Gates muttered, Zeke shaking his head at him.

Vincent sighed. "Alright everyone, get back to work for the day. We'll meet up again later this week to discuss where we're at."

Everyone got up from the table and started heading out of the room. However, they stopped and looked back as Vincent started talking again.

"Before you go. Chris, Zeke, and Gates, I need you to stay with me for a few minutes."

Chris frowned, and Gates and Zeke exchanged looks as Vincent waved the others away. Dorothy came over to join them once everyone else was out of the room.

"What's up?" Zeke asked.

"I want you and Gates to go and see how many people we have signed up for this so far, including your people," he said. "There's paper on my desk in the back there if you want to go and grab that. Add it all up and then start going around and see if you can recruit more people to help us in this fight against Marion and the witches."

"How many do we need?" Gates asked.

"And does it matter how we get them to sign up?" was Zeke's question, a bit of a mischievous look on his face.

Gates gave him an amused smile, clearly on the same wavelength as him.

"Do what you have to, just don't hurt anyone," Vincent sighed. "We need as many people as we can get."

Both men nodded. Vincent indicated to a door on the left of the room that led to his office. Gates and Zeke headed over there, leaving Chris and Dorothy with Vincent.

"Chris, I need your help with something," he said, beginning to walk and forcing Chris to follow, Dorothy not far behind.

"What with?" Chris asked.

Vincent gave him a smile as they headed through one of the doors to the right. "You'll see."

Chris stayed quiet as he followed Vincent down a very long flight of steps with a door at the end. Vincent unlocked the door, opened it, and went in. Dorothy shut the door once they were all through.

They were in a lower part of the castle, walking past what looked like holding cells. They were in the dungeons.

"Don't worry about them," Vincent said as they passed the cells where three people were locked up. "They've broken the law and won't be out for a bit. There are some people we have to keep off the streets."

"Where are we going?" Chris asked as they walked into another part of the dungeons, going down another set of steps.

This reminded Chris a lot of the dungeons in Wonderland, but this was a lot nicer than there.

"We're going to see Alice," Vincent said as they reached the end of the staircase, continuing on through another area. "She won't talk to anyone, and I think she might have a word with you. She seems to know you a lot better than she knows us."

Chris looked at Dorothy. "I thought she was your sister?"

"She's been gone for years," Dorothy said. "She doesn't recognize me. Doesn't trust me."

Vincent unlocked the door in front of him, looking at his two companions. "We have to be very careful around her. She's still quite unstable."

He opened the door cautiously, peering around the corner before entering, indicating for the door to be quickly shut once they were all in.

The room wasn't what Chris had expected. He'd thought it was going to be like the rest of the dungeons, but it was completely opposite. This room looked like a normal room, like the ones they were all staying in. It was furnished with a bed, a desk, a number of different decorative objects, and more. The only difference was that this room had no window, and the only light hung from the ceiling and was currently on.

Alice was sitting in the middle of the bed, and she glared at the three of them as the door closed, but she didn't say a word. They stayed near the door.

"Alice," Vincent said. "I've been told you aren't behaving very well. I brought Chris down here in case you want to talk to someone you know."

Alice switched her gaze to Chris, looking him over before returning her glare to his face.

"Where's Matt?" she asked bitterly. "I wanna talk to Matt, no one else."

"Matt's not around," Chris said, getting a growl from Alice.

She didn't say anything, just continued to glare at Chris. Chris looked at Dorothy who shrugged, so he looked back at Alice, speaking again.

"Look Alice, we need your help with taking down Marion and her two friends," he said. A slight smirk appeared on Alice's face. "They've got an army, and we need everyone we can get to fight. That includes you."

Once again, Alice stayed quiet. Chris sighed, looking at Vincent who was watching Alice cautiously.

"She's not going to talk to anyone who's not Matt," Chris confirmed. "There's nothing I can do."

Vincent gave a slight nod, his gaze never leaving the girl in front of him.

"Well, then," he said, disappointment in his voice. "I guess we need to get Matt back before Alice will agree to help us."

"Is Matt missing?" Alice asked, her voice low and concerned. "Where's he gone?"

"Marion has him," Chris said. "We don't know what they've done to him or if he's still alive. If you want Matt back, then you have to help us take down the people who have him."

Alice narrowed her eyes, but didn't say anything more.

"This is no use," Vincent said, shaking his head. "She won't talk to anyone who's not Matt. Looks like we have to do this with one less person."

Chris nodded as Dorothy opened the door again, and they all stepped out. Vincent shut and locked the door once they were out, hearing a noise in the room. It sounded like something breaking.

"Don't worry about her," Vincent said, putting the key back in his pocket. "She's been smashing things since she got here. By the way, why won't she talk to anyone but Matt?"

Chris shrugged. "No idea, she seems to have a bit of a fascination with him for some reason."

"Alright, well, we'll see what we can do about getting Matt back," Vincent said. "I don't think we'll be able to just yet though. The rate this is going, we'll have to take down Marion first and then try and get him back. If he isn't already dead."

CHAPTER THIRTY-SIX

Recruitment

"So, we've got ... less than one hundred people," Gates said, running the pen down the page as he walked alongside Zeke. "Where do we want to start with this recruitment drive?"

Zeke shrugged, thinking as he halted, forcing Gates to halt too. Gates looked up from the paper, seeing the thoughtful look on Zeke's face.

"What day is it?" Zeke asked.

"First Thursday of the month," Gates said, an amused smile on his face as Zeke nodded, the same look on his face.

"Market day," they both said.

Without another word, they headed towards the town square, knowing that was where they would find a lot of people today. Neither of them had been to the markets since the first incident, deciding that it was safer—and saner—to stay away for a bit.

"So, what's the plan?" Gates asked as they turned down one of the alleyways that led to the town square. "We rock up, get a couple of people to talk to us, and sign them up? What if they don't want to chat?"

"We can start like that. If people don't want to listen, we might have to move onto a different tactic," Zeke said as they reached the town square, coming to a stop on the edge. There were a lot of people around and Zeke watched a few pass by, making sure to keep their distance. "Hmm, we might have a bit of a hard time getting people to talk to us willingly."

"Seeing how everyone's already avoiding us," Gates remarked, watching a group glance at them and quicken their pace as they passed. "Think they might still remember the last incident?"

Zeke scoffed, crossing his arms as Gates looked around.

"Dude, that was three months ago. They should be over it by now."

"You'd think so," Gates sighed. "Alright, what's Plan B?"

Zeke just gave him a smile, before moving off and beginning to push his way through the crowd. Gates wasn't far behind, making sure he wasn't about to lose him in the crowd.

Zeke stopped in the middle of the town square, Gates next to him as people continued to walk around, looking at the different stalls and happily going about their day. Gates made sure he kept a tight hold on the piece of paper with the names on it, the pen still in his hand.

"You know what's great?" Zeke asked, looking at Gates who shrugged. "Being under the Wizard's protection, which means we have free rein with what we do."

Gates shrugged. "He said to do what we had to in order to get people to sign up."

Zeke nodded and smiled as he looked at the area in front of him.

"Alright, everyone shut it and listen up!" he shouted.

People nearby stopped to see who or what was interrupting their day. A few backed up a bit when they saw who was standing in the middle of the town square. The area around them quietened down a bit.

"We've been asked by the Wizard to find people who are willing to sign up for some up-and-coming issues that involve a few unsavory characters," Zeke yelled to make sure people further away could also hear him.

"What if we don't want to sign up?" a man called back. "I know I don't want to sign up and a lot of others won't either. This isn't our war to fight."

Zeke and Gates exchanged a look. It was the man who had accused Gates a few months back.

"Well, that's a very good question," Zeke said, turning to face the man. "What's your name?"

"Gordon Bates."

Zeke looked over his shoulder at Gates who returned the look. "Sign him up."

Gates nodded, looked at his piece of paper, and wrote something on it. Gordon looked at Zeke with shock and anger.

"You can't do that!" he exclaimed loudly.

"I can and I have," Zeke said, the authority clear in his voice. "You screwed us around and hunted us down, and we aren't about to forget that. As punishment, and a bit of payback, you've now been recruited. You're expected to show up when told or you're going into the dungeons. Your choice. Now, who else wants to fuck us around? Anyone?"

"Just remember you'll make the list," Gates input, Zeke nodding as he looked around.

"We need people to sign up," Zeke restated. "We aren't leaving until we have a significant amount of names on our list."

"What are you going to do if no one else signs up?" Gordon sneered.

Zeke looked over his shoulder at Gates.

"There's a woman off to your right who was part of the group that hunted us down. Add her," he said, Gates nodding and looking to find the woman. Zeke looked back at Gordon. "To answer your question, we'll be the ones you answer to. Unlike last time, I'm allowed to set these stalls on fire. There are plenty to choose from too, so either sign up or face the consequences."

"You can't physically make us sign up," a woman in front of Zeke said. "You have no right."

"What's your name?"

"Delilah Adams."

"Congratulations, Delilah Adams, you've just made the list."

He indicated to Gates who wrote her down, much to the woman's annoyance.

"Alright, we're on a roll, that's three so far who have been kind enough to sign up," Zeke said, clapping his hands together as he looked around. "Anyone else want to back chat? Anyone ready to sign up yet or do we need a bit more motivation?"

"You can't legally burn down any of these stalls," Gordon spoke up. "You'll be locked away where you should be."

"Well, sorry to break it to you, man, but we're free to do what we want," Zeke said, indicating to Gates who gave a nod as he looked around for someone else to sign up. "We're under the Wizard's protection, which means we have free rein."

"Who told you this?"

"The Wizard himself," Zeke said matter-of-factly. "You'll be answering to him if you mess up this entire crusade. He doesn't seem to be overly wrapped up in the idea that people don't want to help out. He thinks his citizens will be more than willing to defend this City and this county. I mean, let's face it, if you don't sign up, the City won't be here for much longer. Let's be real here, guys and girls."

"Why?" someone called, Zeke trying to pick them out from the crowd, but unable to find them.

"Because we have an ever-growing threat making its way here," Gates said, stepping up and finally saying something. "Carmen and Heather are preparing an army with someone from Wonderland who we tried to take down before we came here. If they manage to get their entire army up and running, this city will fall, and fast. Zeke and I have seen firsthand what these soldiers can do and we need as many people as we can get or else the Emerald City won't be around for much longer."

"You expect us to sign up and risk our lives in order to stop something that we didn't even start?" someone else said, Zeke once again trying to find them in the crowd. "Most of us can't even use our abilities, and some of us don't even have one, and you expect us to sign up?"

"You don't need to know how to use your ability. We have people who don't have an ability who have already signed up," Gates said, looking around at everyone. "There are people here who can show you and teach you how to use your abilities. We can't do this by ourselves."

Silence fell over the markets as people considered Gates's words.

"Anyone going to sign up?" Zeke asked sternly.

Gates shook his head. "No one's going to sign up, man."

"This isn't our fight," someone shouted, Zeke glaring in their direction. "This doesn't concern us! Find someone else. I certainly won't be signing up!"

A chorus of agreement sounded out throughout the town square. Gates sighed and Zeke shook his head.

"Well, I guess we all need a bit of motivation then."

He clicked his fingers, and the closest stall immediately went up in flames. People moved out of the way very quickly, someone disappearing to get something to put it out.

"There are plenty more stalls," Zeke threatened. "For every minute Gates and I are standing here and no one signs up, I'll set another one alight. Time starts now. Clock's ticking, people."

"Well, I think that went rather well," Gates said as they entered the arena.

There were a few people training like every other day they'd been here, and this was their next stop to sign people up to their crusade.

"How did we go?" Zeke asked as they headed over to three people training with each other.

"Well, we got a good hundred or so to sign up after the first stall," Gates said. "After the other three went up in flames, we got nearly another three hundred, so about one hundred per stall."

Zeke nodded in satisfaction as they halted in front of the group who stopped what they were doing and looked at them.

"Sorry if we're interrupting you," Zeke began. "We've been asked to go around and ask people to sign up for a crusade ... or well, more a war really. We were wondering if you could help us out and be a part of it?"

One of the men nodded and Gates handed him the paper and pen.

"We're happy to help," the man said, writing his name down and handing the paper to the other man. The woman with him waited to write her name down, too. "You're part of the group that came in from Wonderland, aren't you?"

"Sadly," Gates sighed, taking the paper and pen back from the woman. "Thanks for that, we need everyone we can get."

The man nodded, Gates giving him a nod back.

"Everyone will get a notice when they're needed," Zeke said as Gates started counting the people on the list, marking every twenty people. "So, it's best to get a good hold on whatever your ability is now. It might come in useful when this shit happens."

The man nodded again. "Like I said, we're happy to help. The last thing we want is to see the City and the county fall. What are your names?"

"I'm Zeke, this is Gates."

The man held his hand out in a friendly manner. Zeke shook it as Gates continued to calculate the exact number of people they had on the list.

"Nice to meet you. I'm Ben, this is Doug, and Ruby," he said. "We've seen you two here more than the rest of your group. You two certainly know how to handle your abilities."

"Thanks," Zeke said. "We've been working on them for a while, just takes practice."

Gates finally looked up from what he was doing, having written the total amount of people on the end of the page at the last name.

"We've been training here for a couple years but we still haven't gotten to our full potential yet," Ben explained, Zeke nodding as Gates crossed his arms and just listened. "We've trained with some of the instructors, but we've been working on our own for a few months to try and get the hang of it by ourselves. We want to work with Jacob but sadly have never had the chance."

"Well, just keep at it," Gates said, Zeke nodding in agreement. "You'll get the hang of it in time. Can't rush these things."

"We'll work on it," Ben said with a nod. "By the way, we were hoping you'd come by. We were wondering if maybe you guys could help us out with a bit of training?"

Zeke and Gates looked at each other before looking back to Ben and his two friends.

"Well, what do you need help with?" Zeke asked. He looked back at Gates. "Think we have enough people for now?"

Gates nodded. "We can recruit more later. We've got time to stop for a bit."

"Awesome," Ben said with a smile. "We've really only trained with each other, which was why we wanted to know if you'd train with us for a bit. Give us a different, more challenging session. We've seen how you guys train with each other, and we thought we could benefit from your abilities and knowledge."

"Sure," Gates said. "We're happy to help, but you've got to understand that Zeke and I aren't about to go easy on any of you."

"Who does what?" Zeke asked, looking between the three of them.

"It's ironic in a way," Ben said with a bit of a laugh, Zeke raising his eyebrows in interest. "Mine's the air, as lame as that is. Doug can do things with the earth, and Ruby has water."

Zeke's expression fell slightly upon hearing the last one. Gates smiled in amusement as he looked at him.

"There was bound to be one," he said.

"Of course there was."

CHAPTER THIRTY-SEVEN

Helping the Untrained

"Alright, try pushing me back a bit," Gates said, standing his ground as Ben changed his stance, fierce concentration on his face.

Zeke stood back a bit with the other two, just watching.

"Is it going to hurt if I don't?" Ben asked, looking intimidated as the barrier appeared in front of Gates.

"Oh yeah, you've got to learn to defend yourself, man. I don't stand and wait for my opponent to make the first move. You've got to learn to identify your openings and go for it," Gates explained.

Zeke nodded to Chris, who had just joined them.

"What are you guys up to?" Chris asked.

Gates pushed forwards and knocked Ben over. He hit the ground hard.

Gates went for Ben again. Ben quickly scrambled to his feet, avoiding him.

"Training people," Zeke said. "What did Vincent want with you?"

"Alice wasn't cooperating. He thought I might have been able to get her to talk and join us in the fight against Marion," Chris said.

Zeke nodded as Gates once again knocked Ben hard onto his back.

"Are you even trying?" Gates snapped as Ben pushed himself to his feet. "You going to give up that easily when we're in front of a damn army? You make one wrong move, and those soldiers will kill you. They won't wait for you to get up again. Step up your game, Ben. You wanted to train with us, so that's what you're going to get."

Ben nodded, brushing himself down as the rest of them watched. A strong wind picked up around them as Ben tried to push Gates over.

Gates stayed in the same position, but Ben was unable to get past his barrier. Ben was suddenly on his back on the ground again.

Gates sighed and the barrier disappeared.

"Why won't she say anything?" Zeke asked.

"No idea," Chris shrugged. "The only thing she's said since we got back from the other reality is that she won't talk to anyone but Matt."

Zeke frowned as Gates came over to them. "Why only Matt?"

Chris shook his head. "We don't know, but either way she won't be helping. We don't have Matt with us, so there's not really any way we can get her to come and help."

"What's this about Matt?" Gates asked, placing his hands on his hips as Ben joined them, too.

"Chris was saying that Alice won't talk to anyone but Matt," Zeke said. "And she won't help until she's spoken to him."

"Well, that's a person we could have used," Gates said, Zeke and Chris nodding. "Alice would have been a good addition to this fight. Why's she so fascinated with Matt?"

"We don't know. She seems to have latched onto him for some reason," Chris said. "We don't know why she wants to talk to him and no one else. When we were in the alternate reality, she grabbed Matt and threatened him, but after he told her what to do, she backed off. She was iffy around me but not him for some reason."

"Who's Matt?" Ben asked. Doug and Ruby also looked interested.

"Matt's a friend of ours," Zeke explained. "Well, he's more family, really. About three months back we got called out to go and see why Heather was out of her area. Matt volunteered the three of us to go out with the security patrol. Heather had her soldiers out on a test run, but it turned out also to be a trap to catch Matt because Marion claims she needs him for something. We don't even know if he's still alive. We don't even know if he's still alive."

"Very sorry to hear that," Doug spoke up, the first thing he'd said the entire time. "Let's hope we can get him back and defeat this Marion person."

"Yeah, that's easier said than done, mate," Chris said. "We nearly got her in Wonderland, but she'll be healed up now. From what these guys have said, we don't have much of a chance against this army."

"Yeah, you should have seen it," Gates said with a shake of his head. "Only six of them, once Heather had gone with the one that grabbed Matt, and we nearly didn't make it out of there. We wouldn't have if they hadn't just disappeared after about ten minutes. This City really doesn't stand a chance."

Zeke looked at Chris. "How's your ability going?"

"Yeah, good. Getting the hang of it," Chris said. "I can now stop people in their tracks with a flick of the wrist. I don't have to physically touch them now."

"Can you get through the barrier?" Gates asked, a thoughtful look on his face.

He stepped back and put his hands up, making the barrier appear as an interested look crossed Chris's face.

"I don't know. I still have a way to go with it but I can always try," he said, moving to face Gates.

"We were testing the barrier a couple of months back against non-physical attacks," Zeke said. "Nixx could just get through, but that kid couldn't. Were you there for that?"

"I don't think so. That must have been when Matt and I were in the alternate reality."

Zeke nodded. "Either way, it seems the more control you have over your ability, and the more advanced you are, the easier you can get through."

"Come on, give it a shot," Gates said. "Gotta be prepared for anything with this Iron Army. Just make sure that if it works, you unfreeze me afterwards."

Chris gave a nod of confirmation as Gates readied himself.

"I wonder," Zeke said, his tone thoughtful. He looked at Ben and his friends. "Sorry, this won't take long. We'll get back to helping you once we're done with this experiment." He looked back at Gates. "If you push it back and defend yourself against it, could it hit Chris and be used against him? You've done it to me before and nearly hit me with my own fire."

"You stepped out of the way, you were fine," Gates said. "But that's a good question. It may be that it's only physical attacks I can deflect back onto the caster. But it's worth testing with both."

Gates switched his gaze back to Chris, giving him a nod. Chris nodded back and flicked his wrist to the side. Gates held his ground.

"Did it get through?" Chris asked.

Gates shook his head. "Nothing. Looks like you're useless against me for now until you get a bit more advanced. Probably a good thing, never know when you might go darkside."

Chris shrugged as the barrier disappeared and Gates came back over.

Zeke looked at Ben and the two with him.

"You want to keep going?" he asked. The three of them nodded. "Alright, well, how about we split into three seeing as there are three of us now. Chris can help out now he's here. Choose who you want to train with, and we'll go with it."

Ben immediately went and stood next to Gates, and Doug went to Chris. Zeke sighed, seeing that he'd been left with Ruby, the one with the water ability.

"Just my luck."

"How are you going over there?" Gates asked as Zeke stood behind his wall of flames, having created a circle around himself so Ruby couldn't get to him.

"Yeah, we're getting there," Zeke called, only just able to see Gates and Chris through the flames as Ruby tried once again to use her ability to put at least part of the fire out. "She can't break through."

"She has a water ability. How can she not get through to you?" Gates asked with a laugh.

Ruby shot him a glare. Then, without warning, she suddenly turned to Gates and Chris. Gates put his barrier up at the last second as a wall of water came their way.

"Nice try, hon."

Ruby crossed her arms in annoyance as Zeke sat down in the middle of his fire circle.

"Would have thought she'd have gotten through by now," he remarked as Jacob and Abel came up and stood with Chris, Gates, Ben, and Doug. "She's meant to be my one weakness."

"What are you doing?" Abel asked in confusion as Ruby tried again to put the fire out.

Ruby groaned, unable to make even the slightest dent in the flames.

"Training," Zeke said. "I'm probably gonna be here a while."

"Should have thought about that before you did it," Gates said with a bit of a laugh.

Zeke flipped him off and got back to his feet. He looked at Ruby.

"Look, even Abel can get me out of here," he said. "Ben could. Hell, even Doug could reach me here. Maybe even Gates. Ruby, you're disappointing me."

"I can leave you in there if you want," Ruby said, the irritation clear.

"You kind of already have."

She shook her head as Zeke looked at Abel and raised an eyebrow. Abel sighed, staying where he was, far from impressed with having to get Zeke out of his own predicament.

A loud, clash of thunder sounded overhead, making everyone jump from the sudden disturbance. Not long after, a torrent of rain poured down on the entire group, putting out the fire and drenching everyone.

"Thanks," Zeke said as he tried to get the water out of his eyes.

"Any time," Abel sighed, the dark clouds having disappeared with now no sign they were ever there.

Only the area around their group was now completely wet, the dirt already having turned to mud.

Gates ran his hands through his now wet hair. Chris wasn't particularly happy with how wet his clothes were now.

There were scorch marks on the ground where the fire had been, leaving a complete circle around the area where Zeke had been standing.

"What now?" Chris asked.

"We should probably call it quits for the day," Gates said, taking his shirt off to ring the water out of it. "I don't know about the rest of you, but I'm done for today."

Zeke nodded, both of them looking tired.

Jacob switched his gaze to Gates. "Vincent said you guys have the list of people who have signed up for this fight."

Gates nodded as he put his damp shirt back on. "Yeah, we've got it. Might be a bit damp now. You need it?"

Jacob nodded and Gates took the folded piece of paper out of his pocket. He handed it to Jacob, then threw him the pen. Jacob caught it, nodding his thanks.

"We don't know how many others will want to sign up later," Zeke said. "That's the best we could do today."

"Better than nothing," Jacob stated. "We should all head back. You two look like you could use a bit of rest."

"You've got that right," Gates said.

"Hey, thanks for taking the time for us," Ben said.

"It's nothing," Gates said with a wave of his hand. "We're happy to help. If you need any more help, come find us. We'll probably spend a lot of time down here again for the next few days if we're not recruiting."

"We going?" Zeke asked. Gates nodded and Zeke looked at the others. "Alright, we're off. Catch a couple of you back at the castle. Everyone else, have a good night, and we'll see you whenever."

Zeke turned away and he and Gates headed out of the arena.

Jacob looked at Chris and Abel. "We should get back too. It's going start getting dark soon and Vincent wanted to talk to everyone about what we're going to do about finding Matt."

"Sounds like a plan," Chris said.

Ben looked at Jacob. He was obviously the spokesman of his small group.

"If you need help with anything, just let us know. We're more than happy to help out with whatever you need."

Jacob gave a nod. "Thanks, I'll keep it in mind."

CHAPTER THIRTY-EIGHT

Strategy

"We need to figure out exactly what we're doing about getting Matt back," said Vincent.

"Well, we can't exactly waltz on up to the front door and ask for him back," Ash said, snarkily. "We won't be able to get anywhere near the castle, let alone get to him."

"If that's where he's actually being held," Chris input. "We don't know if that's where he is or not. They could have him somewhere else entirely for all we know."

Vincent nodded at what Chris had said.

"You're right, we don't know where he is," he began, everyone turning their focus to him. "We need a strategy on how we're going about this. I don't want to risk anything happening to anyone else. We don't know what's been happening to Matt over the past three months, and the last thing we need is for someone else to end up in his position."

"Well, if you hadn't wanted us to go out there in the first place, Matt wouldn't be gone, would he?" Gates said, a hint of anger in his tone. "You couldn't just send your own guys out. They knew what they were up against. We didn't and now look. For all we know, Marion's already killed him and we're not going to get him back."

"He's not dead," Vincent said seriously.

"You don't know that!" Gates snapped, slapping the table loudly. "It's been three months, Vincent. You really think Marion would keep him alive that long?"

"She's been after him for years," Zeke spoke up. "There's not much chance she's left him alive."

"We need to know for sure," Abel said, Zeke and Gates both looking at him. "We can't just assume he's dead. Sure, we don't know what Marion's done, but that doesn't mean she's killed him. We have to know for sure."

Vincent nodded, looking at Gates and Zeke.

"Abel's right," he said. Gates shook his head. "We'll put a task force together and do a perimeter scout first. Once we know that's all clear, we'll bring the fight to them, and we'll get Matt back."

"You said you weren't going to go anywhere near their territory," Gates said with another shake of his head, not meeting Vincent's gaze. "You said we were going to wait for them to come to us."

"Well, I've changed my mind," Vincent said harshly, getting sick of Gates's constant attitude towards every situation lately. "You want Matt back? We have to go to them. It's been three months, and we've heard nothing from them. Not a sound. No one's been wandering around or setting off any alarms. There's no other way we're getting Matt back or learning more about what they're planning."

"So, you're willing to risk all of us," Gates stated, indicating the group around the table. He finally looked up and met Vincent's stare.

"You know that without us you're pretty well fucked, right? This City will fall if we're all gone. You have no chance without us."

"What do you propose we do? Hmm?" Vincent asked, leaning back in his chair. "Go on, tell us what you'd do instead."

"Send out your task force, yes, but keep us out of it," Gates said, not about to back down from Vincent. He may have been the one in charge, but Gates wasn't one to back down to anyone when he felt strongly about something. "Send them out first to see how big this threat really is, then come back to us."

"What if none of them make it back?" Vincent asked. "What then?"

"That's not my problem," Gates snapped back. "You send out your task force before you send us out. Your task force should be trained enough to be able to handle this kind of threat. If none of them make it back, that's when you get everyone together and push onto them."

"I'm not sending my people out there without someone who knows their ability," Vincent said sternly.

Gates shook his head again. "Are you even listening to what I'm saying? For fuck's sake, your men should know what they're doing. They don't need one of us to go out there with them! It's too dangerous for any of us to go out there with them. Marion wants to kill *all* of us, no matter who it is."

Vincent was looking rather unimpressed as he answered.

"I've already said I won't send them out there by themselves," he restated. "It's safer to have someone with an ability out there with them in case things go wrong. We need everyone to cooperate here, Gates."

Gates shook his head, looking very frustrated with Vincent.

"You don't seem to understand what I'm trying to say," he said. "Marion. Will. Kill. Any. One. Of. Us. Who. Goes. Out. There. With. Your. Task. Force."

"You don't have to spell it out for me," Vincent said with annoyance. "I'm not an idiot and I know exactly what you're saying. I'm not sending them out there alone, and I'm not changing my mind. We send out a task force to establish the threat, and then we push forward with everyone else."

"Who do you propose goes with your people?" Abel asked.

Gates refrained from saying anything as Vincent looked down the table at Abel.

"I want to send you, Chris, and Gates."

"I'm not going out there," Gates said harshly. "I'm not risking my life for a stupid task force that has no idea what they're doing. You two are on your own."

"You're the best person I have who can go out. You can protect everyone else."

"Against those soldiers? Count me out. I said no and I'm not going."

Vincent sighed. "Gates, you have to go, it's an order."

"Oh, an order?" Gates remarked with a laugh. "Save it, I don't take orders from you, Vincent. You might be in charge of this City but you're not in charge of us."

"You're in my City, you're under my rules," Vincent snapped, finally sick of it. "You, Abel, and Chris are going with the task force to scout out the areas around here that Marion and the witches will be coming to. That's final."

"What if I don't? You can't physically make me go, Vincent."

"I may not be able to force you to go, but there are always consequences," Vincent said seriously, the authority displayed in his voice as he stared Gates down.

"You going to lock me up? That what you're going to do?" Gates asked, his tone equally as serious. "Really, Vincent? That's your solution to everything? Someone disagrees with you, and you lock them up? Unbelievable."

"I do what I have to do," Vincent said. "I get that you're against everything I'm saying to do, but in the end, you're not the one in charge. I am. You do as I say or spend time in the dungeons to think it over."

Gates shook his head, glaring at Vincent.

"You're no better than Marion," he stated, watching Vincent's expression become angry. "You don't like people disagreeing with you or stating their more logical opinion, so you lock them away to 'think it over'. You're unbelievable."

Vincent looked at Dorothy at the other end of the table. He indicated to Gates and Dorothy nodded, getting up from where she was sitting. Vincent looked at Gates who just returned the look.

"I hope you know this is the last thing I wanted to do," he said as Dorothy stopped just off to the side of where Gates was sitting. "Take a few days and then maybe you'll realize what I do is for the best for everyone. I won't let this City fall and if you don't want to help, then I need you to step out of the way."

"In other words, you don't want me changing people's minds and showing them how corrupt you really are," Gates said bitterly, violently pushing his chair back as he got up. He looked at Dorothy who'd moved out of the way. "I can walk myself down there, thanks."

Vincent gave him a non-caring shrug. "You made this decision yourself. I'm not corrupt, and you don't listen."

Gates shook his head at him as Dorothy headed to one of the doors on the right, indicating for Gates to follow.

"Let me know how your little crusade goes," Gates said. "Maybe when something happens, you'll put your damn ego aside and actually listen to someone else for once."

Gates shoved his chair back under the table, the chair hitting the table before he stalked off to where Dorothy was waiting, holding the door for him. Once the two of them were gone and the door had shut again, Zeke looked at Vincent.

"Why did you do that?" he asked. "Seriously, he wasn't doing anything wrong except disagreeing with you. He's right, you're unbelievable."

He shook his head, got up, and left the room, not bothering to push in his chair. The door shut silently behind him.

Vincent sighed, shaking his head before turning his attention back to the remaining five in the room with him.

"Before I say anything else, is anyone else against this as much as those two?" No one spoke up, making Vincent nod before speaking again. "Alright, in that case, Chris, I'll just send you out with the task force. Abel can stay here. No use putting everyone in the line of fire. You'll go with them, help them with the scouting, then you all come back here and tell us what you found."

Ash hesitantly put her hand up and Vincent looked at her with irritation.

"What if Marion still wants Chris? Isn't this just handing him to her?" Ash said quietly.

Vincent sighed. "What would she want him for? If she was still after him, she would have tried again by now. Chris goes."

Chris nodded to Ash, "It's fine, Ash. She's really not interested in me. She won't even know I'm out there."

Vincent sighed again and stood up.

"Alright, meet me back here in about an hour and everyone should be ready to go."

CHAPTER THIRTY-NINE

Scouting

"I thought there was meant to be more than one of you."

The group leader looked Chris over disapprovingly as the rest of his team continued making sure they had everything they were going to need.

Chris shrugged, gesturing to himself. "This is all you're getting, sorry."

The group leader still looked far from pleased or impressed as he looked Chris over again. Eventually, he stopped summing him up and looked back at his face. Chris mirrored his unimpressed look.

"Where are the ones we had last time?"

"Well, one of them disappeared due to the group's screw up," Chris stated, the leader glaring at him now. "One of them didn't want to go, which ended with him locked away in the dungeons. And the third one, he doesn't go unless the second one goes."

The leader made some noise in response before speaking.

"Hmm, well," he said, once again back to summing Chris up. "The missing one wasn't much use. The other two managed to do a few things and were slightly useful. I'd rather have them than you on our mission. What can you even do?"

"Well, sorry, but you're stuck with me. Take it up with the man in charge," Chris shot back, feeling offended. "And in answer to your question, I can stop people moving. They can't get anywhere near you if that happens."

"Doesn't sound very useful."

"Too bad, because no one else is coming with us. If you don't like it, then I won't do anything. I'm only here to make sure you lot don't get into any trouble and to try to stop it if it happens. Get used to it."

The group leader didn't say anything more and turned away to look at the rest of the team. There were no more than twenty, and Chris wasn't very happy about it. These men looked more useless than they should have. It made sense now as to why Gates and Zeke had been the only ones to put up any defense against the witches' soldiers.

Chris wondered how Vincent could justify sending these people out there, but he also understood now why Vincent was adamant they needed to be accompanied by someone with an ability.

"Alright, listen up," the leader said with authority. "We only have one extra with us today instead of three. He's not one of the ones we had with us last time. There were some complications and so now we only have one."

He glanced over at Chris who just crossed his arms in response. The leader turned back to his group.

"We have to deal with this as best we can," he said.

Chris shook his head. This man was unbelievable.

"If it comes down to it, our friend here will step in," the leader continued.

"Chris," Chris introduced himself bitterly. "My name is Chris and I'm not sure I'm your friend."

"Yeah, whatever, Chris, then," the leader said.

Chris didn't much like this non-caring attitude. With the rate this was going, this man would get them all into trouble, if not killed.

"If something happens, Chris here will step in and stop it. He may not be as good as the barrier guy or the fire guy, but he can help."

"They have names too, you know."

The leader shrugged. "Not my problem. Alright, we're going to scout the area and make sure no alerts have been set off. Once we've done that, we push into the witches' domain to see what's going on. Be on your guard the entire time and don't let it down for an instant."

Everyone nodded and the leader looked back at Chris. "You ready?"

"How long do you think they're going to keep him locked down there?" Abel asked as he watched the training dummy go up in flames.

Zeke was mad and didn't care who knew. He watched the dummy burn in front of him.

"Who the fuck knows?" he snapped. "He's not letting anyone down there to see him yet, so I don't know what the hell he's doing. Fuck him, fuck this whole place."

Zeke clicked his fingers, and a second training dummy caught fire. It went up in flames in seconds.

It was starting to worry Abel.

"Come on, man, shit like this happens," Abel tried. "He won't be there forever, you know. He'll be back in the game soon and helping us out again."

"At this rate, no one's going to be helping anyone," Zeke said.

Ben, Doug, and Ruby, the three trainees from yesterday, joined them.

"Vincent knows nothing and he's going to end up fucking this whole thing up," Zeke ranted. "I don't get why he was so against what Blaine was saying. Then suddenly, when he's out of the room, he pretty much said exactly what Blaine had said. It doesn't make any sense to me, whatsoever."

Abel shrugged as Zeke gave the others a nod of greeting, looking back at Abel as the fire continued to blaze. He wasn't worried about it.

"I'm sure Vincent knows what he's doing," Abel reassured as Zeke looked at him with an unamused look on his face.

Abel sighed as Ruby took up a place next to Zeke, but he didn't even glance at her. She began trying to put the burning dummies out, clearly up for a bit of practice to see if she could get past Zeke's defenses today.

"Look, Zeke," continued Abel. "What happened last night with Vincent wasn't something that should have happened. Gates was in the right."

"Damn right he was!" Zeke said harshly. "Vincent doesn't know anything. He's completely clueless about this whole fight. Shit, he sent Chris out there when Marion's after him. I'm betting either no one comes back, or Chris doesn't."

"Why wouldn't Chris come back?" asked Ben.

"Because Marion wants to get her hands on him!" Zeke exclaimed. "And Vincent's gone and sent him out there with that useless fucking team, which means he's not coming back. They're going into enemy territory, which is where Marion is currently residing. This can only end badly."

Zeke turned to see what Ruby was doing. The fires were starting to die down themselves; she hadn't had much luck putting them out.

"You'll get it, eventually," Zeke said tiredly before looking at Ben and Doug. "How can we help?"

"Where's Gates today?" Ben asked. "He said he'd be down here with you."

"Gates isn't available right now," Zeke said, trying to refrain from snapping, that brief sense of calm now gone. "He's out of action for a few days. Don't know how many, but it's gonna be a few."

Ben and Doug exchanged looks as Ruby finally stopped what she was doing and joined the conversation.

"Did something happen?" Ben asked.

"It's a long story. Just know that Gates won't be around for a bit," Zeke said. "Abel's here, so he can help out."

"Any further news on this ... war?" Doug asked. "I mean, I know it was only yesterday we were talking, but has anything changed since you talked to the Wizard last night?"

"Well, opinions have changed," Zeke said with an unamused smile. "But no, nothing. Vincent's just an idiot and he's going to be responsible for the City falling if he's not careful."

Doug raised his eyebrows, but Zeke waved a hand to dismiss it.

"Don't worry about it," Abel said. "We'll help you train and let you know what's going on when we know."

The group leader looked around at everyone as they stayed in the cover of the forest bordering the barren wasteland. There was a medium-sized castle not far from where they were, and Chris was sure that was where Marion was holed up.

"Alright everyone, here's the plan," the leader said, addressing the entire group. "We have to get in as close as possible to see what's going on. We need to make sure there's nothing threatening. We have to make sure there will be no attack on the City any time soon."

"I don't think it's a real great idea to get up close," Chris interjected, the leader looking at him. "We're in a pretty dangerous area and getting closer to the castle will probably end badly."

"This isn't your task force, so it's not your decision," the leader said with annoyance. "You do as I say. I'm the one in charge, not you."

"Well, you'll certainly be the one to blame when something goes wrong."

The leader shot him a glare, neither of them saying anything more to each other.

"Boys, please," they all heard from behind their group, forcing them all to look around. "Quit arguing. You're giving me a headache."

Marion gave them all a smile from where she was standing just a few paces away. Hunter and his dog were standing by her side.

The group stepped back a few paces to gain a bit of distance between themselves and Marion and Hunter.

"Marion," Chris said. "Thought you'd be locked inside that castle instead of lurking out here in the woods. Don't recall you being the outdoors type."

Marion smiled but didn't move.

"Well, you're all loitering out here in the woods, too," she said, looking around at the group before looking back at Chris who also didn't move. "What are you doing out here? You wouldn't be planning to launch an attack now, would you?"

"We're out here to make sure you aren't launching any attacks on the City," the group leader finally spoke up.

Marion switched her gaze to the leader.

"We wouldn't dream of it," she said with a smile. She looked at Hunter, who was staring Chris down. "Would we?"

Hunter shook his head, his dog growling in response. Marion looked back at the group in front of her, before focusing back on Chris.

"I'm honestly surprised you're out here with them, Chris," she said, linking her fingers together as she looked at him. "Pray tell, after what happened with Shade, how come Vincent sent you out with this ... useless team?"

"You watch what you're saying," the leader snapped, pointing at her.

Marion rolled her eyes.

"Oh, shut up," she said, waving her hand dismissively at him.

The leader suddenly froze. Chris glanced back at him to find he had turned to stone.

"Oh, my bad," said Marion.

"What the hell?" one of the team members said, horror on his face as he cautiously touched the stone statue that used to be their group leader. "What have you done?"

"All I did was turn him to stone. He was useless anyway," Marion said with a shrug as she looked back at Chris. A smile appeared on her face. "But now he can be useful. He'll look good in the castle garden, don't you think?"

"You're sick, you know that?" Chris said. "Where's Matt?"

"Matt's nowhere that concerns you," Marion said in response as the team continued to stare at the stone statue. It would take them a while to get over this. "He won't be going anywhere any time soon."

"So, you've killed him."

"I never said that."

"Then where is he?" Chris asked again, a bit harsher this time. "We need him back, Marion, and we're not leaving without him."

The smile appeared on Marion's face again as she crossed her arms, looking around at the group before looking back at Chris.

"Oh, Chris. I don't think any of you are going anywhere just yet."

CHAPTER FORTY

Bad News

"I need everyone back in the castle, immediately," Jacob ordered. "We've got an issue, and we need everyone back, right now."

Zeke and Abel looked at the three trainees.

"Alright, we'll have to pick this up again later. Looks like we're needed," Zeke said apologetically. He was disappointed because this had been taking his mind off everything else that was going on.

Ben, Doug, and Ruby all nodded, showing they understood.

"Bring them with you, they might be of use," Jacob called as he began heading out of the arena, followed by Abel.

Zeke looked at the three trainees. "You guys OK with coming along?" he asked. They all nodded. "Alright, I don't what's going on but if Jacob thinks you may be able to help, then I guess it's important."

Abel was waiting outside the arena for Zeke, and they all started heading back to the castle.

Ben caught up to Zeke, walking alongside him. "You don't know what's happening?"

"No idea," Zeke said, his focus on where he was going.

"When we get called up, it's never anything good," Abel said. "Vincent usually wants to talk to us about something but, the way Jacob was speaking, it sounds like something's happened."

On the way to the castle, they passed a few people who moved aside for them and didn't make eye contact. It happened a lot now, mostly because of what Gates and Zeke had done in the way of recruiting.

"I bet it's that no one's returned," Zeke said, turning down another street. "It's been hours since they left. They should all have been back by now."

They all walked in silence the rest of the way.

"We've run into a very serious problem," Vincent addressed everyone, pacing back and forth in front of them in the group room. "Only one person from the task force has made it back."

"I'll take it Chris isn't that person," Zeke spoke up.

Vincent stopped pacing, trying to calm himself as he looked around at everyone. He shook his head, and Zeke looked far from happy as he leaned back in his chair.

"No, Chris isn't the one who made it back," Vincent said. "I've spoken to the one who made it back and he told me what happened."

He stopped talking and sat down on the closest, unoccupied chair.

"OK, so, what happened?" Alex asked as the silence dragged on too long.

"Marion's a lot more dangerous than I originally thought," Vincent continued as Alex and Ash exchanged looks. "My man said that she turned the entire group, apart from him and Chris, into stone."

"Wait, what?" Abel said, the first one to speak up. "Stone? She turned people to stone?"

Vincent nodded. "That's what he said."

"Well, it looks like Marion has an ability after all," Nixx said, a bit of intrigue in his voice. "I mean, I assumed she already had one and had mastered it, but that's not what I actually expected it to be."

"I never even knew she had one," Ash said. "Alex and I lived in the castle for years and not once did we ever see her use any ability whatsoever."

"Well, now she has," Abel said, shaking his head. "This is not good. We really don't have much of a chance against her, do we?"

"Come to think of it, there were some very lifelike statues in the Wonderland castle gardens," input Alex unhelpfully.

"Gates might be able to stop or deflect her ability," Nixx said hesitantly, looking at Zeke for confirmation. "We were working on defending against non-physical attacks. Marion is rather advanced by the sounds of it. Maybe we could work with him to try and deflect it back onto her?"

"When he's out of the dungeons, I'll ask him," Zeke said bitterly, shooting a disapproving look at Vincent. "How long are you going to keep him down there anyway?"

"Until he's learnt his lesson," Vincent said.

"Come on, that's bullshit," Zeke snapped. "He didn't do anything wrong, and you threw him down there. Once he was gone, you pretty well agreed with everything he'd said, and yet you still won't let him out. You're ridiculous and this whole thing makes zero fucking sense!"

"Zeke, I'd appreciate it if you stopped raising your voice," Vincent said calmly. "What I do is always in the best interests of this City. Gates won't be down there forever."

"By the time you let him out, Marion and her friends will already be here," Zeke shot back. "Why would you hamstring your own defense? You need him. He's one of the only people who has a real shot at stopping these attacks. Without him, without us, this whole City is doomed to fall."

"You're saying you're not going to help?"

"Not until you let Blaine out of the dungeons."

Vincent looked unimpressed as Zeke stood his ground, staring him down.

"He won't be down there forever," Vincent repeated. "Now, getting back to the problem at hand, as I was saying, Marion now has her hands on Chris. From what I was told, he went willingly."

"Chris wouldn't do that," Ash said with a shake of her head. "He's better than that. He'd never side with the enemy."

"My man thinks it was a spell of some kind," Vincent said. "We don't know what it was but, by the looks of it, Carmen and Heather have given Marion something that's now caused Chris to side with them, however unwillingly that might be."

"How do we get him back?" Abel asked. "If Marion's somehow corrupted him, we don't have much of a chance of getting him back. To make matters worse, Matt's still missing, and we haven't learnt anything else about what she's done to him. We don't know where he is, if he's even alive, and if we can get him back."

"Apparently, when Chris asked about him, Marion confirmed he wasn't dead. It's a start."

"OK, so we presume Matt's not dead, but what can we do about getting the two of them out of that castle?" Zeke asked, not quite as pent up as before. "By the looks of it, they knew we were coming. Were they waiting for them? If they were, we don't have much chance of getting close to that castle or breaking in to get our people back."

"We'll figure something out. Right now, we just have to wait," Vincent said.

Zeke shook his head once more. "Wait for what? We've waited long enough."

Vincent looked around at everyone in the room, the look on his face telling all.

"We wait," he repeated.

"We can't wait," Abel said. "Once again, we don't know what she's going to do to Matt. We don't know what she's done to him over these past three months. And now she has Chris. We have to figure out what they're going to do and stop them before they can do it."

"It's not that easy," Nixx input. "Vincent's right. We can't afford to lose anyone else by charging in there with no preparations or strategy."

"They have an army, we have citizens," Zeke stated. "We stand no chance against that army. Gates and I were both there and we know what they can do. And that was just the test run. They've probably improved them by now which means it's going to take a lot more of us to defeat them. A lot more effort and time that we just don't have. Half of these people aren't even ability-trained. How the hell are we meant to defeat their Iron Army when we can't even show someone how to put a damn fire out?"

Ruby shot him an annoyed look that Zeke chose to ignore.

"I understand where you're coming from, I truly do," Vincent said. "But for now, we have to wait, and we have to train. We have to wait for them to bring the war to us."

"That's not good enough," Zeke said. "We have to match them."

"How?" Alex spoke up. "You said so yourself, Zeke, they have an army, and we don't. Most of us aren't going to be of any use in this war. I know I won't be. I can't do half the stuff you guys can do. You've already said we don't have any chance against these soldiers. What do you propose we do?"

"We don't have enough time to train people up to their full abilities," Jacob spoke up from where he was sitting next to Abel. "We don't know when they're going to strike, and we don't know what they're going to do. We can train as much as we can, but we don't have all the time in the world. They'll attack and, now that they have Chris, it probably won't be too long before it happens."

Vincent gave a nod of confirmation before looking at Zeke. Zeke linked his fingers together as he looked at the floor and thought quickly.

"What do you think we should do?" Vincent asked. "Jacob's right, they could strike anytime."

"They've had three months to do so, and they haven't," Ash said, Alex nodding in agreement. "We might have more time than we think. You have alerts all around Oz. We'll know when they're coming, and we can act on it when it happens. We train up as many people as we can, as far as we can, and when it happens, we still have people to cover us and help out."

Vincent seemed unconvinced, but he switched his gaze back to Zeke.

"Zeke, I'm putting you in charge here. What do you think we should do?"

Zeke finally looked up, having made up his mind.

"We have to make our own Iron Army."

Also by Daryl Walker

The Other Side of Andy

Motionless series

Motionless in Wonderland